The life of Crosbie Alfred Norr
Jack London, or one of the ch
Buchan's novels. He was born
Norman Garstin, who was one .... .ue
Newlyn School of painters. The third volume in the *Penhales*
trilogy, *The West Wind*, is dedicated 'To Norman Garstin,
dearest of fathers, wittiest of companions, best of friends. Died
June 22, 1926'.

Crosbie was educated at Brandon House School, Cheltenham,
Elstow School in Bedford, and in Germany. He went to the
United States and Canada, where he worked successively as a
horse breaker on western ranches, in threshing gangs, as a
sawyer in the Columbia and North Thompson lumber camps in
British Columbia, and as a miner on the Pacific coast. He then
travelled to Africa, where he became manager of a cattle ranch
and ranger to the Tati Concessions in Matabeleland.

On the outbreak of war in 1914 Garstin returned to Britain and
enlisted as a Trooper in the 1st King Edward's Horse. He was
commissioned in the field in 1915, served briefly as an Intelligence Officer in Ireland, following the Easter Rising of 1916,
and returned to the Western Front in the same year. While at
the Front he wrote the popular *Mudlarks* series, and other
articles, for *Punch*. Following the Armistice he became horse-
master to the XIth Corps and was demobilised in 1919.

His publications include a book of poems, *Vagabond Verses*, *The
Sunshine Settlers*, *The Black Knight* (with Mrs Alfred Sidgwick),
two volumes of *The Mudlarks*, *The Ballad of the Royal Ann*, *The
Coasts of Romance*, and *The Dragon and the Lotus*. *The Owls'
House*, the first volume in his masterly trilogy, *The Penhales*, was
published in 1923. This was followed by *High Noon* (1925) and
The West Wind (1926).

Crosbie Garstin listed his recreations as foxhunting, rugby foot-
ball, and boat-sailing. When not travelling he lived at St.
Buryan in West Penwith, which is the 'St. Gwithian' of the
Penhale novels. He was accidentally drowned in Cornwall, on
20 April, 1930, at the tragically early age of 42.

THE CORNISH LIBRARY
NUMBER TWELVE

High Noon

CROSBIE GARSTIN

ANTHONY MOTT LTD

LONDON

Published by Anthony Mott Limited 1983
50 Stile Hall Gardens, London W4 3BU

First published 1925

ISBN 0 907746 11 X

Printed in Great Britain by
Richard Clay (The Chaucer Press) Ltd
Bungay, Suffolk

CHAPTER I

FROM where Trou Gascon stream met Gros Inlet to the fall three hundred yards above, both banks were blocked with seamen filling water casks. The *Triton's* baby midshipman, a late-comer, tried to find a gap for his men but was blasphemously ordered off by elder midshipmen from the first-rates. They called him "Susan" and "Polly" and told him that if he were looking for his wet nurse he'd better look farther up. He blushed in pretty rage and trailed on up to the fall, his men at heel, shouldering casks.

The *Torbays* occupied the pool below the cascade and warned the *Tritons* to stand clear till they'd finished or somebody'd get a bath. As they out-numbered the frigate's party by three to one, the midshipman called a halt. It was scandalous, he considered, one officer calling another "Susan" in front of his men; he would protest to his first lieutenant as soon as he got back . . . very bad for discipline. In the meanwhile he sat down on a block of lava and, with a thorn, pursued a shred of salt junk which had stuck between his teeth and irritated him all the morning.

Ortho Penhale, pressed man and ordinary seaman, set down his burden and looked about him.

To the east, stretched across the sparkling blue waters of Gros Inlet, rode the main body of the West Indies fleet, thirty-four sail of the line with attendant frigates. The bay was dotted with water boats, speeding to and from their ships, oars striking diamond flashes from the sea.

To the north Pigeon Island rose up sheer out of the glitter. On its crest, to Ortho's knowledge, sat Admiral Sir George Brydges Rodney, in an armchair, under an awning, watching for signals from his scouts.

Under his breath, Ortho consigned the ancient admiral to perdition. He had nothing against him in person but he was an officer and at the moment the seaman felt murderously inclined toward all such—even the pink-and-white infant on the lava block.

Eastwards and at his back the island of St. Lucia humped its peaked backbone skywards, a thirty-mile ridge of wooded cones, wooded right down to the water's edge. A magic island transformed by every shift of sun and cloud; now amber, now dragon green, now deep cobalt, now, ruffled by the Trade Wind, the shimmering purple of a peacock's breast.

Ortho could not see the ridge from where he stood but he had looked on it long and often from the *Triton's* deck, in the full light of day, at dawn and sunset, floating apparently in mid-air under a canopy of fire-tinted cloud. An entrancing island, a magic island, a bright sea jewel.

And this was the first time he had set foot on it, or in the West Indies at all for that matter; and, in the ordinary way of things, it was unlikely he would do so again: the French might be out any day now. In an hour at the most he would be back on the *Triton,* and, possibly, in for another flogging bout—there was no saying.

He turned his back on the sea and stared at the jungle that pressed the stream hard on either flank.

The sight he saw took his breath away. Vast green glades, pierced with shafts of sunlight, hung with trailing strings of flowers, festooned across and across with ropes of flowers, flowers of every conceivable shape and hue. Convolvulus lay in tangles across the lava, a purple trumpet at each joint. Bushes of dark lustrous leaves, crimson spined, and hung with grapes, crowded the underwoods, and between them young palms thrust their plumy jets, like green fountains bursting into spray. Fleshy shrubs covered with great waxen stars, red and white, there were too, and among them drifts of orange butterflies went winging lazily. Above all stood great trees blazing with vermillion flowers, hung with purple tassels, sheeted with silver blossom, which quivered and flashed under the breath of the Trade. And with every gust came puffs of warm, intoxicating scent, sweeter than anything Ortho had ever known—frangipani.

He snuffed delicious draughts of it and, as scent does, it brought memories thronging, memories of the wind blowing over miles of orange blossom in the Sultan's gardens in Morocco City, blowing in at his window. . . . He was a Kaid Rahal then, commanding a regiment of royal lances! Now he was no better than a slave with a back whipped into bloody stripes.

Again his eyes sought the wood glades—so cool, so still. Again the scent of frangipani invaded his nostrils.

Within a few yards lay freedom and a garden of paradise lovely beyond belief; eastwards, floating hell.

Within an hour he would be back on the *Triton,* out on the shadeless bay, sweating up round shot from the hold, cursed at, bawled at; with the sun melting the pitch in the deck seams, scalding his raw shoulders . . . he winced at the thought.

The *Torbays* had nearly finished, some of them were already trundling casks down the beach; a petty officer was barking at the laggards like a dog gone mad, slashing at a poor old seaman with a knotted rope's end. In a minute the *Triton's* plaguy little terrier would be yelping too.

Ortho glanced at the midshipman. He was sitting with his back to the woods, the best part of one hand in his mouth, from his intense expression evidently on the point of harpooning the offending shred. The marine on the far side leaned on his musket, half asleep. The marine on the near side, not ten feet away, was awake though, a big-boned, straw-coloured Scot with pale blue eyes. Again came the breath of frangipani, insidiously sweet, and Ortho made up his mind.

He moved nearer the sentry, drew a coil of pig-tail tobacco from his frock bosom, bit off a chew, screwed up his face appreciatively and winked.

The sentry replied with a flick of a white lash; the pale eyes were those of a child watching another eat sweets. Ortho smacked his lips and replaced the coil, then, as on second thoughts, withdrew it and dumbly offered the marine a chew.

The red-coat shot a quick glance about him and, seeing no one of importance was looking, nodded gratefully. Ortho stepped up to him, tossing the coil from hand to hand, dropped it, stooped as if to pick it up and butted the marine in the stomach, with his head, all his weight and force behind it.

The deluded Scot folded up like a clasp-knife and shot backwards into the pool, taking his musket with him, and Ortho flung himself into the bushes. The second sentry did not know what had happened for the moment. He was aroused from his day dreams of Oxfordshire meadows by the splash his opposite made on meeting the water. He did not see Ortho enter the bushes, and when he fired it was at random.

Other marines, farther downstream, fired as well,

also at random. Their bullets loosed a shower of purple angelim blossom and sent a trio of green parrots flapping and screaming in alarm, but they came nowhere near Ortho. He knew it would take the red-coats a full half-minute to reload and in that half-minute he made a good fifty yards, flung himself flat and crawled sideways. He heard the midshipman yelp, and some more bullets went over, droning like infuriated bees, zip-zipping through the foliage, all wide and all too high. They could not see him: the scrub was thick enough to conceal an army. He jumped up and ran on uphill, keeping the plash of the stream within hearing. He ran for ten minutes, floundered over a ground liane, fell, rose slowly, the breath shaken out of him, and walked on. He must be out of harm's way, he thought. They dared not pursue. Did they put a search party in after him, half that party would desert as well; furthermore, seeking an inanimate needle in a haystack was child's play compared with hunting a mobile seaman through those square leagues of jungle. He was quite safe, he considered; nevertheless he pushed steadily upstream: there was nothing like making sure.

The going became increasingly difficult. What looked like solid forest floor was in reality a network of knee-high roots and creepers, invisible under a coverlet of leaves. It was like wading through an everlasting pig-net, tripping at every step. Lianes like slack rigging trailed from the treetops and caught him in their nooses; others, thick through as ships' cables, barred the way horizontally.

There were dwarf palms which pricked if you blundered against them, and green whip-plants armed with terrible hooks fit to tear the clothes and flesh off you. The stream made no easier road: it came foaming headlong over a series of jagged lava steps and even here the roots did not stop but flung across and across it in obstructive suspension bridges.

At the end of an hour Ortho halted. He could not see the sun for interlacing foliage, but judged it to be about noon. He was beyond pursuit, a free man again. No shrill bosun's calls or raucous speaking trumpets could pester him here in this cool, scented paradise.

He took a long drink from the stream and ate a delicious meal of avocado pears and bananas— rendered all the more delectable by thoughts of the rancid pork and hard peas he was escaping—lit a pipe and lay back smoking in heart-whole content.

He was no spiritless slave, he boasted; they should not drub him twice—curse them!

He had been flogged only the day before, spread-eagled at the gangway and laid into with a waxed cat-o'-nine-tails wielded by a bosun's mate who enjoyed his work. Two dozen he had endured and then fainted. They had brought him round by sluicing salt water over him. And all this agony for laughing—laughing at an officer. Ortho ad-

mitted that it was a foolish thing to do, but not
for the life of him could he help it—Bandy Joe
looked so absurd.

Bandy Joe, officially Joseph Macwhirter, was first
lieutenant of the *Triton,* an elderly but capable seaman with a bald pate and legs so convex that, in the
words of the lower deck, "you could sling a ham-
mock between 'em."

The lower deck had a legend concerning Joe's
legs. For twenty years they had been straight as
spars, the lower deck declared, till one day he was
put in charge of a prize in the Gulf of Darien with
instructions to take her to Port Royal. All went
well until he was to windward of the Rosalind Bank
where he got whisked up by the tail of a hurricane
and the leaky old basket literally dissolved under
him. Everybody was drowned but Joe, who got
astride the drifting main-mast, wound his legs about
it and hung on. For two days and nights he jockeyed
that stick, to be rescued little the worse for wear
save that his legs had become permanently warped
to the curve of the mast—or so the story ran.

On the day in question Bandy Joe had been dining with an old mess-mate aboard Hood's *Barfleur,*
and dining well. He returned to the *Triton* seething
with mixed drinks and dignity, figged out in his
best in honour of the vice-admiral, blue coat, gilt
buttons and all, the whole surmounted by an enormous cocked hat and wig. In the ordinary way
Joseph was not a dressy man, in the ordinary way

a red bandanna bound about his arid scalp was good enough for him. But on state occasions he donned a wig. He bought it second-hand and it did not fit him, being too large by half, but it was a generous, luxuriant wig and the pride of his life.

He came carefully up the frigate's ladder, ordered a taut brace to be tautened; cursed the bosun, who was behind him, for getting in his way, fixed his eye on the poop cabin door and bore up for it.

On the top of the open door sat the captain's spider-monkey, "Yarns," so called from its having the appearance of a piece of unravelled rope, a wistful black and grey beast from Guiana. Yarns was in disgrace. She had just been kicked out of the cabin for taking liberties with her master's sword-knot—she had a passion for bright objects—and was expiating her crime by banishment. There were no bananas to be had on deck and nothing bright to play with. She was desperately bored. All of a sudden she saw Bandy Joe waddling towards her crowned with glory. She stared at the glory, fascinated. Bandy waddled nearer and nearer and made to enter the door. As he did so a thin, thumbless hand shot out, and away went his cocked hat and wig. It was Yarns: she simply couldn't resist that gold lace. Bandy wheeled about and slashed at her with his rattan. She bounded for the overhang of the poop deck and the wig fell out of the hat. Up the mizzen rigging she went (imagining it to be some

sort of tree) chattering with terror, but still clinging to the hat.

Bandy uttered a sob of anguish and ordered the
entire watch aloft to save his festival headgear.

Then he noted that the wind was blowing his wig,
his precious wig, across the deck straight for an
open port; in a moment it would be overboard, and
swallowed by a shark! He emitted a shattered roar,
like that of a lioness that has been robbed of her
surviving cub, and flung himself upon it. Unfortunately the bosun flung himself at the same time
and their heads met.

When some seconds later, Bandy, half-stunned
and wholly furious, rose from his prone position,
it was to be confronted by an ordinary seaman bent
double over a gun breech laughing himself sick. The
seaman was Ortho and he paid two dozen across
his bare back for that joke.

Lying on the frigate's deck, salt water eating into
his wheals, he had promised himself to be even with
Bandy Joe, to shoot or knife him in the smoke and
confusion of the impending action, but now he was
thankful that he had obeyed the impulse of the
moment and run for it. The drawback to his
murder plan was that he might himself be killed before he could lay out the lieutenant. French round-
shot made no discrimination between just and unjust.
But now Bandy would go to battle and, he hoped,
be riddled by De Grasse's sharpshooters, while he
himself lay safe and snug up among these iridescent

hills sucking green cocoanuts, oranges and "midshipman's butter." All was for the best and it was a good world—up here, a wonderland of trees, scent and flowers, beyond his wildest dreams. The farther one pushed inland the higher grew the trees. They were monstrous, astounding, shooting up a hundred feet, some of them, without branch or twig, pillars of a mighty twilit cathedral. Some were smooth and appeared to be made of metal—iron, copper, bronze; others were mottled with lichen, shaggy with tree-ferns and moss; others again struggled upwards wrapped in the coils of python creepers, and on every bough, in every crevice, grew vanilla orchids, scenting the wood with delicious perfume. A moth swung by, big as a linnet, a metal thing in bright blue armour. A shower of jewels, rubies and emeralds, fell from above, dipped across the glade and rose again into the high sunlight—humming-birds.

The deserter sighed in deep content. Two hours before, he had been tugging a heavy boat across the sweltering bay, a beaten slave. A short dash, a little risk—now here he lay, taking his ease in a still, enchanted forest. Vengeance was sweet but this was sweeter.

Bandy Joe and the fleet could go to blazes for all he cared: he had done with them. He knocked his pipe out, hitched up his belt, and pushed on for the peacock mountains, crushing masses of white arum lilies underfoot.

CHAPTER II

ORTHO hauled himself up the ceiba-tree, sending a brace of howler monkeys scuttling, and swung across his favourite bough.

Rotted by rain, the ground in front of the tree had slipped downhill, carrying every sprig of vegetation along with it, so that the bough gave a clear look out to the north and west.

Ortho looked out to the west and swore aloud.

The fleet was still there!

He could see very plainly in the keen light of morning, plainly enough to count the gun-ports in the nearest first-rates.

"They'll go aground on their own beef-bones, soon," he growled. "Why the dickens don't the French come out and draw 'em off?"

He glanced northwards across the St. Lucia channel in the hope of seeing De Grasse's van rounding Diamond Rock. Twenty-five miles away, across the ruffled azure of the straits, loomed the island of Martinique, a purple smudge, with the Piton de Vauclain smoking like a volcano. Off Pointe du Cap was a British frigate, tacking against the trade wind. A few miles farther north was another, and another, a diminishing chain, the head of which was

off Port Royal watching De Grasse's every movement. There was no signal from the frigates, no
sign of excitement on the anchored line of battleships; all was as it had been every morning for
weeks—yards jerking up and down, water boats plying, sail, gun, cutlass drill going on. Another day
to wait. Ortho cursed again. He cursed the French
for not coming out and relieving him of his embarrassment.

The truth of the matter was that he had seen
more than enough of the enchanted forests. He had
been in them for twelve days now and they were not
what they seemed. To begin with, there were the
mosquitoes. These issued, ravenous, with the shades
of night, in swarms and clouds so that the glades
rang with the drone of their million trumpets. Ortho
experimented with a smudge fire and succeeded in
nearly suffocating himself. When he sat with his
head wrapped in smoke, blinded and coughing, they
concentrated on his legs. When the smoke drifted
about his feet they attacked his head. They worked
down his frock and up his sleeves and loose breeches,
bit him through his stockings—everywhere. He
smote ten gorged insects on his right cheek; as he
did so twenty settled on his left. All night long he
twitched and smote and raved.

That was not all. Scorpions and tarantulas
abounded; and there was hardly a bush or plant that
was not covered with barbs and hooks—his hands
were full of them; a chigoe fly had burrowed into his

foot, setting up a sore, and, tripping over a creeper
he had fallen into a manchineel bush, blistering both
palms most painfully.   He was itching tender from
head to heel.   The fruit he had at first thought
ambrosia he now positively disliked.   One can have
too much of anything, and at that moment Ortho
would have given all the avocado pears, bananas and
yams in the Windward Islands to set his teeth in a
chunk of despised salt horse.   Other kinds of fruit
there were in profusion, but he dared eat nothing
but what he had actually seen in the negro bumboats,
having been too often regaled with stories of young
seamen who fell into temptation ashore and plucked
forbidden fruit, followed by graphic descriptions of
their death agonies.

And that did not exhaust the dangers.   One morning he trod on what he took to be a root but which
proved to be a rat-tailed snake.   Ortho jumped into
the air and the snake missed him, its head grazing
the side of his shoe.   He gave way and it made off,
five feet of sluggish, red-brown evil.   It was the
dreaded fer-de-lance.   Next morning Ortho saw two
more.   The undergrowth was wriggling with them,
apparently. He hardly dared stir for some days after
that, but placed his feet with exceeding care, lifting
the mamures leaves in front of him with a stick.

The scents of frangipani, logwood, jessamine and
vanilla bewitched him no longer, the flower-hung
forest enchanted him no more; it was a poisoned
paradise; there was poison everywhere, crawling

double-fanged among the ground lilies, spurting in milky acid from broken shrubs, lurking in thorns, in glowing fruit, even in the most lovely flowers. The forest was like some burning beauty of the Cinquecento, decked out in splendid satins and brocades, a jewelled ring on her finger and in that ring— murder. The woods were getting on the deserter's nerves; he hardly dared put a hand out for fear of getting either pricked or blistered; in every rustle of the undergrowth he detected fer-de-lance and jumped half out of his skin. He had been up to the peacock mountains—so alluring from afar—and come quickly down again, soaked to the bone. They drew every cloud in the Caribbean, those peaks, and then dissolved them in deluges of rain.

He was now established in a glade at the back of the ceiba-tree, under a primitive shelter of plantain leaves, ragged, unshorn, itching, craving for meat, tobacco and human companionship.

Rubbing a swollen shin he damned the laggard French afresh.

"Skulking frog-eaters!" he exclaimed. "Why don't they come out? They've got better ships, more men and metal, leagues of start. What in hell are they waiting on?"

There was nobody present to answer his question.

Anger at the French produced a change of feeling for his countrymen. He nodded towards the anchored fleet.

"Drub 'em sick, you bullies; make shark-feed of 'em!"

It would be a great battle, he reflected, probably the greatest in the world's history. Whether De Grasse wanted to fight or no, the grim old sea-dog on Pigeon Island would bring him to it—sooner or later. It would be a stupendous action, the two paramount fleets of the world at a duel to the death for the West Indies. It would be a wonderful thing to see—and boast about afterwards—always supposing one survived.

His eyes searched out the *Triton,* lying at the tail of the fleet, admired the clean curve of her sheer, her sharp entry and moulded stern. Swift pretty little ship, very sweet to handle. Pleasant memories he had of her on the voyage out, in the sparkling blue weather of the trades, running like a stag under stunsails, a white cloud among white clouds; flying fish skimming the sapphire alongside, silver shining; dolphins caracoling under the bows, brilliant emerald as they plunged, gleaming gold as they leapt into the sunshine. Pretty little ship. He hoped the French didn't maul her badly—or her crew. There were some good fellows aboard—even among the officers.

Time had softened his feelings toward Bandy Joe. Bandy was reputed to keep his brother's widow out of his meagre pay and, as a fact, had saved a top-man from drowning by diving after him off Cape St. Mary, where there are about four sharks to the cubic yard. On second thoughts, Ortho hoped the French sharpshooters would not get the lieutenant; he hoped the little frigate would escape scatheless and see good sport. It seemed rather like treachery deserting her at a time like this, short-handed as she was; but if he went back now the cat would not stop at two dozen, or four, and fainting would not save him. He would be flogged round the fleet. His jaw hardened. No, by the Lord, he was not going back—not alive!

Blast the fleet! He owed it nothing. He had not joined of his own free will but been pressed—knocked on the head and dragged off senseless when within three miles of his own Cornish home. Let them fight their own battles. He would hang on, miserable as he was, until the French left Martinique, and then work his passage home on a sugar ship. Furthermore he was under the impression that he was no longer alone in the jungle. The night before he woke up to hear drums beating and horns blowing. It was too dark to do anything then, but he had marked the direction and intended to investigate early that very evening. It was a party of deserters he felt sure, fellow prisoners of the woods whiling away the time of waiting as best they might. He pictured them sitting before a cheerful blaze, banging and blowing away at their improvised instruments, dancing competitive hornpipes and spinning fabulous yarns. He would join them that night. Twelve days' solitude in those still woods, where the sun never entered and the most tempting things were the most deadly, had crushed his spirits.

Companionship—other men blistering themselves, being stung frantic by mosquitoes, worm-eaten, stuck with thorns—would make the wilderness more endurable.

He shot a last glance round. The frigates were keeping station, glints of white on hazy blue; over the fort on La Vigie headland a flag drooped idly and from Morne Fortunée came the song of soldier bugles. All was as ever. Ortho swung down the lianes and gathered himself a meal of detested fruit. Another day to be got through, and homesickness came on him as never before, amounting almost to physical pain.

At the age of seventeen he had run away with a family of Romany horse-dealers and he had been roving by land and sea ever since. He was now twenty-eight—eleven years wandering and fighting. Perils and hardships he had known a-plenty, yet never during his most bitter experiences such gnawing nostalgia as this. The reason for it was that always before there had been others with him; for the first time he was bearing his troubles alone.

All day long he pined for home, saw heart-wrenching visions of it. It must be about the end of March or the beginning of April, he thought. In the Keigwin Valley thorns were touched with the first hoarfrost of blossom, sycamores were unfolding. Every gorse bush was a yellow bonfire, every orchard twig

tipped with a pink pearl, the hedgerows creamed
with primroses. He saw the old place that had bred
him, Bosula—the Owls' House—nestling in the
crook of the valley, the thatch arching over the upper
windows like surprised eyebrows, the tall chimneys
sending their smoke straight up through the trees;
heard the rooks quarrelling; the everlasting music
of the stream. He thought of his gypsy mother,
ponderous, cynical-eyed; pictured her riding off to
some feast or bull-bait upon her roan stallion,
dressed in flaming colours, barbaric ear-rings shining
like crescent moons in the thick night of her hair.
He saw his brother Eli, that home-loving, home-
keeping yeoman, saw him on the uplands ploughing,
dark and soil-stained against a windy sky, a storm of
crows and seagulls swooping in his wake. Ortho
sighed. Oh, well! he was out of the navy, out of
bondage, a free man again. Before long he would
be homeward bound, and once in his native parish
never again would he stir abroad.

He passed the long hours away in sleep, in cutting roseau thorns from his forearm, climbing for
fruit, playing his right hand against his left at pitch
and toss, whetting his sheath-knife and throwing at
a life-sized mark carved in the bark of a tree. Towards evening he bound his legs with protective
bandages of palm-leaves and fibre and set out in the
direction from whence had come the noise of the
drums. As he went he wondered who the runaway
sailors might be and decided that they were from

the *Russell*. She had been in the Carénage, over-hauling, and had had many desertions.

He headed due east, crossed Gros Inlet River and climbed the highland beyond just as the sun went down, blood-red, into the Caribbean, and the swift tropic night came rushing. Ortho sat and rested. He had reached the point aimed at and there would be a moon before long. The drums would lead him the rest of the way. Crickets, beetles and tree-toads opened their nightly din, fireflies swept from bush to bush. Through a gap in the leaves Ortho saw the eastern sky paling: the moon was coming up. He sucked at his empty pipe and hoped the *Russells* would have some tobacco to spare.

Time crawled by, leaden-footed. Ortho began to fear that there would be no concert that night, or perhaps the deserters had moved away, gone south towards Choiseul or down the windward coast raid-ing plantations. If they were a strong party they would stop at little.

The moon rose higher, shafts of wan light pene-trated the filigree of leaves; the night-blooming cereus unfolded; bats went by. Still no sound, beyond the monotonous serenade of toads and insects, the occasional eerie cry of a pootoo-bird. Ortho scraped a hip-hole with his knife, covered himself with a thatch of giant leaves and prepared to take what sleep the mosquitoes would allow him. It was nearly midnight and the gang had given no sign—

impossible to find them in this pestiferous tangle-wood. On the morrow he would return to the ceiba-tree and bide the sailing of the fleet with what patience he could muster. He was tired and, despite the incessant tickling and itching, fell asleep at once. He woke again almost immediately, to an unwonted clamour. It was the drums, quite close, not more than a few hundred yards distant.

Shaking off his coverlet he went forward, feeling the way with his stick like a blind man. They, whoever they were, were raising a most unholy din, howling, blowing horns and banging drums with no attempt at concerted effort.

"Must have looted a pen and got mad-drunk on rum," he said to himself.

Presently he caught sight of a red glare among the trees. The thought of sitting at a fire, gulping rum, surrounded by human beings again, made him quicken his pace with the result that a trip root sent him sprawling.

Rub-a-dub went the drums, *rub-a-dub, rub-a-dub;* then blaring moans from the horns and more howls.

"Stewed in ripe Jamaica," said Ortho. "Crazed as jackasses." Never before had he heard white men bang drums like that—white men varied their beats. This monotonous thumping reminded him of tom-toms, of snake-charmers summoning audiences in the Djeema-el-Fna and the discordant nights of Ramadan. Odd!

A huge logwood had fallen, carrying all before

it, and in the little clearing thus formed the concert was being conducted. Ortho crept closer, but could see nothing for a screen of guava-bushes and aloes. A delirious voice bawled something unintelligible, was answered by a long-drawn growl from a score of other voices and a crescendo of drumming. Ortho halted. Whatever language was being used, it certainly was not English or any other civilized tongue. There was something mighty queer afoot in that circle. Caution warned him to look before he leapt.

A big cottonwood, its trunk smothered in creepers, stood at his side, forming a convenient ladder. Ortho climbed twenty feet and looked down, but a young cocorite palm obscured his view. He must go farther up. Ten feet higher was the cottonwood's lowest bough, festooned with lianes, projecting over the clearing like a gallow's arm. Ortho climbed on, straddled the limb and, leaning well over, looked down—looked down and gasped. Was it the West Indies he was in or the dark heart of West Africa?

A red fire glowed in the centre of the clearing, with something roasting on it, and round about squatted a score of ragged negroes, thumping eboe drums, blowing on conch-shells and rattling pigs' bladders filled with pebbles. One of them held a mule's jaw-bone and scraped a stick up and down the teeth.

Circling the blaze was a diabolical creature, a

deformed negro, stark naked except for a cape of
monkey skins. On his head he wore a crown of
vulture feathers and round his neck hung the insignia
of the obi-man—cats' ears, wisps of human hair,
fish bones and alligator teeth. His face was daubed
with white clay, leaving black rings about the eyes
and mouth. His protruding ribs and bones were
picked out with smears of white, giving him the
appearance of an animated skeleton.

He reminded Ortho of an old Dürer print seen
in Exeter.

"Death," he breathed. "The Dancing Death."
Grasping the creepers firmly he leant farther over,
so to see better. The witch-doctor cast some salt
on the flames, which sputtered and burnt blue,
then he went round and round the fire on all fours,
growling, snuffling, baying from time to time as
though he had been a bloodhound on hot scent.
Suddenly he flung himself in the air, writhing, shrieking like a thing in a fit, champing blood and foam.
The surrounding negroes appeared possessed by
a sort of diabolic ecstasy; they drummed and
moaned, uttered bestial cries, their eyeballs rolled
drunkenly, sweat streamed from them. One toppled forwards on his face, apparently insensible.
Some revel of the damned, it seemed, in the ghastly
blue light.

"Escaped African slaves holding a devil-dance,"
thought Ortho, and shuddered. Filthy swine, stupe-
fied with palm-wine, maddened with noise, worse

than wild animals—and in another minute he would
have thrust in among them—phew! What in the
name of Satan, their father, were they up to now?

He craned forwards to see, lost his balance,
clutched a creeper which snapped under his weight
and, emitting an involuntary yell, down he went
into the middle of them.

But he did not reach the ground. The trunk end
of the liane broke, but the outer—laced about the
gallow's bough with a dozen pliant offshoots—held
firm, with the result that Ortho swung right across
the clearing and back again, went on swinging back
and fro like a gigantic clock pendulum. He missed
the ground by a yard, but not the witch-doctor,
whom he caught a terrific blow in the chest, knocking him into the fire. Five swings he made across
the clearing, whooping as he swung. When the
liane came to a standstill there was not a soul to
be seen and Ortho dropped to the ground.

From the dark forest round about came the noise
of bushes being burst asunder, twigs snapping, thuds
of men running blindly into trees, tripping headlong.
Somebody shouted, "Duppy! Duppy!" and was
answered by sobs of terror. Then silence. They
were gone, scattered broadcast. Ortho smacked his
thighs and roared with laughter.

"They called the Devil down in fine shape, that
time," said he and laughed again, highly pleased
with himself—what a story to tell at home! He
must have looked somewhat odd swooping out of

the sky, whooping like seven screech-owls, his rags and tatters flying in the breeze—odd, to say the least. Well, the black heathen had gone leaving him the feast—and just done to a turn, too. Meat at last!—and sufficient for a week—excellent! He licked his lips. The adventure had turned out very prettily. What was the dish? Barbecued pig, or what?

He examined the thing on the spit. No, not pig; shaped all wrong for pig. It was a monkey, by the Lord Harry! He did not know apes of that size grew on the islands. Never mind, monkeys were very good eating, he had heard. He took his knife out, then hesitated—a monkey without a tail! His memory gave a twitch. He had seen something like this before. Where? When? Then he remembered, remembered a day in the Rif Mountains of Morocco and a party of obdurate rebels in a patch of dry thorn. They, the Sultan's forces, had set fire to that thorn. Afterwards. . . .

His laughter died suddenly, puffed out like a candle. A spasm of cold shudders possessed him, sweat soaked his forehead.

"I'm going out of this," he whispered, "out of these curséd woods—*now*."

CHAPTER III

AS a jackal draws to a campfire Ortho Penhale drew to the Great House.

The sugar-mill, slave-cabins, workshops and cattle-pens were huddled together in a clump of abba-palms and pepper-trees, but the Great House stood alone on a knoll at the head of the savannah, dominating its village like a feudal keep. Embowered in double jessamine and convolvulus though it was, the house had the truculent air of a fortified place, being built with all its rooms facing inwards on a central court. The windows were barred with heavy iron grilles, loop-holes pierced the walls. A strong house built in the days of the Spanish occupation when a man lived in dread that any night his slaves might rise, machetes in hand, maroons swoop from the hills or buccaneers from the sea.

Ortho Penhale drew closer. The main gate was open, revealing an empty courtyard, but light shone through the shutter chinks of one window. Somebody was up and about, but all was quiet: there was no dinner party tonight. There had been a dinner party a couple of nights previously, a cheerful affair. Sounds of revelry had reached the lone deserter hidden in the bushes: thick voices uplifted in song, whoops, a pistol shot and brays of laughter.

Later by the light of the moon he had watched the more abstemious guests depart, convivial gentlemen in white, crowned with red bandannas and palm-leaf hats, who hiccupped pleasantries to each other, were hoisted on mule-back and maintained there by attendant slaves. Others left the morning after, and that same morning there was an incident.

Ortho was sucking his fruit breakfast in the bushes when suddenly there came an incoherent bellow from the house, the roar of a savage animal, deep-chested, shattering, and out of the gate rushed a slave pursued by a huge man in his shirt and drawers. The negro ran, but the master bounded, bounded like a tiger, flaming head sunk in his great shoulders, freckled hands outstretched. He gained on the slave, two feet to one, and sprang upon his back, bearing him to the ground. The pair rolled out of sight behind the bushes and Ortho heard the negro scream. The big man rode away south an hour later with a trio of revived guests, laughing and talking: he seemed a genial fellow. The little black vultures attended to the negro.

But on this night all was quiet at the Great House; the festivities appeared to have been transferred to the slave village, whence came a prodigious noise of singing and drumming.

"Rum," thought Ortho. "They've broached a puncheon. The whip all round one day, drink the next—faugh!" He had been four days in the bushes now and knew a good deal about the plantation.

The management was slipshod, to say the least. One morning the drivers would be hounding the slaves afield at sun-up, kicking and abusing them; the next morning there would not be a soul stirring until the day was far advanced. The white book-keepers and overseers quarrelled like dogs over the young negresses and lived openly with them; mulatto and quadroon children were as common as black in the village—a large proportion of these had red hair.

"They'll be drunk tonight, every one of 'em," said Ortho, thinking of the overseers, "sitting at the fires with their black wenches—the trash! I'll go steal a duck."

Duck there were in plenty on the stream below the mill. At night a boy called them in on a conch-shell and shut them in a wicker hut. Turkeys and pigs abounded also, but they would be too much of a handful. A duck would do very nicely. His lips moistened at the thought of a duck spitted through the middle and roasted over a red ash fire. Meat again—he craved for meat.

Since little danger threatened from the village, one thing remained and that was to make sure of the Great House—and there was the mystery man besides. The mystery man was a person who came and went by night stealthily and unattended. Twice Ortho had seen him. He came from the south, from the direction of Marquise, tied his mule up in a clump of guava-bushes on the fringe of the savannah, and made his way towards the Great House, slipping from shrub to shrub.

On the first occasion he had almost surprised Ortho. It was getting on towards dawn and the deserter, who had been on the prowl, was creeping back to his hiding-place, when he heard a stone rattle and stepped behind an orange-bush just in time to avoid colliding with the enigma. As it was, he passed within a few feet, and in the light of the old moon Ortho saw him plainly—a mere boy of about his own height but more slenderly built, with clear-cut, sensitive features—a good-looking lad. He went by in haste, glancing furtively over his shoulder, and was swallowed up in the guava-bushes.

Ortho wondered what his game was. It was clear that he was up to no good and therefore could hardly give a fellow-trespasser away. Still, a meeting was to be avoided if possible. Up to that moment he had not arrived; at least there was no mule secreted in the scrub. Ortho determined to steal his duck and return to cover while the coast was clear. He crept round the bushes for a last glance at the Great House before making the attempt.

Light still showed through the shutter cracks, but there was no movement anywhere, nobody stirring, as far as he could see. A candle lighted and forgotten, probably. Now was the time!

He stepped out of cover and as he did so there

was a hurried patter of light feet, something white rushed out of the darkness, and a pair of soft bare arms went round his neck. Ortho was so startled he could make no move. The last thing on earth he expected to meet was a white woman; he had no idea there was one on the estate. He had come to steal a duck and instead found himself passionately embraced by the lady of the house! He had reason to be surprised. His first impulse was to throw her off and run for safety, but somehow he could not bring himself to it, the arms about his neck were so silken soft, and moreover the woman was in trouble, weeping brokenly, hugging herself to him as to a refuge.

Ortho rather specialized in pretty women in trouble—a little sympathy yielded such bountiful results. Instinctively his arms went round her. "I believe I shall see some fun tonight," he said to himself, and stroked the lady's head.

"O Raoul, I thought you would never come!" she sobbed against his bosom.

"Now I know who I am supposed to be," thought Ortho, "and why that young man comes and goes by night."

"Raoul, Raoul, speak to me! Say you love me still!"

"Time to end this," Ortho decided, crushed her to him and slipped a hand over her mouth.

"Scream and I'll choke you," he said in her ear.

"Keep quiet and you shall come to no harm, no harm whatever, neither you nor yours."

For a moment he thought she had fainted, so quiet she kept, then suddenly she began to fight, to wrench crazily this way and that, beating on his chest with her closed fists, moaning behind the gag of his fingers.

"You'll kill yourself before you hurt me," he warned. "Keep quiet; I mean no harm, do you hear?"

Still she struggled. Ortho was afraid she would work herself into hysterics, and crushed her closer, so close she could not move at all. This had the desired effect. The tattoo on his chest ceased; he heard her gasping for breath and eased the gag somewhat.

"Now will you listen to me, Fury? Will you?"

The woman mastered her nerves with an effort, looked up, her eyes wide with mingled terror and astonishment, and nodded.

"Very good. I am an Englishman, a "run" seaman from the fleet over yonder. I mean no harm to anybody; I am only hiding till the fleet sails. I would not have touched you if you had not rushed into me. I am going to release you in a moment, but before you go I must warn you that I have been in the bushes close by these four days and I know your secret, madam. If you give me away I will share it with—with whoever is interested. If you say nothing, I say nothing, and all is as before. Do we understand each other?"

There was a pause; then she nodded slowly.

"May I take my hand from your mouth, then?" Again the sign.

He released her. She sprang back, turned as if to run, and then hesitated.

There was no moon, but the unclouded night was bright with jewelery of stars, fragrant with blossom, warm as milk, and there were fireflies everywhere, spangling the bushes, sweeping hither and thither like sparks blown on a wind, glints and glitters of living emerald. The woman was dressed in white and Ortho could see her plainly enough where she stood, the fireflies sweeping round her. A young woman, a pretty woman, it would seem; he admired her slim uprightness, the proud poise of her little head. He squared his shoulders and gave thanks that his beard had grown past the stubble stage. If only he had a presentable coat on his back now instead of rags and tatters! He smiled at her and spoke in his smoothest tones.

"I regret I was rough with you, madam, but I was surprised, and be taken and returned to the fleet I will not—not alive."

She made no reply for a moment, then she said: "What do you want here?"

Ortho laughed. "To speak the whole truth, I came to steal a duck."

"A duck! Why?"

"Because I have not tasted meat for weeks and I am neither horse nor ape to thrive on grass and fruit."

Came another pause. Ortho could feel the woman's eyes fixed on him and bore the scrutiny unflinching. His clothes hung in strips, but no matter, he stood six feet one and was as slim-run and taut-muscled as a greyhound. He was a fine figure of a man and well he knew it. Let her look. That duck should be his yet—and more perhaps.

The woman spoke again. "Your speech is not that of a common seaman."

Ortho bowed. "I thank you, lady. I am a land-owner in Cornwall, and in Barbary I commanded a regiment of lances. The press took me."

"Why did you leave the fleet?"

"We had trouble, a Punchinello lieutenant and I. He lost his hat, his wig and his dignity all at the same moment and I laughed at him. He had me flogged for it, so I ran into the woods at Trou Gascon with all the marines in the squadron firing at me. If they do not improve their aim Monseer de Grasse has little to fear."

He picked up her hand and pressed his lips to it. "Bella Donna," said he, "have I your permission to wring that duck's neck? A week more of my present diet and I shall either neigh or swing by my tail."

She snatched her hand from his grasp, but he knew she was not offended.

"Are you very hungry?"

"A dried pea would rattle inside me as in a kettle-drum."

Silence again, a long-drawn, awkward silence, and then the woman spoke, her voice sounding oddly strained, as though she were forcing the words against her will.

"I can offer you something better than raw duck, I think. And possibly a bottle of wine into the bargain. How like you the sound of that?"

"She wants to gag me with good living," said Ortho to himself. "She shall." Then aloud, "How like I the sound? Madam, I have heard violins and harpsichords, the band of the Horse Guards and the bells of St. Mary's Redcliffe, but nothing near so sweet as the words you utter—but how . . . ?"

"Yes?"

"How am I to obtain these delicacies? You will bring them here?"

She stamped her foot. "Huh! am I a slave to fetch and carry for you?"

"I crave your pardon. But how then shall . . . ?"

"You will come to the house, naturally."

"The house?"

"Why not? There is nobody there. They are all drunk in the village. Is Don Desperado afraid then?"

Ortho considered rapidly. The house was a trap. There was but one exit. Once in he might find it impossible to get out. On the other hand what motive could the woman have for betraying him; she had her secret to guard. He decided that she was to be trusted.

"Madam," he said "a hunted man is cautious by habit, but in the presence of such beauty I fear nothing." He bowed low. "Lead on when you will."

She turned and walked rapidly towards the house, Ortho at her heels, his knife loose in its sheath, ready. They passed through the gate into the court. No dog challenged, no servant stirred. It occurred to Ortho that it was not deserted by accident, that the mistress had sent the slaves away to clear the coast for her lover, the lover who had not come. He momentarily wondered why the boy had not come. Had he scented danger anywhere? And, if so, what was the danger? Husband, father, brother? Whatever it was it could not be imminent, else the woman would not have led him into the house. It would have been perfectly simple to let him take his duck and disappear. There was no danger assuredly. Nevertheless he determined that he would not stay long.

His hostess crossed the court and threw a door open. It was a small room but high and without any ceiling: mahogany beams supported the roof-tiles. The floor and furniture were of mahogany also, the latter hasped and hinged with heavy brass fittings and of crude construction, obviously the work of the estate carpenters. A bare white room,

broken up with masses of dark polished wood and
glints of brass. Light came from a pair of heavy
silver candlesticks round which moths fluttered and
insects buzzed.

The woman motioned him to a chair and was
gone.

Ortho looked about him. There was a sofa in
one corner littered with odds and ends of sewing.
A *prie-Dieu* stood against the wall with a sacred
picture above it. Not the dining-room certainly,
but, for all its austerity, an intimate, feminine room.
Since she intended to feed him he wondered why
he had not been shown into the dining-room. Oh,
well, it was her house; doubtless she knew best.

A small mirror in a gilt frame hung over the sofa.
In it he had the first look at himself for weeks, and
the sight was less shocking than he had expected.
If his hair was longer than he liked, the short beard
and moustache rather suited him, made a frame for
his fine teeth. He smiled, displaying his teeth, and
admired the white gleam of them.

"You have the young moon in your mouth," an
old gypsy woman had said to him, adding sourly,
"and moonshine."

Ortho was pleased with his reflection. Not so
bad, all things considered. If only he had a sound
coat to his back! "Don Desperado" she had
called him; well, she had good cause. He looked
desperate enough in all conscience, with his long hair
and earrings and clothing hanging in strips—a

veritable wild man of the woods. Ortho smoothed
his new moustache and winked at his reflection.

He heard a step at the door and whirled about.
It was only the woman bringing food, half a cold
capon and a mountain mullet. She set these down
and went out again, returning with some ribs of
pork and two bottles of wine. She wagged her
finger at him.

"What are you waiting for? Eat, eat if you are
as hungry as you said."

Ortho laughed. "Indeed I am even hungrier—
now I see all these delicacies."

He fell on the mullet as a famished dog falls on
a beef bone, finished it and picked the capon to the
bare shell. The woman poured out a glass of wine
and passed it to him and when he had drained that,
another, and another.

Ortho polished off the pork and lay back in his
chair replete.

"More?" she offered. "You have only to
say . . . ?"

He shook his head. "I was hard put to stow that
last. Never have I enjoyed a meal more than this,
madam. If hunger got the better of my manners
just now, I crave indulgence—also for my appearance. I have seen rough weather of late and, as
you will perceive, my paint-work is somewhat tarnished."

"But not your audacity, it would seem."

Ortho laughed. "No, madam, never that. I

carry royals in all weathers. Not for any gale that blows will I strike my royals."

"You have a stout heart, sir," said the woman, with a hint of cynicism.

"Indeed it is all I have at the moment," said Ortho, and tapped his knife. "That and a sharp friend here. No matter. Today is a beggar, but tomorrow may be a king. I trust to those royals—but my manners again!" He raised his glass. "To my lovely benefactress!"

She made acknowledgement with a slight bow.

A pretty woman, Ortho thought, older than he had surmised from the slenderness of her figure, in the late twenties maybe, or even the mid-thirties —these Creoles aged devilish quick—but still very well worth a man's civility. Her bare arms were beautifully moulded and she carried her head like a queen. Masses of thick dark hair she had and big eyes like troubled pools. She must have been a real beauty in her day, Ortho imagined, a flame to set men burning. But now there were faint creases and shadows here and there about the eyes and mouth, silver streaks in the piled tresses, and her pallor was deathly. Summer turning, he thought, beauty on the wane, clutching at any little straw of admiration, even that of a boy ten years her junior, she who in her day had spurned half the gallants of Kingston or Port of Spain. Madeira and good feeding made him sentimental. How sad it was that **all soft** and lovely things were so short-lived!

Women, roses, rainbows—a year, a day, a second—
then pest! all gone. Very sad!

He consoled himself with another glass of wine.
When he looked up it was to find his hostess had
left the room. She returned a moment later carrying something over her arm which she handed to
him.

Ortho examined the offering. It was a single-
breasted broadcloth riding coat, heavily frogged
and of excellent quality.

"Madam! . . . for me?"

She nodded. "You have need of something,
sleeping in the woods. Put it on."

Ortho hustled into the coat, to find it overhung
even his tall frame.

"The man who wore this must have been well
grown," he said.

"Hello, there is money in the pocket, pistoles by
the feel of 'em."

"They are pistoles and I trust they may be of
service to you," said the woman.

"You overwhelm me with kindness, madam. I
do not know how to find words to thank you."

"Do not try," she said drily. "The bottle stands
beside you, pray help yourself. The night is yet
young and I presume you have no pressing engage-
ment elsewhere."

"If I had, it would no longer press me."

"You are gallant, sir."

"I am on fire, madam," Ortho replied and, seizing her hand, kissed it again.

He was getting on famously, he told himself, making a great impression. He had only known this woman an hour and yet here she was piling food, drink, clothing and money on him, entertaining him alone in her fine house at eleven at night. So far, excellent. A little farther and even better. He proceeded to make himself attractive, told stories of his smuggling escapades in Cornwall; of his voyage to Barbary in the hold of a pirate xebec and slavery in Sallee; of cavalry raids in the desert and hand-to-hand encounters among the Atlas crags. A pleasant voice he had, vivacity, and the trick of story-telling. He had held the whole larboard watch of an Indiaman tense with his yarns and seen soldiers fight for a place beside his campfire, but, charm he never so wisely, he could not hold this woman's attention. She sat before him white and rigid as marble except for her restless eyes. When she laughed her laughter came in mechanical jangles and at the wrong time; her comments were inapt. She was not listening—to him. This irritated Ortho; he was not used to having his best stories so treated. The woman seemed to be uneasy, on the *qui vive*. At the slightest sound, the rustle of a creeper outside, the whine of a shutter hinge, she cocked her head and drew breath sharply. He became uneasy himself and rose to leave.

"The hour advances, madam. I . . ."

She placed small ringed hands on his shoulders and pressed him back. "Chute! where are your manners, sir? I have not yet dismissed you. Do you so much prefer the *croch-chien* bushes and the fer-de-lance to my company? Sit down, I pray, and entertain me further."

"Madam is expecting somebody?"

She glanced at him sharply. "What makes you say that?"

"You appear to be listening for something . . . footsteps perhaps?"

"Did you spend half your nights here alone you, too, would be listening for footsteps," said the woman with bitterness, "footsteps, very soft and stealthy. It is on still nights like this I think I hear them, creeping through the gate, across the yard, up to the door, hundreds of bare black feet. I tell you every time the night winds stir the latch I can barely keep from screaming." She hid her face in her hands. "Four years I have been here."

"This woman is a little mad," said Ortho to himself. "but nevertheless exceedingly comely. She will serve my purpose very well, till the fleet sails." He placed a reassuring hand upon her shining shoulder, felt it quiver beneath his touch. "There, there, have no fear. You are alone no longer. Maroons shall not molest you while I am about. Maroons! Why I fell headlong into a party of 'em up yonder and, stap me! they all fled screechin'. Maroons . . . ha-ha!"

Sitting again, he opened the third bottle and lifted his glass. "To the Queen of the Antilles!"

She bowed. "My thanks, King of Flatterers—then you will not desert me for the allurements of the guava-bushes just yet, hein?" She sparkled at him, the coquette all over, the horror of the previous moment wiped clean.

"I protest, madam, that had I my way I would never leave you."

"A pretty speech, so glib methinks it is not the first time you have made it. Continue your history. Tell me about Bombay and the East. You had gay adventures there? Tell me."

Her eyes danced, her mouth curved roguishly, quick colour flushed her cheek—and was gone as quickly. "Ah!" An alarming change came over her; stiff she went and ashen pale. She drew a long breath as a swimmer before plunging, closed her eyes and swayed.

"Swooning," said Ortho, catching her in his arms, and as he caught her knew that she was not swooning. She clung to him strongly enough, her head on his shoulder facing the door. He could feel the furious beat of her heart, the tremors that shook her from head to foot. He laughed in triumph. His, his, the proud lady! Two hours ago an outcast in the thickets, now wrapped in snowy arms! Rags and tatters went for naught against a bold and merry spirit. Women—he knew the way with women. It was a rich good world, full of spice and laughter. He kissed the ash-pale cheek and felt fire beneath the ashes; kissed the bent neck, the silver shoulder, glanced up and saw a face in the mirror, a great freckled, bestial face surmounted by a blaze of red hair.

Ortho pushed the woman from him and whirled about just as the other charged. The red man came for him in a blind headlong rush, so headlong, that Ortho avoided it without difficulty and went dodging through the furniture, the great brute groping after him.

"Hold fast! Let me speak! There's no harm done!" Ortho implored. As well to treat with a stag royal that finds another among his hinds. The man caught up a chair and struck at him. Ortho picked up a second to guard himself. They thrashed the two chairs to splinters and went on again, overturning the table, trampling the broken crockery to powder. All the time Ortho's inner voice was saying, "She *must* have known he was coming; *must* have known. Why did she do it? What is the meaning of this?" Twice he was forced into a corner but managed to get clear by sending lefts and rights to his opponent's face. He caught a glimpse of the woman as he backed round, crouched under cover of the heavy *garde-robe,* heard her hiss some advice he could not grasp, felt her hand snatch at his belt. Then he fell, a rug slipped on the polished floor and down he went with the red man on top of him.

They rolled over and over among the broken bottles and splintered chairs, feeling for holds. The red man fought with a dumb, senseless fury that was terrifying. Never had Ortho encountered such crazy strength. He hoisted Penhale as though he had been a hay-truss, banged him against walls and furniture, tumbled on him, crushed him against the floor, wallowed on him and hoisted him again. One cannot take the offensive against a tornado. There was but one thing for Ortho to do and that was to grip tight and keep the freckled hands off his chin, from snapping his neck as they had that slave's. He wove himself about the great body, dug his chin well in and hung on with all his twelve stone of weight, praying that the red brute was human and would tire. But the other showed no signs of weakness. He got one hand on Ortho's forehead and tried to break the grip, then suddenly butted him against the corner of the *garde-robe*.

The corner took Ortho between the shoulder-blades and on the back of the head and the candles went out—snip! He woke up convinced that he was dead. Then he noticed that there were two candles burning. When he left earth there were two silver candles burning, and now in the hereafter there were two silver candles burning—odd coincidence! There was a curious booming in his ears, too, and something heavy sprawling over him. He wondered if it were his earthly body, sloughed like a snakecast. What was that against the light?

A woman. Why a woman? Oh, yes, of course. Consciousness returned almost as abruptly as it had gone. Of course. He was lying in that room with his neck broken, neither quite alive nor quite dead. He remembered a lancer in Morocco falling from his horse, breaking his neck and living for days. Why was his murderer lying on top of him like this, clawing him? He could do no more harm.

"Are you going to stop there forever, fool?" came the woman's voice from a long way off. "Get up, can't you?"

"Can I?" said Ortho stupidly.

"I know no reason why you should not."

Ortho was amazed. Wasn't his neck broken? He turned his head cautiously this way and that and found all intact. Strange! The man was still sprawling on top of him, but there was no power in his grip. He struggled free, stood up, found his hands all over blood, his thighs and chest smeared in it. There was blood everywhere. The spot where he had fallen was slimy with it. "Lord!" he gasped. "How? Where . . . ?" Then he saw that there was a knife sticking into the giant's back, a sailor's sheath-knife with O. P. carved on the haft—his knife!

The man on the ground made a convulsive movement and turned over on his side, blinking his eyes as though facing too bright a light. The woman went down on her knees beside him. "Adieu, Olaf. A small return for fourteen years' neglect, insult and brutality here and elsewhere. Adieu!!"

"Look you," said Ortho huskily, pointing to the knife. "I had no hand . . . You, you did that."

The woman nodded calmly, her mouth drooping in scorn.

"Certainly. But who will believe you?"

Ortho stared aghast. "You mean?"

"I mean that in a quarter of an hour I shall recover from the swoon into which I fell on witnessing my beloved husband's murder and shall then give the alarm." She bent and wrenched the bedrabbled knife free. "O. P.," she mused, reading the initials. "I should advise you to run, O. P."

"That I will not, you she-devil," Ortho raged. "Oh, I understand now. You lure me in so that your husband should find me with you, and when he did it would be a case of kill or be killed for me— eh? You wanted a clear way for your puppy lover, your precious Raoul. But I didn't stick your husband. You snatched the knife from my belt and did it yourself. *You* did it and I shall say so. See?"

The woman shrugged her shoulders. "Certainly I did it, since you could not. But who will believe you—Runaway?"

Who *would* believe him, the "run" seaman, ragged, bearded, smothered in blood? How could he explain his presence in the Great House at that hour, the wreckage, the knife-wound,—anything? Ortho saw in a flash that he had not a leg, not a toe, to stand on. She had him trapped, the little slim woman. Instead of making her his tool she had made him hers, and never for an instant had she considered him as anything but a tool to be used and thrown away. She had used him as one would a mastiff, a silly fighting animal. Of all the blows he had taken, that at his vanity stung the most. He fairly quivered with it.

"Give me that knife!" he demanded, hitching his belt.

She shook her head. "Your sharp friend? No, I need it as evidence. If you come a step nearer I shall begin screaming at once, and, I warn you, I can scream very loud. I should go if I were you."

Her face relaxed, her lips trembled, tears filled her eyes. The last traces of youth dropped from her; she looked old, haggard and pathetically frail.

"You had best go," she stammered. "I shall scream soon . . . I cannot help myself . . . fourteen years' bondage all over . . . run, O. P.!" She stood swaying, one hand pressed to her heart, one clutching the knife. At her feet among the shattered bottles and upturned furniture the red bondmaster lay sprawled, redder than ever. Moths danced round the silver candlesticks, shadows nodded across the walls. From the slave-village came the *rub-a-dub* of eboe drums and the squeal of a pipe.

"Run!"

Ortho came out of his daze and ran, out of the

grim house across the court and into the bushes. Every second he expected a scream, but it did not come and the drums went on undisturbed. "She has swooned in good earnest," he thought, and fought his way through the thorns and creepers upwards and westwards over the hills. Not till he had been running half an hour did he remember that he wore the murdered man's coat and carried a pocketful of his money. He tore the coat off and pitched it furiously aside.

"Pest!" he cried. "That she-devil thought of everything!"

"Push off! Push off!" brawled the pinnace midshipman. "We're last as it is. D'you want to be left behind? Shift yourselves, you scum! Hello! Lord save us, what's this?"

A man, naked but for a few rags of clothing and his belt, lacerated with thorns from head to heel, burst out of the scrub and staggered down the beach towards them, hands extended, shouting, "Stop, stop!"

"Avast," said the midshipman to his rowers. "Who are you?"

"Deserter from the *Triton* frigate," panted the wild man, splashing through the shallows towards the boat. "Want to rejoin, sir. Please take me aboard."

The officer grunted, *"Triton's* ten leagues to

the north'ard with Byron. But I'll take you. Come aboard and get forrard."

Ortho tumbled aboard and went forward as bidden, noticing for the first time that there was an unwonted stir in the fleet. Sail was a-trip on all the great first-rates and they were hove short on their cables ready to weigh.

"French out?" he whispered to the bowman.

"Aye, out and gone. Signalled at eight bells."

"What boat is this?"

"The *Duke's.*"

Ortho whistled. He was in for the battle, after all.

CHAPTER IV

ORTHO was roused from his slumbers between two lower-deck guns by the sudden electric excitement running through the ship. What was the matter? Matter, God save us! why the French fleet were broad on the lee bow, standing south, and there was a lame first-rate in tow of a frigate not two leagues distant. Fleet action at last!

He rubbed the sleep from his astonished eyes and ran to the upper deck to witness for himself what dawn had revealed. Sure enough there was the enemy away to the northeast, a clump of six line-of-battle ships with a huge three-decker in the centre, the rest of the fleet scattered away to the horizon. Close at hand was the cripple with her frigate, toiling painfully before the wind for shelter in Basse Terre. Right into their hands!

It was incredible. For four days the slow old British ships had been pursuing the fast French along the shores of Martinique and Dominica, baffled by calms and contrary winds. There had been a brush off Prince Rupert's Bay on April ninth, but on the evening of the eleventh De Grasse had been nearly out of sight. And what had Rodney done? Gone after them? Not he. Manœuvred up and down the Saintes Passage all night with lights out and lured them back to pick up laggards. Now, at dawn on the twelfth they were almost within touch. As Ortho watched, four of Hood's smartest broke out of the rear and made to cut off the cripple.

Would De Grasse sacrifice the *Zélé* or come to the rescue? All eyes in the British fleet were fixed on the great three-decker, *Ville de Paris*. Would he accept the challenge? Would he? He would. As they watched, the French admiral ported his helm and made sail, firing signal guns to call his fleet up. Cheer upon cheer rang out from the British line.

An old tar beside Ortho gave a cackle of joy. "He's formin' on the port tack—he's done, done."

"How?"

"Weather shore, blangetted by that island, o' course," pointing a shapeless finger at the coast of Dominica. "Head on into the calms, the heathen!"

They were piped down to breakfast.

The veterans of Barrington's, Byron's and Hyde Parker's days munched with deliberation—the galley fires were already doused; it would be the last meal before the battle was over, for better or worse —but the younger men were too excited, anxious to be on deck and watch developments.

The veterans dredged the messkits to the bare bottom, and, after the kindly manner of old hands, hailed each other for the benefit of boys on the threshold of their first action.

"Ahoy there, Ned—very full of spirit our young laddies are just now—eh?"

"Aye, the pretty pap-suckers."

"How d'y think they'll be lookin' an hour on?"

"White as suds, George, white as suds."

"I warrant—where they ain't splashed with t'other's guts. We'll see some comicals then, Ned."

"You're right, George—Doctor Grasse'll serve 'em pills they won't throw up."

"Shiverin', are you?" an aged salt enquired of Ortho, tobacco-stained mouth gaping with malevolent enjoyment. Ortho shook his head.

"I've seen enough blood to float this trow," said he. "Hand-to-hand and none o' your cut-and-run cannonading." He looked the wizened mariner up and down. "In the army I come from we'd have set you with the baggage, you bilge-rat!"

He spoke a great deal more boldly than he felt, determined to keep his feather high as long as possible.

The rolling war-drums beat to quarters, producing a sensation in Ortho as if the very sticks were thumping on his nerves—thud—thud—rumble—thud.

Yards were slung in chains, battle-lanterns hung, decks cleared and sanded over. Down in the magazines powder-monkeys were busy filling cartridges and running them up to the guns. Down in bilge-stinking cock-pits surgeons and their loblolly boys sat in the feeble light of dips and waited the grisly inundation, joking with bedraggled women.

Ortho's business was running powder and ball to the marine sharpshooters on the foretop. Having to wait his turn at the after magazine he could not go aloft immediately. When he did, all was in readiness. On all three decks the guns were run out, pig-tailed crews grouped about them, stripped to the waist, with handkerchiefs knotted over their ears to deaden the noise of explosions. They were like boys before a hurling match. They sang, they danced, put last touches of polish on their pieces and, charging their rum tots with gunpowder, drank them off to "old Rod," to the French admiral, and blowsy inconstants left behind years ago on Portsmouth Hard.

On the quarter-deck Alan Gardner and his officers were parading in their best gold lace as for a levée. It was a foible with these gentlemen to appear, if needs be, before their Maker as gentlemen.

Ortho, slung about with flasks of powder and bags of bullets, went up the foremast shrouds into the top.

The two fleets were approaching fast on opposite tacks. The British were in line of battle ahead, one cable's interval between ships, but the French had not yet formed: De Grasse in his spirited determination to save the *Zélé* and the *Astrée* had been too impetuous, the weather shore was baffling him.

Drake's division of twelve formed the British van, with the *Marlborough* 74 in the place of honour.

The *Duke* was seventeenth in the line. Immediately following her was the centre flagship, Rodney's *Formidable*, with the huge lion rampant on her bow and the white ensign flying at her main.

On came the French fleet, on and on. Thirty-four towering ships of the line officered by the flower of the old French noblesse. The Comte de Grasse flew the white. Bougainville, the circumnavigator, was admiral of the van, the Marquis de Vaudreuil of the rear. The explorer La Perouse and the Comte de Vaudreuil, first lover of the disastrous Gabrielle Yolande de Polignac, both had commands. Bruix and Decrés, later Napoleon's ministers of marine, were midshipmen. Serving in the fleet as cadets were Magnon, L'Hermite, Troude, Williamez and Bourayne, all destined to be admirals under the First Empire. Aboard the *Astrée* was the great Marquis de Bouillé, commander-in-chief of the French army in the West Indies. And that is but to mention a few; nobles and notables crowded the French fleet that fateful day, a debonair and gallant company.

They pressed their beautiful big ships to meet the enemy, forming line as best they might.

Old Rodney, too racked with gout to climb his poop ladder, sat in an armchair on the quarter-deck and watched them grimly, rubbing his hands.

Three days before he had backed his topsail and challenged the *Ville de Paris* to combat—declined. This time, M. de Grasse would have no option; they would cross swords, admiral and admiral.

Ortho Penhale, high on the *Duke's* foretop, watched the enemy too, but with different emotions.

He could see nothing of the British but the next ahead—Lord Robert Manners' *Resolution*—so perfect was the alignment, but the French were in full view and never had he seen a more lovely sight. So filled with their splendour was he that he forgot they were lethal engines bent on his destruction.

Southwards they swept under all plain sail, the foam sparkling along their black water-belts. Blue bulwarks they had and the lashed port lids showed scarlet. Their canvas shone white, three towers of ivory to each ship. Sunshine gleamed on the varnished yellow sides, glittered on the gilt figureheads. To windward swam the pretty frigates, graceful as girls. The beauty of the scene brought Ortho's heart to his throat.

"Oh, *ziné, ziné,*" he muttered in Arabic—"lovely, lovely!"

Fifteen miles away to the north the little Saintes Isles broke out of the blue sea; behind them loomed the heights of Guadeloupe. Northwest lay the flats of Marie Galante; southwest and close at hand Dominica with the mighty cone of Diablotin smoking with morning mists. Fairy islands in a jewelled sea and two trim fleets hastening to wreak bloody havoc on one another.

Below, the *Duke's* band had struck up "Hearts of Oak." Waisters and upperdeck gunners huzzaed and sang with it. The big drum boomed, side-drums rattled, wind instruments blared bravely.

In the French fleet the bands were playing "Vive Henri Quatre" with no less vigour.

A sort of grim elation possessed Ortho. Seventy line of battleships, not to speak of frigates, coming together bent on wholesale murder. In a minute this entrancing scene would be one mad maelstrom of thunder, lightning, smoke and flying iron. It was terrific and he was in it. Whether he lived or died he would have seen something. Ahead a gun slammed, two, three, then several together.

"French thirty-thix pounderth," lisped the Welsh midshipman in charge of the top, a plump gentleman in the mid-twenties. "We'll hear from Taylor Penny in a minute."

More guns, desultory, followed by a broadside, but still no reply from the *Marlborough*.

Below a bell chimed eight brazen notes—eight o'clock.

The four leaders of the French van came in sight on the port bow, all of a huddle, standing due south.

The midshipman damned them for runaways. "They're holdin' their luff!" he cried. "Pay off four pointh an' let uth get at you, you filth!"

A loud huzza came up from the deck—the Welsh-
man clapped his palms together. "Red flag hath
broke," he announced. "Penny ith in touch—
Yah!"

Crash! went the *Marlborough's* first broadside,
every gun in unison. Crash! went the *Arrogant,*
crash! and crash! again; and the *Alcide* took up
the tale and so on down the line as each ship came
up, put her helm down and sidled along the French
rank, lashing broadside after broadside into the
opposite vessels as they hove, one by one, out of
the smoke. Battle was joined.

Ortho lay stretched on the top platform, peering
ahead. In a minute or so it would be their turn.
Leaning across he shouted in the ear of a marine,
"I'll give you a month's pay for your musket." But
the man shook his head and cuddled the stock lov-
ingly to his cheek. A three-decker lolled towards
them, the entire hull wrapped in vapour, nothing
visible but her topsails and royals, the former riddled.

"Here comth ourth," sang the midshipman.
"Whoo!"

The fog that wrapped the enemy ship was jagged
with myriad tongues of fire, the foretop was swept
with a shrieking storm of iron, and at the same
moment came a detonation from below as if the
Duke had burst asunder. Ortho saw the Frenchman's mast-trucks reel. He lay on the top, clutching the grating with both hands, dizzy, scared,

stunned with noise, expecting the whole perilous
fabric that bore him to go toppling over. A block
came down, the end of a topsail buntline and a man,
turning over and over like a circus acrobat. Again
the *Duke's* smashing broadside, again and again,
rocking the entire ship.

Then the voice of the midshipman exulting, "By
the holy thath thickened 'em! Right into his
porth!"

Seizing his speaking-trumpet he bawled to some
yard-arm men to throw gaskets round the clewed-
up course.

"Here comth the next!"

The upper canvas of another enemy approached
through the murk. Ortho clung on, both eyes closed,
awaiting the shriek of the grape. The ancient salt
he had rebuked so boldly earlier in the day would
have got his own back then—he was frightened
stiff. It was the fall he particularly dreaded. Going aloft in a squall on the tall East Indiaman for
the first time had been bad enough, but there had
been sound spars under him. Now everything was
shredded and splintered. A couple of true shots
into the foremast and they were by the board,
pitched headlong. The French always fired high to
wing their opponents; they were bound to go.
Every time the *Duke* jarred with the recoil of her
broadsides he thought his last moment had come.
Another ship loomed up, loosed her iron hurricane,
and passed on. A marine, leaning against the top-

mast ratlines, gasped, let his musket fall, turned slowly on his heel and dropped out of sight. The musket fell against Ortho. Mechanically he picked it up and loaded.

Two-thirds of the British were in action now; the cannonading was ear-splitting, incessant thunder-claps; the pouring smoke stung tears from the eyes; one breathed sulphur, smelt burning. Nothing was to be seen but upper canvas above and leaping tongues of flame below. The ships fumbled for each other through a hanging fog. Ortho could not discern the deck of his own vessel. Admiration filled him for the men in the cramped gun-decks, choked, blinded, pounded unmercifully, yet never faltering for an instant. As each enemy hove up, the *Duke's* three decks vomitted fire together, three volleys for two. And the officers—Rodney, old and sick—walking the swept poops in their blue and gold, groping inflexibly ahead through pit-dark and hell-fire. Pride rose up in him, pride for the company he kept.

Sighting the musket with care he fired for the opposite foretop, saw a Frenchman reel—or thought he did. He loaded and fired into the next, went on firing, coolly and rapidly. All fear was gone from him now. Ortho Penhale vanished, a frigid autom-aton took his place, firing, reloading, firing, re-loading, oblivious of all else. The foretop sail was shot adrift at the weather clew; it flogged and thrashed above him like an animate, wounded thing; but he took no notice.

Grape from a swivel killed the man beside him, fleshed the midshipman and seared his own shoulder; he paid no heed, but picked off a man in the opposite main-rigging, a masterly shot.

The midshipman sent him down with a message to the first lieutenant. He laid aside his musket with reluctance and was back inside of eight minutes.

The lieutenant was on the main-deck at the moment and Ortho had to go below to find him, plunging down from the brown fog of the upper deck into a black sulphur pit. Battle-lanterns hung here and there, mere feeble stars, illuminating nothing.

Invisible quarter-gunners, hoarse with saltpetre, shouted for cartridges, quills and flints, barked orders. Unseen gun-crews yo-hoed, gasping, at the tackles. Powder-monkeys skurried hither and thither, yelping, "Way! way!" Carriage-guns rumbled as they ran out. Handspikes thumped. Wounded, lying anywhere and anyhow, groaned for loblolly boys, water.

Suddenly the whole deck lit up with one blinding red flash. Ortho had an instantaneous vision of half-naked men standing braced as against a blow, arms thrown up over their heads, matted chests black with powder, drenched with sweat; the lieutenant right before him, eyes shut, teeth clenched; a dismounted gun lying on top of a beastly crimson

mess, its crew; the lanterns jumping on their hooks
all together.

He fell over on his hands as the ship recoiled,
convinced that he was deaf for life. When he
looked up the smoke was pouring back through the
ports and all was dark again—but the gunners were
already reloading. Having delivered his message
he scampered for daylight as fast as he could, but
they fired two more volleys before he was clear and
a French double-shot came through close beside
with a crash like the world's end. He could see
nothing, but he heard a gun-captain cry out in the
darkness that his crew was gone.

Regaining the top he found the midshipman hopping about and waving his hat at an oncoming
enemy.

"Bong jaw, Moothoo Grath! Come for a bit
o' parley voo, Moothoo l'Admiral?"

It was the *Ville de Paris* unmistakably: the big-
gest ship in the world, mounting 110 guns. Half
seen in the fog bank, she looked enormous, devas-
tating; but the *Resolution* cheered undismayed and
slashed three broadsides in as she went by. So did
the *Duke*, but the flagship astern gave her four,
double-shotted. The leviathan quivered throughout
and wallowed on, barely replying. Old Rodney
hobbled to his cabin and drank a lemonade on the
strength of it.

"Moothoo le Comte hath the belly-ache . . .

beaucoup malade!" chirped the midshipman and ran aloft to supervise the fishing of a chipped spar.

Ortho picked up his musket again and fired into the fo'csle of the *Couronne.* The *Eveillé* went by, terribly mauled, then the *Sceptre,* and up came the *Glorieux.* The *Duke's* first rounds staggered her, the following finished her off. She swam up a proud ship, dropped astern a sheer hulk, all three masts trailing overside; captain dead; sides gaping, showing the carnage within; deathly silent except for a heroic sergeant of Auxerrois infantry yelling defiance over the taffrail. All round her the sharks crowded, thrashing, fighting, tearing for the bodies of the top-men. The French threw their dead over as they dropped and the sea was alive with sharks, hanging in dense packs about each ship like wolves round a foundering stag, ready to rush.

The midshipman came sliding down the topmast ratlines, the expression on his face of one who has seen the wonders of the Lord. "Three masth at onth—one, two, three . . . like that . . . clean thweep!" he panted. "Hallelujah!"

Four more ships went by; then, without the slightest warning, the wind shifted to the south and came in a strong puff throwing the French out of formation. They had either to swing head-on to the enemy or be taken aback. They swung into bow and quarter line, echelon—those that were smart enough.

The midshipman danced and crowed, too full-

hearted for coherent utterence; went hand over hand
to the topsail yard to get a better view and screamed
aloud. "Through, through! Old Rod hath luffed
up! He'th breakin' their line! Through!" In his
excitement he lost his footing, only saving himself
by a miracle. It was as he said. Seizing the shift
of wind the admiral had headed the *Formidable*
through the gap between the *Glorieux* and the
Diadem.

Alan Gardner followed suit. Round came the
Duke, blazing with all port and starboard batteries
together; to the men on the top she seemed split
transversely by a solid sheet of flame.

The French ships replied gamely, but they were
done, hopelessly huddled, their line cut in three
(later, by the inspired blundering of the *Bedford*,
in four). But still they fired, indomitable to the
bitterest of bitter ends.

A lame attempt at a volley sang over the *Duke's*
waist, a spatter of grape whined through the foremast rigging. A bullet flicked the midshipman on
the knuckles. He took no notice, but leaned against
the mast, wiping the sweat from his fat face, too
moved to speak.

The marine beside Ortho jerked his musket in
and polished the breech with his sleeve, observing,
"Well, they won't join up with the Dons *now* . . .
nor get Jamaica. Hello, where did all this blood
come from?"

"Me," said Ortho feebly. "That last volley . . . I . . . I think I'm . . . dying."

He was no longer the cold automaton but Ortho Penhale again, no longer the impersonal unit of a vast machine but one poor lonely man in mortal pain.

"Don't throw me to those sharks—yet . . . I . . . " his voice dwindled into a whisper and then ceased.

"What did you say?" the marine enquired.

He got no answer.

The marine went on polishing his musket. "Thought he said somethin' about 'Owls.' "

CHAPTER V

THE Comte de Grasse dined on board the *Formidable* as Rodney's guest the day after his defeat and sailed on the first convoy to England, where he was hospitably entertained and had his sword returned to him by King George. The same reception was not accorded this gallant but unfortunate man in his own country: he was banished from Court and nearly torn to pieces by the Tuileries mob.

Rodney took his battered ships to Port Royal and there received orders to hand over to a non-entity named Pigot and come home—virtually in disgrace. He returned home to be rewarded with the thanks of the nation, a peerage and £2000 a year. The reason for this surprising *volte face* was as follows: Rodney was a Tory, Pigot a Whig and the Whigs had come into power. Rodney was the first sailor of his age, Pigot had not been to sea since he was an undistinguished captain; but no matter, Rodney was a Tory, Pigot a Whig, so the Government replaced the former by the latter, *pro bono publico*. Two days after Pigot had left London, news of Rodney's staggering victory came to hand. The Cabinet saw apoplectic citizens, bunting

in hand, hanging perilously out of upper windows
while anxious families clung to their coat-tails;
heard the guns of the shipping in the Pool emulating
those of the Tower, and the wild cheers of the mob
in Whitehall cheering that England was England
yet—and the Cabinet bit their thumbs. They
strained every means to recall Pigot, but that gentleman was well away, racing westward to reap the
fruits of political acumen. So, with the agility which
distinguishes a British Cabinet when its existence is
at stake, the Government turned about face and
loaded Rodney with honours, but with the worst
grace they could accomplish, for, though the fellow
had saved his country, he was still a Tory.

However, the vicissitudes of admirals mattered
little to Ortho Penhale, ordinary seaman.

All the way to Jamaica he lay in the *Duke's*
cavernous sick-berth, floating in and out of consciousness, on the twilit borderland of life and death.
Around him lay men without legs and arms, blinded,
horribly charred and lacerated. The tight-packed
hammocks jostled each other every time the ship
rolled, and the men groaned miserably. The surgeons and boys did their rough best for them, but
it amounted to little.

Ortho was not nearly as badly wounded as he
thought. A shred of grape had entered his right
shoulder and torn its way outside the ribs without
injuring anything vital, but he had lost a bucketful

of blood before they could sling him down from aloft, and fainted from sheer weakness.

It was eighteen days before the fleet saw the Palisados and heard the Kingston merchantmen thundering their royal salute, and by that time Ortho was on the mend.

At Port Royal he was sent ashore into hospital and at the end of July informed that he was to be returned home and discharged at the first opportunity—his mother and Eli had been busy. He had heard no more of the affair on St. Lucia and did not expect to. They were probably still beating the woods for him, little dreaming that he was eleven hundred miles away. The last place they would look for a deserter was back in the Fleet. Even were the matter pursued the bearded wild man of the forests was hardly recognizable in the shorn, emaciated convalescent of Port Royal. Ortho was not frightened of being brought to book, nevertheless he felt that an ocean placed between him and the scene of his supposed crime would add somewhat to his comfort and was therefore relieved when sent aboard the *Harwich*, frigate, under orders for England.

The *Harwich* left Port Royal on August 23rd, and brought up in Negril Bay on the following evening. A fleet of eighty home-bound merchantmen had collected in the bay under the protection of a second-rate and some frigates and sloops of war. The convoy sailed on August 27th by way of Cape San

Antonio and the Florida stream. It was slow travelling. Many of the merchantmen were poorly found, trailed a foot of weed and were overgrown with barnacles. In light airs they were immovable, in blowing weather they split canvas and blundered foul of each other. Off Grand Cayman, with the wind fair, a lot of them hove to and set to work capturing green turtles with which the sea was covered. The two-decker plodded inexorably on, under short canvas, firing testy signal guns. The frigates and sloops rounded the merchantmen as collies round sheep, when curses availed not, passing out tow-ropes and dragging laggards bodily into the fleet. Despite their vigilance two Liverpool vessels fell behind off the Cuban coast during the night and were captured by privateers.

It was not until the middle of October that they were in soundings on the Newfoundland Banks and there fog and squalls came upon them, scattering the traders broadcast. On November 10th they spoke a Falmouth packet, outward bound. The three-year siege of Gibraltar had terminated in the repulse of the combined forces of France and Spain, she told them. The "old cock of the Rock," General Eliott, had set their floating batteries ablaze by firing red-hot shot at them. Further, there was talk of peace with the revolted American colonies.

Next day they were in soundings and the shipping for the St. George's and Bristol Channels broke away. The remainder of the fleet rounded the Scilly

Islands during the night of the fourteenth and on the evening of the eighteenth the *Harwich* swam past the green shores of Wight on the flood-tide and dropped anchor on the Motherbank, twelve weeks out from Jamaica.

Four days later Ortho was paid off. Negotiations with the Americans were actually taking place in Paris and general peace was in the air. The press tenders let merchantman after merchantman pass them unsearched, and quantities of naval seamen were discharged as unfit who at other times would have been sent to man lower yards.

Ortho, along with a score of these gentry, West Country men all, took passage in a coaster for Falmouth. They laid in a plentiful store of liquor, no edibles to speak of, and hired a fiddler to accompany them. Some had lost eyes, others limbs, but this did not damp their spirits. They were both boisterous and mischievous, like so many lads home-bound after long bondage. They set the fiddler on the capstan, bade him scrape his best, and, manning the bars, hauled the anchor out of the ground in no time, singing and stamping. Chronic seasickness having claimed the fiddler, the evening was consecrated to eating and drinking.

Next morning the wind had gone round to the westward. The captain was for sheltering under Portland Isle but his arbitrary passengers would not hear of it. "Work to windward, you shore-crab!" said they. "Drive her at it. If you don't we will!"

As they outnumbered his adherents by three to one
the wretched man complied and was pitching about,
leg and leg, off Portland Bill for twenty hours without making a yard of headway. Then, when the
wind took a southerly slant and the brig was bowling
comfortably past Start Point, he was suddenly ordered into Dartmouth—the passengers discovered
they were out of victuals.

Here, however, the exasperated ship-master's
troubles ceased, as far as the seamen were concerned,
for all went ashore.

Curses be on his worm-eaten trow! they said:
they could go faster and easier afoot; moreover, a
stretch ashore would enable the fiddler to give an
aural, rather than an ocular, demonstration of what
was in him. Whereupon they cut ash cudgels (in
case the press should change its mind and attempt
to take them back again) and set off for Plymouth,
waddling bow-legged, hobbling, limping, the woebe-
gone musician at the head of the column, playing
"Come ye all."

They slept at Totnes that night; and next morning, after beating the Watch and rescuing two of
their comrades, took the road again, their numbers
depleted by a cook's-mate, who saw no reason why
he should walk to St. Austell when there was just
as good flip to be obtained where he was, and a
marine, who suddenly remembered he had a wife in
Kingsbridge and thought he would pay her a visit
before joining his previous spouse in Lostwithiel.

On the other hand, three flamboyant ladies joined
the party and marched at the head of the shambling
column, arm in arm with their temporary affinities,
singing shrilly. By dint of turning aside to steal
dogs and fowls and stopping at every inn to drink
and dance, night saw them no further on than South
Brent. Next morning the three ladies had gone
and so had the money of their admirers, who, however, took their losses with admirable philosophy
and, by borrowing left and right from their comrades, were very little out of pocket.

Ortho Penhale broke away at Ivybridge. The
company had ceased to amuse him and at the rate
they were going he would hardly see West Penwith
before Christmas.

He put up at a sailors' lodging-house in Plymouth
that night, sharing a bed with a seaman who told
him that there was a Mount's Bay smuggling craft
at that moment lying off Cawsand; but as he did not
know whether she was bound home or back to
Guernsey Ortho decided to push on afoot.

His bedmate, a hardy fellow, informed him that
he was second mate of a local privateer lately in
from cruising off Vigo. Before getting into bed he
drew two loaded pistols from his pockets and laid
them on the floor within easy reach, explaining that
his Moll had turned sour on him because he had
given another girl a pair of red shoes (a harmless
enough action in all conscience!) and he thought she
might inform on him for a certain little affair. He

then produced a flageolet and played "Dumbarton's Drums Beat Bonny O" and "The North Country Lass," lying back on the bed, one knee crossed over the other.

Came a thumping on the wall.

"What's the matter?" the musician demanded.

"There's a door hinge squeaking to and fro," growled a voice. "Put a drop of oil to it, for God's sake!"

"Squealing, quoatha!" the mate exclaimed, jerking upright and addressing the wall at the top of his lungs. "Come round here, you bachelor's brat, and I'll show you which of us two can squeal the loudest. You — — — !"

The invisible objector replied in kind and a bawling-match ensued, ending in a vocal victory for the privateersman, who took up his instrument again and addressed Ortho.

"I'll play you the sweetest little stave you ever heard. 'Philomel' 'tis called. Listen."

He blew noisily through his pipe and started work, faltered, stopped, and started again. This was repeated several times.

The musician sighed, "In irons. Hung in the wind, can't cast neither one way nor t'other. Tum-tee-tum, tum-tee-tum tee, de . . . no. Oh, dang it, maybe 'twill come later."

He rummaged in his inexhaustible pockets, brought forth a sausage, polished it on his sleeve, broke it in two and offered one half to Ortho. The dainty being declined he ate both halves himself, kicked off his Greenland boots, snuffed the candle and rolled into bed.

Ten minutes later he leapt out again, exclaiming, "Got it, got it!"

"What?" Ortho growled.

" 'Philomel'! Sweetest little stave you ever heard. Where's my flageolet?"

Ortho groaned and buried his head under the pillow.

The concert finished, Ortho had barely closed his eyes when he was aroused by the explosion of both pistols followed by appalling howls of anguish. The mate and he both jumped out of bed and relit the candle. An elderly man of nautical appearance was lying prone in a crimson puddle, yelling out that he was murdered.

"You've burst him wide open," said Ortho to his companion.

"He's squalling very lusty for a burst man," the culprit observed, tapping the lintel. "Moreover, here's the two bullet holes over the door. I thought it was the constables."

"But look at the blood!"

The mate looked at the blood, then bent down, dipped his finger in and smelt it.

"That's not blood; that's claret," he said. "The old sot had a bottle of claret on him when he fell. Rise up, cully, you're not nearly so dead as you think."

The landlord appeared, candle in trembling hand. "Lawks, 'tis Captain Townsend!" he said. "What are you doing here, Captain?"

"Lodge—here," stuttered the corpse. "'S my bed."

"No, it's not," said the landlord, "and hasn't been for a week."

"Tha' show?" said the dazed mariner. "Then where d' I lodge now?"

For answer the privateersman took him by the slack of his coat and hove him bodily down stairs, slammed the door and took up his pistols once more.

"What are you doing?" Ortho enquired.

"Reloading, of course. If those plaguy constables . . . hello, where be going?"

"Outside to get a bit of sleep," said Ortho.

As he ran downstairs he passed Captain Townsend going up again, on all fours, mumbling "'S my bed. I know 's my bed." He was evidently a man of one idea.

Ortho crossed the Saltash ferry at dawn and got a lift to Liskeard in a farmer's gig. For his share in the defeat of its enemies, a painful wound and nine months' service, a grateful government had rewarded him at the rate of twenty-two shillings and sixpence a month, less deductions for desertion, slops, tobacco, etc., and enforced contributions of sixpence a month to Greenwich Hospital, fourpence for the chaplain and twopence for the surgeon (valuable evidence as to the exact ratio of value between soul and body). Of the small surplus there was little remaining and he was husbanding it for a grand finale. Ortho believed in a strong finish. However disastrous his ventures may have been in the past, he had always marched home with the honours of war, with drums thudding and flags flying, so to speak. And this should be no exception. He would tramp it all the way to Marazion, if needs be, so that he could ride the last three miles in a carriage and make an impression on Penzance. He breakfasted at Liskeard, swung along the Fowey valley and, leaving Bodmin on his right, took the pack-track to High Cross, lay down in the hedge and made a meal of bread saved from breakfast and onions obtained from a street barrow when its owner was not looking.

It was mid-afternoon. He had done nearly twenty miles on his feet and intended to do no more. As he was now on the main road he thought it would be strange if he could not pick up a lift of some kind.

A carrier's waggon lumbered by, a huge tilted wain drawn by six horses whose bells rang a pretty peal; the carrier himself sitting astride a diminutive pony, cracking his whip and encouraging his team with a ceaseless stream of clucks and whistles. This was followed by a Jew peddlar, bent double under his wooden pack, a human snail. Then, with a rat-a-plan of hooves, a rumble of wheels, and a jingle of chains, its four bay horses soaped with lather, a black-and-yellow coach swung by, crowded with passengers, the Lisbon mails (whipped ashore that morning from a Falmouth packet) stacked high on its swaying roof. No luck so far.

Ortho lit a pipe and lay back in the rusty bracken, taking his ease. He had hoped to get to Truro that night, but now he felt he would be lucky to see Blue Anchor or even Indian Queens.

A horseman came up the hill, a plump, red-headed farmer, bestriding a grey mare with a sway back and one wall eye.

"Hulloa!" Ortho shouted, sitting up.

The grey mare shied and capered across the road, the farmer hanging round her neck.

"My dear soul and life! What do 'e mean hollering so outrageous?" he demanded, wriggling back into the saddle.

"Didn't mean any harm," said Ortho.

"No harm! My blood's curdling yet. What did 'e do it for?"

"I want a ride."

"A ride, sayest? And what'll I do, jump off and walk?"

"Walk, no. I'll get up behind. That's a fine long-backed filly you've got. There's room for a boat's crew."

The farmer examined Ortho with a shrewd blue eye. "You'm a bold one. What are 'e? Sailor?"

"Yes, navy. Just paid off."

"Navy! Did you meet my son 'Zekiel, there?"

"Maybe. What's his name and ship?"

"His name is Harvey and his ship is the *Latona,* frigate, Lord Howe's Western Squadron. His girl crossed en so 'a went to sea to spite her. Though how she would be spited if a cannon-ball took his head off—seeing she married another—do pass my understanding."

Ortho smote his thigh. "My stars, the *Latona* is my own ship! Ezekiel Harvey . . . Ezekiel Harvey . . . why, dang it, I know him well! Chap with sandy hair and blue eyes, and, let me see, is he a gunner or a top-man?"

"Nayther," said Ezekiel's parent. "He's a cook's shifter, and black as pitch; takes after his ma. You backed the wrong dog that time, sailor."

Ortho laughed. "Seems I did. No matter. Are you going to give me a ride?"

The farmer stroked his rusty chin. "I've got a soft heart for sailors, 'count of 'Zekiel, so I'll put 'e as far as Ennisworgey turning—for two shilling."

"To hell with you!" said Ortho. "What do you think you are—a po' chaise?"

"One and sixpence, call it?"

"No!"

"Shilling?"

"No!"

"How much will 'e give, then?"

"Sixpence—and no more, you old bloodsucker!"

The farmer rubbed his chin again. "Call it ninepence."

"No, I tell you!"

The farmer grunted. "Hand over the money first, then."

Ortho gave him the sixpence and swung up behind.

An alarming change came over the drowsy old mare; she gave a sudden squeal, bounded into the air, then, tucking her head and tail well in, lashed out furiously with both hind legs.

"Whoa! whoa!" her master cried, vacating the saddle for the mare's neck.

"Tally-ho! Tally-ho!" cried Ortho, taking his place.

"Stop tormenting she!" yelled the farmer, sliding farther down.

"There's a gad-fly under her tail I expect." Ortho laughed.

"Gad-fly! This ain't the season for . . . hey, you'm pushing me off!"

"Well, somebody's got to go, seemingly."

"Whoa! Steady, you whimsey daffock! Hey! Help! I'm going!"

"Good-bye," said Ortho.

And with an extra high kick on the part of the grey and some assistance from Ortho, he went.

When the apoplectic yeoman picked himself up from the roadside nettles Ortho was slipping his knife back into its sheath and the mare had regained the horizontal.

Ortho smiled upon the farmer. "Want a ride as far as Ennisworgey turning, do you? Well, I've got

a soft heart for farmers, on account of my old shipmate Ezekiel, so I'll take you—for sixpence. Hand
over the money and jump up behind."

Ortho got as far as Blue Anchor that night and
slept it out in a barn, in company with the Jew peddlar and a wandering tinsmith.

CHAPTER VI

THE companions of a night parted at dawn next morning; the Jew going north, the tinker south, Ortho west. He walked as far as Nankervis, where he was picked up by a young squire in a black and scarlet cabriolet drawn by a perky chestnut cob and rattled into Truro in style. All the way he entertained his benefactor with brisk stories of adventure, retaining the best until they were jolting over the town cobbles. The cabriolet was at a standstill in the Red Lion yard before he had reached the climax, so the boy invited him to dinner to hear the end—which was precisely as Ortho had designed. It was a merry meal. There were several other young bucks at table; Ortho expanded until the whole room was his audience and carried off his stories with a flourish. At three o'clock he sang what he described as a negro love song (but which, in reality, was pure gibberish composed on the moment and garnished with blood-curdling howls) and tearing himself from his protesting hosts, went forth to seek a west-bound conveyance.

He had no sooner set foot in the yard than a dirty old woman ran straight into him, shrieking that her daughter was hanging herself in the stable. Ortho rushed to the rescue, the beldame imploring haste, an excited rabble tumbling at their heels. He found the girl dangling from a beam, choking and kicking with the utmost violence, and despite her struggles he managed to support her in his arms until an agile knife-grinder cut the rope. The crone wept upon his chest; the girl lay gasping on the straw, her eyes closed, both hands to her throat. She had evidently waited until the ostler was out, mounted his stool, hitched the rope about her neck and over a harness hook and then kicked the stool away.

Eight tired coach horses champed their oats imperturbably, presenting stolid rumps to the drama. The crowd pressed about the unfortunate, clacking like a poultry yard, exquisitely thrilled; but Ortho looked upon the girl with something like awe. With battle, murder and violence he had rubbed elbows from boyhood, but this was the first time he had met suicide (or the impulse) face to face, and he stood appalled. Death to him was the bland end, a shutting out of sunlight, movement, colour, laughter and melody; of all things sweet and precious. Death spelt everlasting darkness underground where blind worms crawled and stale water oozed, to be fought off to the last snatch of breath and flicker of strength. He had known hard days in plenty but never had life been anything but desirable did it come to the point. If one hadn't one thing one had another—and there was always tomorrow; hope in his breast sprang eternal with dawn. The idea of anybody voluntarily cutting adrift from this entertaining world struck him as uncanny, terrible. He drew a sleeve across his brow and turned on the mother.

"Here, damme! what's wrong with the poor wench?"

She poured out a moving story, common enough in the England of those desperate years.

The girl's husband, a Thames waterman, had been pressed on Tower Hill on his wedding-day and incontinently despatched abroad, leaving two families unsupported. The girl had done her best to keep the household together by hawking in the streets, but had been unmercifully beaten by rival barrow women. A baby arrived and with it the news that her husband had been killed in action. The waterman's old mother died of shock, the wife almost. When she recovered sufficiently they had gone on tramp, lured by the rumour that there was plenty of work to be had in the West. There was no work to be had, and three days before the baby had died, of malnutrition and exposure, under a hedge outside St. Austell.

The story pricked Ortho to the heart, brought tears to his eyes. "Damme! that's bad, bad!" he muttered huskily, and glanced at the girl stretched out in the straw. Not an uncomely woman by any means; handsome, in fact. His heart was still more deeply wounded.

"Hell's bells, that's shameful!" said he, aloud. "A sailor's widow! I am a tar myself. What battle was he killed in, madam?"

"The twelfth of April," the old woman sobbed.

"My stars, I was there! I am one of Rodney's men!" Ortho exclaimed. "Now, by thunder, I will see to it that one April widow does not sleep under a hedge this winter's night, or for many nights to come." He pulled off his cap, pitched two silver half-crowns into it, kicked the door shut and set his back against it.

"Anybody that wants to get out of here will have to pay," said he, defiantly, jingling the coins in his hat. "There was a Thames waterman stood up between you and the French round-shot and got cut to ribands and hove to the Caribbean sharks for it, while you sat snug at home and got fat as hogs on the famine prices. You'll loosen your purses for that waterman's widow now, or have me to deal with. Come on."

There was indignation trembling in his voice, a dangerous sparkle in his eye. The money rattled in. Some paid up from fear of the tall seaman; others, the women, from sheer pity. Peace with the new United States of America was a fact, peace with France and Spain expected, and it was the great battle of the Saintes that had made these blessings possible—some few paid from the less common motive of gratitude.

It was a sum approaching four pounds that Ortho emptied into the girl's lap. Her eyes followed him as he strode out of the stable and across the yard, strangely glowing.

Ortho rode to Penryn on the Falmouth mail and walked as far as Long Downs Inn that night. He might have made the whole distance into Helston had he not stopped to help an old woman ring a litter of pigs. He slept late next morning, was constrained to assist the landlord's buxom daughter at the churn and lecture her father (who was also a farrier) in the Moorish manner of shoeing horses, with the result that he did not reach the scene of his short-lived schooldays until shortly before one o'clock. The grammar school bell was clanging as he halted opposite its gates, and a swarm of day-boys raced past, ki-yi'ing, swinging satchels and trying to trip each other up, little guessing that the bronzed sailor leaning against a gate-post was none other than the great Penhale, that legendary hero who had fought a pitched battle with an usher in his own classroom, ironed him out and run away with gypsies.

A couple of Ortho's old masters went by, strangely shrunken, he thought, and wondered how he could ever have been over-awed by the scrubby little rats. They did not recognize him and he did not announce himself. To appear at his old school in the garb of

a common seaman would be to suggest failure.
When he went back it would be in a cocked hat, with
Valenciennes at his throat and silver buckles on his
shoes—even if he had to borrow them.

It was Saturday and Coinage Hall Street was
moderately enlivened with country-folk doing their
week-end shopping. As Ortho approached the
Angel Inn, there was a sudden rush of people to the
opposite side. By a judicious use of weight and
elbows he worked his way to the front of the ring,
hoping to see a fight, but it was a woman in an
epileptic fit. He had seen those seizures before. A
carpenter on the Indiaman was subject to them and
a Berber in his Moorish regiment had a trick of
tying himself into knots during thunderstorms, but
neither of them approached the violence of this
woman. She writhed about in an incredible manner,
bending her limbs backwards under her and assum-
ing attitudes it would seem impossible that the
human body could attain and remain in one piece.
Her face was horribly distorted and she mouthed
a heavy white foam.

Some of the crowd appeared amused, but the
spectacle did not entertain Ortho: he detested ugli-
ness.

"The poor slut'll break her back in a minute!" he
cried. "Stop her, somebody!"

"If she'd bite 'e when she's like that thee'd go
mad," a voice warned.

" 'Ess, surely," said another; "poisonous like a mad dog."

"Dash a bucket o' water ovver she," a third recommended.

Ortho had had enough of it. "Oh, fetch a doctor to her!" he said, throwing down a coin. "There's something to help pay." As he elbowed his way out again he heard the jingle of many coins on the pavement.

He turned in to the Angel and ordered food. The meal was nearly over, the dining-room empty but for a Leghorn fish-merchant who made a vast amount of noise embarking his victuals, but was otherwise inarticulate. Ortho did not dally, gulped the food down, paid up and stalked out again, a certain amount of swagger in his walk to impress a rosy chambermaid who peeped at him through the banisters. Having one eye cast over his shoulder, he nearly collided with a trio of women hurrying in. They were swathed in long travelling cloaks with hoods and there was a post-chaise drawn up at the door.

Ortho passed on to the yard and found the ostler hauling a bleery postillion out of the litter.

" 'S my birthday," the fellow protested. "Fifty-two year and not a tooth missing. . . . Seven . . ."

"I don't care if you are fifty-two hundred!" said the ostler, shaking him. "Jim's away to a funeral at Sithney and Dickson's sick. Stir yourself!"

"S-seven children I've raised—counting three

d-dead an' one still-born," the postillion informed Ortho.

"There'll be another death in your family if you don't get harnessed," the ostler threatened. "Smart—or I'll fetch the master to you!"

"Where's that chaise for?" Ortho inquired.

"Penzance, soon as the ladies have ate."

"Think they'd share?"

The stableman eyed Ortho's costume contemptuously. "Not with the likes o' you, Admiral Salt-horse. They're quality, by their looks. Roast your soul, you—!"

He turned, broom in hand, on the post-boy, who had sunk upon a bench and was weeping bitterly because people called him names on his birthday.

Ortho shrugged his shoulders and walked out of town and over the Cober stream. He had not climbed two hundred yards up the hill on the far side when he was arrested by a low whistle from the hedge and, looking round, he saw a woman seated on the bank.

"Hoi!" she called. "Come here, sailor."

He crossed the road and saw to his astonishment that it was the girl of the Truro stable.

"You?" he exclaimed.

"No other," she replied. "Hold out your hand."

He did so and she dropped two half-crowns and a shilling into it.

"What's this for?" he asked.

"Your money."

"I gave you two half-crowns—but this shilling?"

"You gave me just now."

"You! How d' you mean? You weren't the girl up there throwing a fit?"

She nodded.

Ortho stared. "Well, I be keel-hauled! I didn't recognize you."

"Like as not. Pretty shape I should find myself in if I let folk recognize me. Think you'd know me again?"

Ortho took a long look at her. "Yes, anywhere."

The girl's features suffered a hideous convulsion and the face that looked at Ortho was that of another woman.

"And now?" she tittered.

"Peste!" said he and rubbed his eyes. When he had finished rubbing them, the face had altered again.

"And now?" the girl taunted.

"Good Lord! Here, stop it, do!"

"Look!" she commanded, and he watched her features slip back into their comely lines, the true face drawing through the false, an uncanny spectacle.

"Think you could swear to me at an Assize?" the girl enquired.

"No—nor anybody else. You give me the gooseflesh," said Ortho. "You'd win a fortune in a Merry Andrew booth."

"I was born in a Merry Andrew booth during

Bartholomew Fair," said the girl. "And it was there I learned the art, contorting my face and limbs on a wooden stage. But as for fortune, I declare to you that if we went hungry to bed but four nights in the week we thought ourselves passing lucky."

"See here," said Ortho. "You weren't bobbing just now, were you? That fit you threw was genuine, eh? Those twistings, that foam—?"

The girl shook her head. "I have double joints, and as for the foam, a morsel of Castile soap in the mouth will bring that very speedy."

Ortho scratched his raven curls. "Your husband, the waterman, killed at sea—was that—?"

The girl drew herself up indignantly. "Hey, do I look the piece that would take up with a common waterman, my faith? I have two silk dresses at home where I lodge, I'll have you know, and more money hidden than you've ever seen. Waterman, faugh!"

"Then why, if you are so rich, do you throw fits, in the gutter?"

"I have my living to earn and I prefer to earn it respectable," said the girl, haughtily. "Would you have me to keep a bagnio or turn bawd and trapse the streets at the mercy of every bezzled guardsman?"

"That hanging was a bamboozle, too, then?"

"Surely!"

"My stars, you may overdo it some day and hang too long. What then?"

"I am used to hanging by my chin from trapezes," the girl replied; "and I never kick the stool away till I hear the rescuers at hand."

Ortho threw himself back on the bank and roared. "By rights I should break your neck for this—an' I would if it weren't so shapely and I could stop laughing. But harkee," he said, sobering, "why do you tell me all this? *Me?*"

The girl shifted nearer and turned her steel-grey eyes upon him admiringly: he was a handsome person.

"'Tis a hard life at sea, ain't it? And poor paid?"

"Shameful!"

"Mmh, so I have heard. Myself, I do very comfortably. Yesterday with one hanging and two fits I gained little short of five pounds. Today I have made eight shillings and three pence already. In London, where I live, it is a poor morning when I cannot pick up a pound; and during May fair, Bartholomew, Smithfield or the like, I think myself disgraced if I cannot touch the treble of that."

"Begob, the public is more generous than I supposed! You increase my opinion of human nature, Pet," said Ortho. "But what of it?"

The girl placed a hand upon his forearm and leaned lightly against him. "A poor female has need of protection on the road, Honey-heart, and I have taken a great fancy to thee. Come with me and thou shalt have all the tobacco and flip you desire and we will live very loving and genteel. 'Tis very tedious all alone."

"But your mother—"

"Mother!" the girl exclaimed. "That old blowse! I hired her in Exeter and discharged her last night. She was vastly too fond of gin, she was. I am partial to a drop of cordial myself—at the proper season—but that dawkin was forever tippling during business hours and getting mixed in her mind. At Plymouth she said I was in trouble to a drummer killed at Brandywine, which, all the world knows, was a matter of five or six years ago. I hardly escaped the crowd with my life."

She rubbed her soft cheek against Ortho's shoulder. "Now if thou was't to come stampin' in, all fire and tenderness, like at Truro, shouting that I was the widow of thy old shipmate, waving thy cudgel and shaking half-crowns together—why we'd win a fortune, my dear."

Ortho snorted.

"Was you ever in London?" the girl enquired.

"But once. I landed at Blackwall from an Indiaman, but there was a hot-press on, so I ran out of it quickly. I am for and of the country."

"Myself, I find the country vastly tedious and the rustics little better than their own hogs," said the girl, sniffing.

"I wonder you venture so far amongst us, then," said Ortho.

"Faith, never again—not after I have visited the Land's End."

"Why that poor rock?"

"To stop the boasting of Mrs. Figg, with whom I lodge. I love Mrs. Figg like my life and there is no lady in the land has genteeler manners for all her father was a chairman and her husband transported. We are like sisters, I assure you, but last Michaelmas she picked up with a party of paid-off sailors in Tower Hamlets and they hired a hackney-coach and drove off for York. At Grantham they set the coach alight, so hired another and drove back again; but to listen to Ann Figg you would declare she had visited the Indies. There is nothing I can do or see in the town but what she can better me with the experience of her travels. So I am determined to overreach her once and for all by coming to the Land's End—for nobody can go further than that."

Ortho laughed. "And then—London?"

"Surely—and you with me, eh, love?" She snuggled against him bodily and his arm went round her—his arm had a habit of encircling pretty women, and pretty she undeniably was, in a sharp-cut, aquiline fashion.

"We will live very genteel in London, my heart," she cooed. "I will buy you a red coat, richly laced like a military captain, and make of you a fine bully beau. And we will go to the shilling gallery at Covent Garden and the bull-baits and blunt play at Hockley-in-the-Hole and the cock-fights in Red Lion Fields and Punch's Opera and the mechanical pictures in Little Piazzas. Oh, you will soon forget your country, for London is very curious and pleasant to one that hath the way of it. Every day there is something fresh to see and admire—processions and fashionables, harlequinades, public raffles and hangings. That is better than going up and down the cold sea—not?"

Ortho gently disengaged his arm. Across the valley he could hear the sound he was awaiting.

"Madam, you have a charming nose (among other things) and I am prodigiously honoured, but it cannot be done," said he. "I should not shape favourably as a town beau—alack! A month's idleness and my belt would cry for mercy." He slapped his lean middle. "Two months and my buttons would fly like grape-shot and the fine red coat burst at every seam. Further, I should grow carbuncles. Picture to yourself a fat sot in a split coat with carbuncles! You would not love me then. Though the parting be bitter let us part while our affection is still bright. Adieu!" He bent and kissed her on the charming nose.

"Come back!" the girl implored.

"I dare not."

"My Honey-dear!"

"My fairest bloom!"

"Plague take you!" shrilled the girl, seeing there was no stopping him. "I hope the sea drowns you thrice over and the Frinch cut your liver out, you . . .!"

Until he turned the corner her abuse followed him: selected gems of invective got from the rich mines of Rosemary Lane and the Cloisters. He recorded some for future use; walked on until he was out of sight; then climbed over the hedge and waited.

Far off down the hill he could hear the rumble of approaching wheels. They approached but slowly. That fuddled post-boy must be asleep or else the horses were tired, Ortho reflected. Another fourteen miles or so to Penzance and it was after three o'clock. They would be lucky if they got in before dark with the roads in the state they were. The chaise lurched round the corner; mud-splashed to the roof, the postillion hunched up in the saddle like a wizened ape, both eyes closed.

Ortho waited until the carriage had lumbered by, then swung quietly over the hedge and climbed up on the luggage lashed behind. It was hardly a comfortable perch but would serve as far as Marazion. The chaise crawled over Sithney Common and then plunged helter-skelter into the Portleven valley. Ortho had to cling to the valise ropes to save himself from being jerked off. The frightened women inside rapped at the windows, but the postboy took no notice; his reins hung loose, his eyes

were sealed in slumber; only his knees, from lifelong
habit, held him to the saddle. The horses, impelled
by the weight behind them, went downhill at a gallop.

"We shall pile up in a heap at the bottom," said
Ortho to himself and prepared to jump.

But the lofty providence which watches over
babies, drunkards and seafaring gentlemen pre-
served that postillion. There was no accident at
the bottom and Breage hill cooled the furious pace.

A window dropped, a hooded head popped out,
and a voice—cultivated, middle-aged and profoundly
agitated—besought caution of the post-boy, who
took no notice whatever, but sat bowed over his
horse's withers in the form of a mark of interro-
gation. They passed through Breage still walking.
An urchin, noting Ortho on the luggage, shouted,
"Whip behind!" but the post-boy did not hear him.
Ortho scowled and shook his cudgel at the brat, who
fled howling to its mother. Antron, and still at a
walk. The road was execrable, a mere chain of mud-
holes narrowing to a twelve-foot slough between
hedges, broadening to a hundred yards on the moors,
the wheeltracks running far and wide to avoid pit-
falls and outcrops. A terrible road, nevertheless
with careful driving it were possible to maintain a
better speed than this. On two occasions Ortho was
on the point of climbing along the roof and giving
the post-boy a slice of his mind, but reflecting that
it hardly became a stowaway to vilify the captain on

the conduct of the ship, he restrained himself, lit a pipe and cried patience to his soul. At all events it was not costing him anything and he was saving his feet—unaccustomed walking had made him footsore.

They rocked and splashed over Tresowas Green to Kenneggy Downs. On a moonlight night, thirty-one years before, Ortho's father had first met his mother on these same uplands, dressed in tumbler spangles, munching a turnip—but Ortho did not know that. The chaise slumped into a mud-hole and stopped with a jar that brought the horses up all standing. The post-boy's head toppling forward met his mount's jerking up and the blow on the nose woke him. He rubbed the nose and looked round stupidly.

The window dropped again and out popped another hood, the occupant of which admonished the horse-man in good sturdy Somerset. Ortho judged her to be the maid. The post-boy replied with a string of unmentionable epithets and lashed into his horses. They flung into their breast-straps crazily and the off horse snapped a trace. The post-boy dragged it to him and battered it over the ears with his whip-butt. It started to kick.

Three women descended into the mire, crying to the sodden brute to have done. He cursed them and battered on. The near horse backed up in fright, tripped over a slack trace and came down. The women whimpered and clung together.

Then out of the desolate moor, out of nowhere, appeared a tall sailor, who seized the postillion by the scruff of his jacket and the slack of his mole-skins, held him spectacularly at arm's-length, and then tossed him head-first into a gorse bush.

"Stir a finger or breathe a word and I'll throw you into the sea! It's a long throw but I'll do it," the sailor threatened; and turned to the astonished women, bowing, smiling, entirely conscious that he was the *deus ex machina*.

The maid stood slightly in advance of the others, as though in their defense: a heavy limbed whole-some daughter of wholesome soil. The remaining pair Ortho took to be mother and daughter and obviously "quality." He could see nothing of their clothes for the long travelling cloaks, but those were of expensive material, and so were their shoes. The mother had a flat face with no distinguishing fea-tures except an incipient moustache, the face of an amiable nonentity; but the daughter caught Ortho's attention. A little thing and slender, exquisitely chiselled and coloured. Her eyes were big and of the deep brown of peat streams, and the little face was delicate as a peony petal, creamy white, pink-tinted at the lips and cheek-bones.

She reminded Ortho of a china figure he had seen years ago in a house in Penzance, a Trianon shep-herdess leaning away from a supplicating shepherd, her head bent coyly sideways, a hand upraised. She had haunted him for some time—he was young then. In his dreams he had seen her poised above him, a fairy thing, graceful as a flower, tinted pink and white. On his lonely night rides she went before him, her head bent coyly sideways, her hand upraised. He fancied himself coming upon her suddenly some May morning, grazing her beribboned sheep in the Keigwin woods; pictured her running in alarm (coral shoes twinkling through the bluebells); made prisoner by the briars, bending coyly from his kisses, her little pink mouth pursed up and a rain of May blossom showering over them. . . . A mere toy, yet sufficient to build his boy dreams on—for a week. Then a mine captain's daughter flashed her saucy black eyes at him and he thought no more of the shepherdess.

But he thought of her again now. The girl before him might have been made of china. There was a gloss, a bloom, a crispness about her almost too delicate for common flesh and blood. He could fancy some master-potter shaping those exquisite curves of nostril, lip and chin with a loving thumb; touching in hints and tints of colour with a gossamer brush. But enough. His fine-china shepherdess was standing in the mud of the highway with evening coming on. He made a low sweep of his hair cap.

"Pardon me, ladies, if I dismissed your servant somewhat abruptly, but I should not have done so could I not provide a better in myself."

The maid eyed his sea-clothes doubtfully.

"I have commanded a regiment of lances in my

day and should be match for a pair of post-nags,"
he informed her. "You are for——?"

"Penzance, the Ship & Castle Inn, good sir,"
said the old lady. "We should be vastly obliged
if——"

"You shall be there before dark," said Ortho;
bowed again and set to work. He slipped the trace,
got the near horse up without difficulty and repaired
the broken trace with rope cut from the valise lash-
ings. Then he backed the chaise up a foot or two,
dropped a big stone in front of the bogged wheel
and pulled out sideways with ease.

"You can call for your horses at the Ship," he
shouted to the furze bushes, as he drove off. A
snore answered him. The road did not improve, but
the team was moderately fresh and with careful
steering Ortho managed to keep them going at a
trot until Marazion was behind, but the heavy beach
track slowed them down. Dusk was sweeping on.
The afterglow still lingered in the western sky, bar-
ring it across and across with tiger stripes of muddy
purple and misty orange. Below the glow Paul Hill
stood like a sombre wall, one window in the high
church-town blazing with reflected fire.

Penzance, a cataract of grey houses, slid down her
long slope to the sea, mysterious with twilight, a
tracery of ships' masts rising like wintry trees about
the base of St. Mary's. Besides the labouring chaise,
along three miles of beach, tired waves launched

themselves gripped at the shingle with grey foam fingers and slipped back sighing.

Home again. The great bay on his left, the old hills on his right, and in his nostrils the smell of salt and seaweed. Ortho let his horses pick their own pace, nursing them for a last burst. He was finishing strong. It was Saturday night: the town would be full of country folk, and next morning outside little moor churches and meeting-houses people would be telling each other how Ortho Penhale of Bosula had come home from the wars, riding full-gallop through Penzance, postillion to a parcel of quality ladies he had rescued on Kenneggy Downs. A notable return, well up to form. He would make a night of it in town with his old cronies and go back to the Owls' House next morning.

The chaise lumbered over Ponsandane River. At the Cliff Ortho lifted his team to a trot. At the bottom of Market Jew Street he rubbed the thong in and took the hill at full tilt, whooping tally-hos, snapping pistol-shots on his whip, scattering the mob to right and left. A party of festive miners cheered as he went by, and all the way up the street the crowd made a lane for him and carried on the cheer. They thought some high notable had come to town. Ortho rounded the corner with a flourish (tipping over a "lily-banger" stall and sending gingerbreads flying) and drew up before the Ship & Castle.

"Hulloa, landlord! Hulloa, ostler, boots!—

every mother's son of you!" he shouted, and banged another fusillade on his lash.

The inn staff came out at the run. The ladies descended, bowed to their amateur postillion, and swept indoors—the shepherdess stole a glance at him over her shoulder as she went. A ring of loafers collected round the smoking horses, and a dozen prosperous yeomen, ship captains and young bloods pressed out of the tavern to see what the noise was about.

Ortho, still mounted, greeted them heartily, "Hello, Harry, my buck! . . . Hello, Carclew and Cap'n Jem! What news? Here am I back again! Been fighting you lubbers' battles for you, I have— with Rodney. Send Jacka to me and bid 'em roll a puncheon out of the cellar, for begob, we'll make a night of it. How are we all?"

The squires nodded to him, grinned and waved their whips; but Ortho sensed an uncomfortable restraint in their manner—one whispered to a friend behind his hand and there was some nudging and furtive grimacing.

"Can't stop tonight, Ortho," said young Teage, uncomfortably. "I've got . . . er . . . business."

"No, not tonight," old Trebilcock mumbled, and turned away. Carclew with him. "Go home, Penhale."

"What in hell's come over you?" Ortho demanded, his black brows puckering stormily. "Turned Quaker, have you? Here's a pretty welcome, damme!" The landlord, Jacka, thrust through the idlers and caught his stirrup.

"Mr. Penhale, go home, sir," he said earnestly. "Your mother—"

Ortho slowly bent and caught him such a grip by the shoulder that he winced under it.

"What do you mean, man? Is she—?"

No need for words; he read the answer in Jacka's eyes.

"When?" he demanded huskily.

"Wednesday, sir—buried this morning."

Ortho slid out of the saddle and walked towards the yard.

"Give me a fresh horse," he said. "I'm going on."

All his fine finish had come to nothing.

CHAPTER VII

ELI PENHALE sat on the granite drinking-trough outside the house of his fathers and scraped the mud from his boots with a piece of stick. Ortho paced the yard before him, a straw dangling from his teeth, thumbs hooked in his belt. A shaft of white December sunshine lit the yard and the rain-wet place suddenly winked and sparkled. Every bare twig was outlined with shining beads, the dribbling tree-trunks gleamed. Ortho's brass belt buckle turned to gold. A cock stood on the wall beyond, shaking his bedrabbled feathers; his translucent comb and wattles became living rubies, drops of blood. The yard puddles brimmed with quicksilver for the instant. Then the sun clouded over and silver changed to lead.

"Can't think how mother came to fall off her horse," Ortho remarked.

"She didn't," said Eli. "Horse fell with her; both its knees were broke and its nose skinned."

"But how?"

"How? I don't know. Horses do fall. Stumbled, I s'pose."

"That Prince horse is as sure-footed as a mule."

"*Was*—but he's getting on and I guess mother

pushed him too hard. She didn't leave the Tinner's Arms till after eleven and by all accounts was a bit . . . well . . .''

"Yes, yes," Ortho cut in hastily. Both brothers evaded the fact that their mother was probably drunk when she died.

"You know what Kelynack Hill is like," Eli continued. "Steep as a roof. The old nag struck a stone and came down all of a bundle and Ma breaks her neck. That's the way I figure it."

"U-m-m!"

Eli glanced up. "If that weren't the way of it, what was? If you'm thinking of foul work, who did it and why? As far as I know, she hadn't an enemy, and there was two pounds, four shillings and some odd pence in her pocket when picked up. What's troubling you?"

"Oh, nothing," said Ortho. "What you say is true enough. Yet she's been coming home at all hours over worse roads for years and never a bruise."

"You can't play the fool forever," said Eli. "She was fifty-two and mighty heavy, and Prince is rising nineteen years. You're fretting yourself needlessly."

"I ain't fretting," Ortho disclaimed. "Only— Oh, well, say no more about it."

Eli tossed his stick away and rose. "There's no more to be said that I can see. Are 'e stepping up along for a bit of dinner?"

Ortho nodded, accepting readily.

Teresa had been far from a model mother. As soon as her sons were weaned she took no further interest in them—until they grew up, when she manifested a strong dislike of Eli because he openly withstood her extravagances, and a certain mild affection for Ortho because he did not—openly. Neither son was consumed with filial sorrow at his parent's death. Eli knew very well (though he kept his teeth shut on it) that, but for an accident which sent Ortho in his stead, he would have been stunned and trussed by the press-gang on Zawn-a-Bal beach, and that his mother had arranged it all: a piece of knowledge that caused him to lie awake at nights— a man does not expect treason from such a quarter. Ortho had, latterly, been much the favourite of the two, but even he felt no heartbreak. From the days when he began to toddle to the age of eighteen she had only noticed him when he had got in her way and then to snap at him as at an obstructive dog, and though he tried to put the notion from him it was a suspicious fact that the days of his popularity with Teresa coincided with his days of affluence.

Ortho was not heart-broken, but solitary meals at home were little to his taste; for though the carnal Teresa lay in the Penhale vault at Gwithian, spiritually she still pervaded the Owls' House. For thirty-one years she had been the moving force of the place and her memory was not easily erased. Ortho constantly found himself glancing sideways expecting to see the vast sombre woman brooding in her rocker by the fire. Did a shadow darken the doorway it was his mother homing. The dead do not altogether die. A widow came up from Monks Cove at dawn and went home before dusk—scurrying to avoid the clutch of buccas and witches. After that Ortho was alone.

The old house was full of uneasy sounds. Draughts soughed down the tall chimneys, whistled under the doors, and little whorls of floor-dust suddenly rose, danced and subsided. In the closed west wing rats scampered, loose boards creaked, and in the hush of midnight lumps of plaster fell with earthquake crashes, while in the woods round about the owls cried to one another, the grey owls and brown from which the place got its name: "Wha-hoo-ooo! Te-wheet-we-e-e! Whoo-hoo!"

And day and night the stream gushed and gurgled, like some one chuckling with malignant laughter. No place for a lone man. Bosula was a family house; for almost the two centuries of its existence it had been hiving its swarms. Between 1500 and 1700 the low-water mark in children born to a Penhale of Bosula was four, the average seven—sturdy, well-fed, rosy youngsters all, growing into good yeomen and good wives of yeomen. Then in a single year (1698) the scythe swept. One sailed with the disastrous Paterson settlement to Darien, strolled into the woods one evening to shoot a gay bird and never came back; two were drowned in each other's arms off the Bucks, pollock fishing; and of the direct line but two were left, a childless daughter married to a Kerrier farmer and one son, Ortho's grandfather.

The old house was desolate. The empty rooms yearned for their dear departed and perhaps were answered.

Perhaps it was not altogether rats and draughts that Ortho heard in the closed west wing.

The majority of past Penhales lay content in the soil they had tended (they were a home-keeping race) but there were others, bold boys or dreamy, who followed the drum-taps or sat on the Luddra Head watching sail-crowded ships go over the sea-rim and in due course followed them and found alien beds. Barren of the living, the old house called home its dead, and perhaps they came, the outcàsts, bloody from Sedgemoor field, glistening with the frost-rime of Hudson Bay, dripping with Gulf Weed. Ortho heard them, or thought he did, slow feet shuffling on the stairs, blind fingers fumbling for latches, heart-weary sighs in the dark.

One night he woke convinced there was some one in the room with him, sat up in bed, every hair prickling, whispered, "Who's there?" No answer. He struck a light, dreading what the light might reveal. It revealed an empty room. He lay back, calling himself a fool, but he did not sleep for an hour and the next night he took the yard dog up to bed with him. For the moment the place was on his nerves and he seized every opportunity of getting out of it. He had had two shocks—his mother's

death and Eli's marriage to the Penaluna girl and
desertion to his father-in-law's farm. The loss of
either had been outside his calculations; both going
at once left him stranded. He had no blame for his
brother. Eli was a landless man and had to look
out for himself; he could only rejoice that Fate had
transferred him no farther than next door.

He set his cap on his head and strode uphill beside
Eli over deep tilled fields and trim hedges.

"You've got everything in fine shape," he commented.

Eli nodded. "Not so bad, but I'm right glad
you're back. It's been hard work tending two places.
Simeon Penaluna isn't what he was—rheumatics.
You'll find a bit of money in hand, by the way.
Prices have been in the tree-tops, but I expect they'll
drop now with peace coming on."

"How much money is there?"

"Mother's debts and funeral paid, about a hundred and eighty pounds."

"Then you take a hundred," said Ortho.

"What for?"

"For your trouble, and—and a wedding gift."

Eli jerked a tansy plant out by the roots and
tossed it into the hedge. "And what of your
trouble, that wound and all? You handle the
French and I the profits, eh? No, thank you. I
snatch your maiden and you offer me wedding-gifts
to boot. Again no, thank you."

Ortho spat. "Oh, pshaw! That's all sunk astern

these months past. 'My maiden'—nonsense! Why, she wouldn't look at me!"

"Yes," said Eli, wonder in his voice, "that's true; she would not. It's a puzzle to me how . . . "

Ortho laughed and clapped him on the mighty shoulders. "Don't vex your head puzzling why Mary chose a good man for a bad, my dear. The ways of women are notoriously strange."

"So they are," said Eli, and his tone expressed thankfulness.

The brothers lapsed into silence, walked on over the high land and came in sight of Roswarva nestling amongst its stunted sycamores, chimneys smoking cheerfully. The contrast between his own comfortable home and the forlorn Owls' House stirred Eli to speech.

"I'm right sorry we can't give you a bed, Ortho, but with the new hind sleeping in, and the woman, and the boy coming and all, there ain't space for a mouse."

"Don't you trouble with me, I'm well enough," said Ortho. "So it's going to be a boy? Sure?"

"Mary says so," Mary's husband replied, his tone implying that that was sufficient for him.

"You're working well to wind'ard o' me, aren't you?" said Ortho. "Good home, good wife, sons; while I've got nothing but six wounds and an empty house. And you the younger!"

"But look at all you've seen and done!"

"It h'ant brought me much, though," Ortho

grunted. "You haven't noticed me dragging handfuls of rubies and diamonds out of my pockets, have you?" He snapped a whitethorn twig out of the hedge and bit on it thoughtfully. He was thoughtful throughout dinner and unwontedly silent, but his dark eyes were busy.

How was it going with his brother? Eli, a beggar as to material possessions, had married substance. How was he being received—as a beggar or a partner? He watched jealously for any hint of patronage, but failed to detect it. Mary scolded Eli for some trifling delinquency, laughter in her voice, affection glowing in her brown doe eyes. Old Simeon raised a sharp argument over some question of pasturage, got the worst of it and deferred to his son-in-law's better judgement. The hinds accepted Eli's orders without question. All was well with his brother, Ortho decided; very well. No poor dependent here but a beloved husband and son. Nevertheless his pride rebelled at a Penhale of Bosula going empty-handed to his bridal. Beyond the hundred and eighty pounds he was penniless himself, could do nothing for Eli at the moment, but he swore that some day he would make it up to these good folk, some day Eli should lay down pound for pound. He glanced round the farm kitchen. It was just as it had been when last he was there, ten months before, fruitlessly courting Mary.

Clean whitewash on the walls, clean sea-sand on

the floor, and polish everywhere. The big copper
pans gleamed with it, the brass-faced clock, prancing
china cavaliers and gilded dogs.

"Spruce as an admiral's barge," he said to himself; "everything just as it was and always will be,
world without end, amen. If Rodney had gone to
the sharks with all hands and the whole West Indies
blown up in spouts of ash and sulphur that clock
would not miss a tick or Mary delay her milking.
Peace, this is thy abode."

The fresh, white, sunlit place filled him with sudden disgust for his dingy dwelling. "Must see to
it," he thought; "get somebody proper to see to it."

He studied Mary and Eli again, under lowered
lids. They made a comely pair, big-boned, deep-
chested, serene. "That nephew of mine will be a
man of his hands, seem me," he meditated, looked
eighteen, twenty years ahead and pictured a brown-
eyed boy jumping into the Gwithian wrestling ring,
proud as a roe buck, the blue of the Atlantic behind
him and all the parish shouting, "Up, Penhale!"

"Eli has got the luff of me, sure enough," he
thought, scraped his chair back and stood up.

"Reckon I'll go into P'nzance 's afternoon. Anything you want, Mary?"

"Bring me a bottle of hartshorn, please, and a
packet of snuff for Pa. That's all, I believe."

She picked some money from under a china dog
and counted it out on the table. "I'm real sorry

we can't give 'e a bed here, but you know how it is. You're brearly welcome to meals anytime."

"Thank you kindly," said Ortho; "but Bosula's my home and I've got to get used to it, so I'd best start now."

Mary smiled meaningly. "Make a proper home of it, Ortho . . . but look, in the meanwhile why don't 'e have Naomi Davy in to fit for 'e? She's a respectable, clean woman; used to cook for the old parson before Tom Davy took up with her. That widow Pender from Cove can just about fit swill for pigs."

"God preserve the pigs," said Ortho, making a wry mouth. "But Naomi lives too far away—and there's Tom."

"Have both to live at Bosula then. They've no childer, and if you put 'em in the west wing you'll never notice 'em. Eli'll rent their cottage for his new hind—eh, Eli?"

"Glad to," said Eli.

Ortho rubbed his chin. There was something in the idea. He knew his hind's wife, a stout, energetic woman of neat appearance. "That's no bad notion," he said.

"Of course it edd'n; all the smart notions up this way do come from me," said Mary. "If there's a rock to be shifted or a field to be tilled, leave it to the poor dumb animals, I say,—the men and the oxen; but if it is a question of brains, well, 'tis me or nothing. That's what we women are for. Now begone do 'e, and remember a bottle of hartshorn and a packet of snuff."

Riding the bay mare's filly, Ortho was in Penzance by three o'clock and, turning in to a tailor's ordered two fashionable coats with knee breeches and waistcoats to match. After that he visited the barber's and was in a mind to have his head shaved and buy a wig, but when he looked on his glossy black curls in the glass he could not bring himself to part with them and compromised by having his nautical pigtail freed of its casing of spun-yarn and tied with ribbon. While this operation was being performed he tried to glean a little tittle-tattle from Solomon Triggs the barber; but Solomon, that fount of trivial information, was not spouting for once. Solomon had a passion for soused pilchards, a devotion which was not reciprocated. That noon, greatly daring, he had dined on soused pilchards and the consequences were dire. His narrow face was chalk pale, his bleak nose a dyspeptic vermillion; these, with the fantastic peruke he wore, gave him the appearance of a bilious old cockatoo. Periodically he caressed his sprigged waistcoat with a trembling hand.

On the subject of visitors Ortho elicited little information and that of no value. There was a John Company *typean* lodging at the top of Quay Street who insisted on being shaved in bed, cursing the whole time in the Hindoo tongue; and a modish old lady on the Green, bald as round-shot but possessing a wig by the famous Mr. Stewart of London, author of "Plocacosmos, or the Whole Art of Hairdressing," a wig *a la Cybèle* which must have cost thirty pounds if a farthing. Right grey human hair throughout, drawn over a tow body, with curls, bobs, ties and . . ."

Solomon was fast waxing lyrical concerning the wig, when the pilchard manifested itself again and brought him groaning back to earth. He folded up over a chair-back and spake no more.

Ortho continued down the street to the Ship & Castle, strolled into the tap-room and, ordering a pewter of burnt ale, took up a position commanding the passage. By four o'clock, his vantage having yielded nothing, he went on the prowl and finding a door ajar on the second floor stuck his head inside.

A chambermaid was dreamily caressing the floor with a dust-cloth tied over a broom. He whistled softly. The girl jumped and then turned on him, flushing.

"What is it?"

"I want a word with you, Blue-eyes."

"I've got work to do—and moreover they ain't blue."

"Ain't they? Well, then forget-me-nots ain't either." He slipped quietly into the room and chucked her under the chin. "See here, do you stand in need of a bunch of ribbons, Miss Pretty?"

The maid eyed him suspiciously. "What's tied to t'other end of 'em, Mr. Penhale?"

"Nothing that's going to send you to the apothecary, my Blossom. D' you remember that party I drove in last week, by any chance?"

The girl grinned. "Their post-boy walked up nex' morning in a fair mess, looking for his horses. Swore he'd have your blood, he did."

"He hasn't had any of it yet that I know of," said Ortho. "But never mind the post-boy; there's a thing or two I want to learn . . ."

Five minutes later he had discovered that the china shepherdess was a Miss Nicola Barradale of Bristol, that the amiable nonentity was not her mother but a duenna, and that the party had left the inn two days before for a house in Chapel Street. The chambermaid had evidently been on excellent terms with Miss Barradale's maid; her tongue, once started, ran on and on.

Miss Barradale had suffered a slight indisposition and been ordered into the mild west for the winter. Mr. Barradale kept a carriage and a negro servant and indulged his darling's every whim; such dresses she had! Paduasoy, Irish and Italian polonese, flounced Georgia silks and gold-net—hey! Beckford was the name of the duenna, and the maid's Vashti Pool. She was the widow of a clergyman who had died of apoplexy preaching No-Popery too soon after dinner. Mrs. Beckford that was, not Vashti Pool. She got ten pounds a year and pickings, and was betrothed to an ostler at the Bell, Taunton—Vashti Pool, not Mrs. Beckford. Mrs. Beckford never rose till ten of the clock and had a lap dog which was more trouble than the rest put together. Miss Barradale was very genteel. All her hair was her own and so long she could sit on it. Vashti Pool made a pretty penny selling hair-combings to wig-makers. The house they had gone to was opposite the church, that one with a green door and brass knocker.

Ortho pressed a coin into the girl's palm and patted her cheek. "My thanks, Rosebud," said he, turning away.

She looked at the generous florin, then at the donor. "They axed about you, sir," she called after him.

Ortho spun about. "Eh? Which?"

"The maid first, sir, and methinks the lady set her on. Then Miss Barradale herself. I was at her bed with the warming-pan and she undressing, and she says to me, she says, 'That gentleman who drove us the other night, Mr. Penhale, he is a notable person in these parts, I am told.' 'Oh, yes, m'am,' says I, 'he is a most notable rake-hell.'"

"The devil you did!" Ortho exclaimed.

"Well, there is no harm in that, sir," the girl retorted. "For my part I consider a man without a trace of roguery very indifferent company. I would as lief walk abroad with a sheep."

Ortho bowed. "I stand corrected, Pansy. I

perceive that you are a woman of spirit and discernment. But in your own case be you wary, for there are many cruel deceivers about. Your consistent rogue is very rare. Many men assume a roguish mien in order to lure romantic young females to church, but once the prey is in their toils they settle down, souls of tedious domesticity. The sheep in wolf's clothing is vastly more common than the fleeced wolf—and far more deadly. Beware! So you said I was Lord Nicholas Satan—eh? God bless you!"

The girl stared at him, bewildered, and then plunged on. "Then Miss Barradale says to me, she says, 'He is greatly travelled, I hear.' 'Oh, yes, m'am,' I says. 'He has visited Muskovy, Boston and both the Americas'; and I tells her how you and King Nick led the smuggling in these parts and fought the dragoons and the King's cutters all to once, and had to flee to Barbary and was a general there and ran off with a queen, and went and visited the Tsar of the East Indies, and how you were just back, mortally wounded, from sinking the Dutch with Admiral Boscawen."

"Hmm," said Ortho. The story of his adventures had been astonishingly embellished. "Hm-m . . . change thy duster for the ink-well, Bluebell, thy broom for the pen, then shall Mr. Defoe weep with envy and Dean Swift hide his minished head. And what did Miss Barradale say to that?"

"She didn't say naught, sir. Sat before the glass,

her hands in her lap, till I'd finished, then she up and told me I talked too much, if you please."

"Angry?"

"Oh, lor' no, sir. Ladies are like that. They ax the gossip of you and then say your tongue runs too free. She gave me a shilling and a sugar comfit."

"Did she?" said Ortho. "You must be in the fair way to a dowry. I would I could pay court to you myself, but I fear I cannot: I have flaws in my character which are a great nuisance to me and would be still more to you—specks of honesty, flecks of diligence, occasional—very occasional—pricks of conscience; I could never live up to your ideals. Farewell, my Sunflower!"

He bowed low over her coarse hand, saluted it and was gone.

The maid looked after him sighing. "Pansy—Pretty—Blue-eyes!" Were her eyes really blue?—She examined them in the mirror and sighed again.

CHAPTER VIII

ORTHO stood undecided at the door of the Ship & Castle, whistling through his teeth, switching his boot with his riding whip. Somewhere upstairs somebody was tinkling out a Handel allegro on a spinet and making poor weather of it. From the cock-pit behind the inn came the shrill crow of a triumphant bird followed by the cheers of its backers. Dusk was closing and with it the rain. Chapel Street lay deserted except for a pair of fish-wives waddling harbourwars, creels slung across their foreheads, and one dejected hound rat-hunting along the sewer, apparently without hope.

A sodden ride home and a dismal night. Ortho thought of the Owls' House among its dripping trees and grimaced. A solitary supper, a pipe or two before the fire with the old clock ticking and the rain soughing, and so to bed—heigh-ho! No ·existence for a live man. He must move the Davys in as soon as possible. Even then . . .

The house with the green door and brass knocker. He glanced down the wet street. It would be lit up by now and the shutters, perhaps, left unclosed. He might catch a glimpse . . . his china shepherdess, tinted like apple flower.

He became aware that something was plucking at his sleeve, and, turning, saw a scarecrow figure of rags and hair which he recognised as Cully John. Cully John was the town wastrel, the disreputable son of a respectable coal-heaver. He was generally supposed to be half-witted but there were those who maintained that, so far from being deficient, he showed more intelligence than most, in that, though sturdy beyond the common and capable of supplying his own needs, during the forty-odd years of his life he had kept his hands unsullied by any form of toil. This was not altogether true. He had his lapses. Though Cully John was blameless of the more expensive vices, clothed himself from dustbins, lodged gratis at the house of the coal-heaver, and might be supposed to have no need for (and therefore a soul above) money, he had his little weakness, a passion for sweets, which occasionally drove him to turn a penny in the lighter branches of labour, such as horse-holding, bottle-fetching, limpet-gathering, and the drowning of pups and kittens for soft-hearted old ladies. When not thus engaged he spent his days propped against the sunny side of the Market House, scratching his populous back against the cornerstones.

Ortho stared at Cully John, who was no whit embarrassed. The middle-aged wastrel was clad in a derelict coat so big that the cuffs dangled flipper-like below his fingers and the skirts covered any deficiencies he may have had in the way of nether

garments. On one foot was the gaping wreck of a
sea-boot, on the other the ruin of a Hessian. His
face was a mat of brindled red hair pierced by a
pair of remarkably sharp little eyes.

"Well, what is it, Beau Nash?" Ortho enquired.

Cully John uttered a long-drawn, guttural whine.

"Good dog," said Ortho. "Now wag your tail."

Cully repeated the noise, drawing it out into a
sort of wail.

"Wha-ow-ooo," Ortho mimicked; then, "That's
enough. Now go and tie yourself up in your
kennel."

He turned his back on Cully John, but the tug
on his sleeve was repeated. Ortho slewed about,
snarling, "Get away, will you?" Then he remembered the little weakness. "Oh, your sugar tooth
aching—eh? Here, go fetch!"

He jerked a coin into the gutter and enjoyed the
spectacle of Cully fishing for it in a foot of rushing
filth.

Cully recovered the penny five yards downstream
and returned to pluck at Ortho's sleeve with slimy
fingers. This time he caught the riding-whip full
across the shoulders.

"Will that teach you?" Ortho enquired.

Apparently it would not. Cully withdrew out
of range, but not from the scene. He circled to
and fro before Penhale, flapping his ludicrous sleeve
and whining dismally. The plaintive expression of
the hairy face, the little twitches at his clothing, the

whimpers, all reminded Ortho of an old spaniel
he had once possessed. She used to behave like that
when there was anything amiss with her puppies.
"I wonder if there is anything at the back of this?"
he pondered; then aloud,

"What *is* it you're trying to say?"

Cully flapped a cuff in a southerly direction,
shambled a few yards down the street, glanced over
his shoulder and whimpered again.

'Well, God knows what you want, but here goes,"
said Ortho, and followed. The house with the
green door lay that way. It was just possible . . .

Cully waddled ahead in the wet dusk, looking like
some vast beetle, wings folded, his misfit boots clip-
clopping on the flags, and turned to the left by the
Abbey.

Ortho hesitated. This was not the road to the
house of his hopes. Cully was twitching at his sleeve
again, whining, gesticulating more vehemently than
ever. Ortho chewed his lip. There must be something behind the halfwit's insistence. Perhaps it
might mean a rendezvous with the maid. Fine
ladies employed such methods for getting in touch
with admirers, he had heard. He decided to go
through with it, whatever it was; no harm could
come anyhow. He signed to Cully to lead on.
Cully emitted a whimper of satisfaction and clip-
clopped downhill. Below them lay the dark harbour with a dozen bleached coasters lying this way
and that, blurred lanterns dangling from their fore-

mast stays. A stench of stale mud and decayed
seaweed rose up on the wind.

Cully turned left-handed again into an alley of
mean cottages, and plunged into a passage, Ortho
at his heels. In a room on the right a woman was
working on a net with a wooden needle, while an
old man sat bowed to the candle scratching the picture of the Eddystone Lighthouse on a sperm whale
tooth. A mangy cat slunk by, a cod head in its
mouth. Upstairs a child wailed and wailed. The
passage was as dark as the pit.

Ortho, following Cully's heel-taps, blundered full
into a couple. A deep male voice exclaimed,
"Teufel!" and a girl cursed, exuding a smell of
cheap gin. Cully's fingers came out of the darkness
and plucked him by the sleeve into a yard beyond.
From the noise behind, Ortho deduced that the
lady had clawed her admirer in mistake for him.
The yard was littered with empty barrels, broken
oars, frayed cables, maritime rags and bones. Beyond it was an outhouse with a ladder leading to
the upper story. Cully's great boots thudded like
mallets on the rungs and Ortho went up behind him.
This was not a rendezvous. A self-respecting lady's
maid would not be seen dead in such a place; but
his curiosity was aroused—and there could be no
harm in it. Cully was no thieves' decoy, whatever
he was.

The loft at the top was as black as the passage
had been, except for a screened light, a mere

glimmer, at the far end. Again Cully's fingers found
him and led him on. They groped across the dark,
the crazy floor protesting under them, and his guide
pulled the screen (a patched sail) aside.

A tallow dip was stuck in a bottle neck and by
its light Ortho saw a man lying on a pile of nets
in the corner, a drab blanket drawn to his chin.
In the opposite corner, stacked against some shattered crab-pots, were five poles, four bolted together
in pairs, the fifth gaily painted; also a rope. Cully
shuffled up to the bed, indicated the visitor with
a flick of his abundant cuff and growled, whereupon
the man withdrew a thin hand from the blanket and
let drop sixpence through his fingers. "My last,"
he said.

Cully John examined the coin, bit and pocketed
it, writhed against a roof-prop as a cow chafes
against a scratching post, grunted and withdrew.
The clump of his boots rang on the ladder and
diminished down the passage.

"So that was the price of his insistence," thought
Ortho. "For that he took a cut across the back
and would have taken a dozen—sixpence! The
sugar craving must indeed be acute!

"Well?" he demanded.

The man turned his head slowly and looked at
him. He was an elderly man, with a week's stubble
of white hair on his chin. His eyes were pits, his
cheeks cavernous, and there was a ghastly blue tinge
on his lips.

"Good God," Ortho muttered.   "The fellow's dying, dying here and now!

"That fool has made a mistake," he said, speaking with some gentleness.   "It's a doctor you need, not me.   I'll fetch one immediately."

The man raised a hand in protest.   "No, no doctors.   You are Mr. Penhale?"

"That is my name, but——" He leant forward, striving to recognise any feature of the deathly countenance.   "But, have we met before anywhere? Do I know you?"

"No."

"Then why do you want me?   A doctor or a clergyman would be more suitable to your case. You look pretty sick, my friend.   Let me send some one."   He rose to go.

The skeleton hand lifted again.   "Stop, I pray!"

Ortho halted.   He was annoyed at being drawn into this embarrassing scene and promised Cully a drubbing later on, but decency held him.   The dying have their privileges.

"Well, what can I do for you?"

"Bear with me . . . a moment."

The man thrust his head back among the nets and closed his eyes; the blue lips were tight-locked, the jaw muscles bunched in knots, his throat worked; he seemed to be mustering the last reserves of strength.   Above them on the slates the rain beat a muffled, monotonous roll, descended through a leak in fat drops, plop-plop, as regularly as a clock-tick.

In some crib down the street a fiddle began to squeal
and an unsteady male voice quavered through one
verse of "Nancy Dawson" and then broke utterly.
A draught stirred the sail to indolent life, threaten-
ing the candle, whereat the shadows leapt out of
hiding like covert beasts pouncing on their enemy
and as it recovered, sneaked back again. Ortho
chewed his thumbnail, sulky with impatience. The
candle was nearly out; presently he would find himself alone in the dark with a strange corpse. A
charming situation! The fellow was asleep, he believed. He would slip out quietly and send up one
of those sluts; it was their house, their affair. He
took a stealthy step backwards and lifted the edge of
the sail.

"Mr. Penhale!" The voice spoke with startling
vigour; the reserves had mustered.

Ortho dropped the curtain. "Er—yes?"

"I crave your indulgence, sir . . . I shall not be
long!"

"At your service."

"I have a story to relate to you."

"To me! Why?"

"Because though you don't know me I know
something of you and I understand that in these
parts there is no gentleman more sprightly and
forward in gallant affairs. Well, sir, I also have
known love in my poor fashion and the way of it
was somewhat curious and I think should prove of
interest to you, to you in particular."

Ortho sat down heavily on a crab-pot and stared. A love story here—now—in a dripping loft, from one on the brink of eternity. A bizarre setting indeed!

"Speak on," he said.

The man regarded Ortho in silence for a second; there was a queer glint in his half-closed eyes, an ironic twist to his mouth. Then he spoke.

"You must know, sir, that I am by profession a rope-dancer. At one time, and I say it without boast, there was no Italian to match me. I could stand on my head, balance and make French postures on the slack-rope against any man in the three kingdoms. I have danced between the top-masts of a ship in London Pool with both banks black with people admiring. I was sober, diligent and saving; at the age of thirty I was on the point of buying a fine booth of my own and having people to work for me. Then enter Love.

"It is, as you know, sir, the fashion with poets to call Love 'the tender passion.' Believe me, it is nothing of the sort. Love, as I know it, is a lightning-stroke, a consuming flame. I met a girl on Bagshot Heath, a vagabond like myself, playing a guitar from tavern to tavern. She was thin, ragged, snarling like a beaten dog, and no man would look twice at her, but her scowling dark beauty lit a fire in my breast, an eternal fire. When tomorrow and a thousand years from tomorrow I lie mouldering underground, dust in dust, there will be one little

spark of me still alight—love. I bought her clothes
and food and we travelled together. We went a
circuit of the fairs and made good money, she playing while I postured on my rope. I gave her all
she asked for, but she was cold. Patience, I cried
to myself, she will come quietly to my arms in the
end, patience.

"She filled out on the plentiful food, wore the
spangled dresses with an air, laid aside her scowl.
Men began to look at her twice, and she at them,
slily, out of the corners of her eyes. This maddened
me and at times I beat her—and afterwards, for
fear she would leave me, wept for forgiveness and
showered on her gifts of clothes, food, money. We
made good wages, I say, but spent it faster. We
slept at inns where we should have slept in barns,
drank ale when we should have drunk water, ate
white bread instead of black. Come six months and
all the money that was saved for my booth is gone,
but my girl has her beauty in full bloom now and
men are looking at her more than twice.

"At Ashburton market my rope broke suddenly,
and I think she had been at it. I had beaten her
the night before for making too free with a horse-
dealer. Howsobe, I fell on my hip and could not
mount my rope again for weeks. I was in a sore
plight, a stiff hip, no money, and I knew that the
only thing that held her to me was money.

"'Let her go and the devil take her,' you say.
Indeed I said it myself twenty times a night; but

I could not let her go. Love had me, I tell you. As well bid a man pluck a cancer from his bosom. I *could* not.

"So we were at Ashburton, the money was out, and I could not dance. What then? I, who had been honest and diligent all my life, took cudgel, limped out into the bye-ways and robbed drunken drovers and farmers on their way home. I did this at Tavistock, Launceston and westwards; and all the time, though she would not bear a hand herself, she urged me on and gobbled every farthing I earned. I had to keep on robbing.

"Then one night I met with a lusty yeoman who was my undoing. We battled for long, evenly matched. A move on her part would have turned the scale, but she did nothing, sat in the hedge and watched. In the end he beat me senseless. When I woke up it was dawn; he had gone and she with him.

"That is over thirty years past. She set him afire as she had me, but she married him; he was a man of substance. I went my way, but I was finished. In my trade a man must make his money before his limbs stiffen. I was thirty-two and there was my hip. My booth was gone. I saw her from time to time at fairs where I was showing, but she never spoke a word or threw me a penny, not once."

Ortho stirred uncomfortably, setting all the crab-pot withies a-creak. From the harbour came the sigh of the flood-tide creeping up the shingle. In the house beyond, the child wailed on. The flame guttered wildly.

"Have patience, sir," said the mountebank. "We approach the end. Neither I nor my story shall outlast that candle. Not long ago, not so long ago, I was at a certain fair on my rope and I could do no good; the crowd was very contemptuous, for which to them small blame, for my antics nowadays are a sorry matter. I did this and I did that but could win no applause from them, nothing but contempt; and then, looking down, I suddenly perceived that she was in the forefront, leading the scoffing. 'Pah!' she says. 'See the old scaramouch totter! Hark how the skeleton creaks!' Anger rose up to my head like wine, anger and pride. 'A moment, my lady,' I said; 'watch and I will show you that you do not know everything,' and throwing my pole aside I essayed the cart-wheel, a movement I had not dared for years. But my hip gave and I came down to the ground in a heap. I can hear her laughter still. I lay on the grass for some time and a charitable woman gave me a sup of cordial from a bottle, and the tinners a capful of pennies to console me for my hurt, but I knew the end was come. When night fell I took my way out of the field and along the road, and there where a little hill goes down to a stream I sat and bided the hour.

"About midnight along the road rides my lady, and she descends from her high horse and is gathered quietly to my arms as I said she would—

in the end. All night she lay in my arms, very quietly, and I said, 'Ah, my dear, I have had the first of you and the last of you and what has gone between matters little.' And all the sweet things I had thought of to tell her when we were young, but had not, I told her then, and she lay quiet all night, her head on my shoulder. Then the stars went out and dawn came up golden, and I kissed the dew from her face and crept away, leaving her sleeping in the shining wet grasses—nobody would have thought she was dead!"

"Dead!" Ortho exclaimed. "What d'ye mean? How . . . ?"

"I hung my rope across the road. Horse tripped . . . she fell."

"Tripped! Fell! Dead! By Jesus you—you ——!" Ortho yelled, leaping to his feet; and at that second the candle went out, and out of the darkness came a wrenching cry:

"Teresa! Teresa!"

CHAPTER IX

ORTHO found the Davys agreeable to the change and installed them in Bosula without further ado. Followed three weeks of house scrubbing, whitewashing and painting. The amount of dirt, dust, cobwebs and fallen plaster that was removed was astonishing. Two of the three tall chimneys were found to be chock-a-block with generations of jackdaw nests; rats had honeycombed a wall on the river-side and worm was in the beams here and there. Ortho and Bohenna, his leading hind, effected the repairs themselves, with an adze, shaping new beams from oak trees felled in the valley, emptying the rat-warrens by means of ferrets, and plastering them up. The jack-daw nests they cleared by dropping stones, set fire to what remained and polished the job off by following the time-honoured receipt of "putting a goose through," with disastrous results, however, for the bird got stuck and they were the best part of a day getting it out.

But when it was all done Ortho hardly knew his old home, so changed was it. During the thirty-one years of Teresa's rule the floors of the five occupied rooms were occasionally swept, the more obtrusive cobwebs removed with the twirl of a broom, but

Ortho never remembered seeing anybody get down on their knees and scrub. Not a penn'orth of paint or lime had gone to the walls; a stain on the furniture remained till obliterated by another. Now, modelled on Roswarva, all was trim as could be. One thing lacked. Ortho took axe and laid into the trunk of a big ash before the house.

Bohenna remonstrated. "Trees don't grow overnight. There's plenty timber behind the barn."

"I know that."

"You let in the sou'west gales."

"*And* the sun," said Ortho, making the clean chips fly. "Stand clear!"

He felled two ashes and a couple of sycamores and the sun came through, flooding the south rooms. Ortho, full of pride, led Bohenna within; but the old moor-man displayed no approval. Like all open-air animals, his first demand of a home was that it should exclude his native element. He screwed up his mouth to spit, met Naomi's terrible eye and gulped instead. He never entered the house again, except of necessity. There was no comfort in a place where one could not spit.

Mary's child appeared on the 19th of January. It arrived promptly, without causing undue trouble, weighed ten pounds at birth, slept regularly, ate heartily, kept its woes (if any) to itself, in fact exceeded all the high expectations formed of it with the basic exception that instead of being a boy it was a girl. Mary made no secret of her disappointment. Eli said he was pleased, but looked as if somebody had kicked him in the face. Ortho cared little one way or the other, but would have preferred a boy. He had looked forward to putting a sturdy young nephew up to a wrinkle or two in the way of riding and shooting. He had no interest in girls. Only the grandfather, old Simeon, approved the baby's choice. Mary had been more than a regiment of sons to him, he said, and now there were two Marys. Hosannah! He hurried into Penzance and bought the child a coral teething-stick surmounted by silver bells, also a spelling book with woodcuts. He weighed it daily, drew up a diet table (disregarded), and built a rocker for it out of teak salvaged from a Dutch Indiaman. He was completely happy.

Two days after the baby's birth Ortho went into Penzance to fetch his new clothes. Only one suit was ready, a mahogany coat with wide lapels faced with buff, and tight buff breeches. He put it on straight away and walked twice the length of Chapel Street, which meant passing the green door four times, but there was no flutter at the window. Perhaps they were peeping at him from behind the curtains. He hoped so. That done, he returned to the Ship Castle; over a pot of ale commiserated with young Teage, who had fallen out with his father and his mistress at the same time; called for his horse and set out for home.

It was a windless evening after storm. Vast

rounded continents of cloud hung becalmed across
the west—rose, orange, underlined with violet. The
long thin arm of the Lizard lay along the east, pink-
flushed, a reptile basking on a sheet of glass. Out
of Newlyn crept the fishing fleet, oars curdling up
the bronze reflections of their sails.

There were many people on the Green, snatching
air and exercise after long confinement. A group
of old sea-captains stood under the flag-staff, tele-
scopes levelled on a barquentine off St. Clements.
Muffled visitors tramped up and down, discussing
their ailments, gentlemen in all manner of wigs and
hats, cloaked ladies with huge calashes, like waggon
hoods, pulled up over their heads. Gossiping maids
patrolled the turf, dragging reluctant children.
Small boys bowled hoops. On the waste ground
by Redinnick some apprentices were playing pitch,
and on a small eminence stood the town's solitary
sedan-chair its door open to allow passage for a
gouty leg completely encased in bandages.

Ortho went on, playing lightly with the filly's
mouth, legging her up to make her show herself.
That, as far as he knew, there was no one worth
impressing, did not deter him from making an impression. He swaggered from pure love of it. The
filly crossed the Green snap-kicking and pig-jump-
ing. She was peculiarly thin-skinned, the touch of
a rowel at her belly and up she went. It looked
dangerous but was not. Ortho sat her gracefully,
smiling, pricking her on to fresh antics, aware that

the sea-captains had turned their backs on the sloop, the servant-girls were staring open-mouthed, and the fashionables raising quizzing glasses. The apprentices, after the manner of their kind, cheered loudly. Penhale, the local daredevil, riding a fiery monster!

"Youp, Penhale! Give it what you gived De Grasse!"

Ortho enjoyed his scamper.

Then, just as he reached the Laregan end and was easing up, he caught sight of the grenadier figure of Miss Barradale's maid, preceded by someone shorter, slimmer . . . Miss Barradale, for a hundred pounds! And they were passing with fifty yards between! He laid his left leg and spur hard in and the filly bounded sideways to the right as if drawn on a string, snorting, tossing her head, shrinking from the rowel. A woman, well out of danger, screamed. Another flung herself into the arms of a portly stranger, nearly knocking him over. The apprentices yelled. Dogs barked. The grenadier maid made a clutch at her mistress and was repelled. Miss Barradale awaited destruction unmoved.

The exasperated mare suddenly got her head down and bucked properly, a manœuvre outside Ortho's calculations. He was very nearly off. By the time he was back in the saddle they were a good deal closer to the mark than he had intended to go. When he checked the filly up there was not a yard to spare. Well, a miss was as good as a mile. He swept off his new cocked-hat quite unabashed.

"A thousand pardons! My mare is young . . . shied at something, a child's hoop, I think. I trust you are none the worse?"

Miss Barradale was none the worse; the little gloved hand stroking the filly's nose had not a tremble in it.

The maid was anxious. "Stand back, Miss; the beast is vicious!"

"You speak when addressed, Vashti," said her mistress, and looked up at Ortho.

"I am devoted to horses and riding. You sit strongly, sir."

Ortho shrugged. "Oh, well, it is my business. I was a lancer once."

Miss Barradale twinkled. "And a post-boy."

He laughed outright. "Yes, that also—once. You remember, then?"

"Naturally. Would you have me so ungrateful? Had it not been for you we might have stayed on that moor all night and been murdered. Both Mrs. Beckford and myself have been waiting an opportunity to thank you."

"Oh, pshaw!" said Ortho. "A pleasure, I assure you."

Pretty he had thought her before, lovely he thought her now, her tinted face upturned to the warm glow of sunset, framed by powdered drop-curls and white gauze. That foot peeping out from beneath the many-hooded Artois cloak—how tiny, how neatly shod! That slim uplifted hand—how perfectly gloved! Never among the many women he had known had he met with anything so elegantly gowned, coiffed and perfumed, of such outstanding quality.

He backed the mare and vaulted to the ground. "You are stepping homewards?"

"Yes, but——"

"May I accompany you to your door?"

"I am honoured . . . but you were bound in the other direction."

"I *was*, but there's no one to fret if I do not arrive either tonight or this day se'n-night," said Ortho, fitting his pace to hers. "Tell me how does it strike you, our rugged West? You are not terrified of being broiled and devoured by us wild Cornish —eh?"

They proceeded back across the Green, laughing and talking; Vashti bringing up the rear.

Ortho, timing himself with care, was in the middle of an enthralling and largely fictitious story of how he and King Nick had hoodwinked the Preventive when they arrived at the Chapel Street house, whereupon he bit the tale off short, bowed low and made motions of departure.

But Miss Barradale shook a finger at him. "You have not yet given Mrs. Beckford her opportunity of thanking you, Mr. Penhale. Furthermore, I shall not sleep till I learn how you outwitted those dragoons." She ran up the steps and threw the green door open.

Ortho tossed his reins to an idler and followed, protesting that he had not meant to intrude, that he really must not stop for more than a minute.

He stopped to supper: he stopped till ten o'clock.

Mrs. Beckford expressed gratitude—not without some prompting from Miss Barradale, however; she appeared to have forgotten the incident. But she warmed to him later when he expressed admiration for King Charles spaniels and for her Rupert in particular. Ortho finished the story of the Preventive's discomfiture and was half-way through another when supper was announced, so stayed to finish that.

It was a well cooked, well chosen meal; the wines likewise were superb. Vashti waited with inconspicuous perfection. Ortho noted the rich Irish napery, the Waterford glass, the heavy Barradale silver, with an appreciative eye. Everything of the very best, everything. His late model, Roswarva, depreciated. Clean and adequate it might be, but here was real class. He wondered how much those dishes cost, those cut-glass decanters and things. A pile of money doubtless. This Barradale must be as rich as an earl.

Urged by Miss Barradale he refilled his glass, informed Mrs. Beckford of a cure for Rupert's eczema and told a story of a former occupant of the house, an old lady who, her orchard suffering from juvenile thieves, set her gardener to watch, armed with a blunderbuss. As, after three nights, the apples were still going, she thought the man must be asleep, and crept forth to catch him, but received a full charge of buckshot instead, fortunately in that portion of her anatomy best able to withstand it.

From that, warmed by good food, excellent wine and an attractive listener, he swept on in a flood of anecdotage. An observant eye and a sense of humour had gone with him on his travels, likewise a feeling for the picturesque. He bounded from continent to continent; leapt oceans between breaths; was describing Sallee with the Rovers coming into port amid a crash of drums and guns at one moment, at the next the flower jungles of St. Lucia. Now Table Mountain rose, cloud-wreathed, before them; now the silver ramparts of the Atlas. Now it was an Arab powder-play, tribe after tribe thundering by, in line, flying clouds of dust and white burnouses; now it was the negro dances at the Spring Path cemetery in Jamaica, women in a host of petticoats stamping and kicking, men rattling tins filled with pebbles. They saw a great Indiaman wallowing like a drunken thing in the dark night off Agulhas, dipping her yard-arms, her three trucks pointed with St. Elmo's fire; heard the temple gongs of Ind and saw bejeweled rajahs riding in gilded howdahs. Nor was the victory of April forgotten.

Mrs. Beckford sat toasting her slippers before

the fire, Rupert snoring in her ample lap. She was perturbed without being interested. Barbary and Bengal were one to her, Cape Town and Kingston. They were "abroad" and that was sufficient; the good housewife had enough to see to in her own home. God, working in a mysterious way, had created "abroad" and foreigners, but He had also created the English Channel as a sign to His Chosen to keep themselves to themselves. Mrs. Beckford did not condemn foreigners — the poor things couldn't order the place of their birth—but she did not approve of them; they were either papists or insufficiently clad. She did not think this talk of Moors and negroes suitable for delicate ears. The terms "Moor" and "infidel" were synonymous, and negroes went about practically naked—she had seen pictures. That battle too. It had been a famous victory and she was sure everybody must be very grateful to dear Admiral Rodney, but there was no need to go into details. "When our officers went aboard the *Ville de Paris* they stepped over their shoe-buckles in blood"—ugh! Most unsuitable!

She made a murmur of protest and got promptly snubbed by Miss Barradale. Mrs. Beckford relapsed into uneasy silence, her conscience itching. Nicola seemed very taken up with this young man— and who was he? A few weeks ago he had appeared to them in the garb of a rough seaman—providentially, no doubt, but still. . . . Now he was dressed like a gentleman. She admitted his handsome looks and the ease of his manner. He had been very nice about her little dog, which was unusual with gentlemen—even her late samt had hurled books at it. But his way of life seemed to have been most irregular and so had the circumstances of his introduction. Dear Nicola's impetuosity needed curbing. There was also the young man to consider; he must not be allowed to imagine a vain thing.

But how to curb dear Nicola? She was the self-willed daughter of an indulgent father and had a sharp way with her if countered. Did she, Mrs. Beckford, apply that curb she might speedily find herself in the street, bag and baggage. It was a case of penury on thirty pounds a year versus the Barradale flesh-pots. Mrs. Beckford sighed and fondled the spaniel's ears. How poor Rupert would miss his chickens! Also there were the strongest reasons why dear Nicola should not be upset. With these and Rupert's comforts in mind Mrs. Beckford decided to let matters slide for the time being. Mr. Barradale might be down any day now and at the worst she could always drop a hint to the young man.

As for dear Nicola, she knew nothing of what was passing in the mind of her duenna—all her eyes and ears were for Ortho. Like an Arabian djinn he spoke his magic and the great, redolent, vivid outside world came home to her, temples and palaces, argosies and caravans. All her life she had been cloistered from this marvellous world, in "select seminaries," by governesses, duennas and hosts of servants. Yet all the time it had been brushing her elbow—had she only known. Her father's captains came up to the house to dine when they docked after long voyages: gruff gnarled old gentlemen mostly, suffering agonies of embarrassment in her presence. But once she had withdrawn there were tales told, she imagined. Rumbles of deep laughter sounded in the dining room. The black butler, Pericles, went in and out loaded with full and empty bottles; the open door showed a haze of pipe-smoke. She had seen the guests depart, reeling unsteadily through the dusk, arm in arm. Sometimes they sang. On one occasion a befoozled master had collapsed in the hall, dragging Pericles down with him; another had tried to kiss her maid. Disgusting old beasts, she had thought them. Now she saw differently. She saw them heroic on the poops of ships running down the Trades, spy-glasses alert for the glint of a Bordeaux privateer; labouring among the snow-squalls off the Banks, gear frozen solid; tumbling in the Calabar surf, dizzy with heat and fevers—and all to keep her snug, to pay for her finery. Her heart softened toward the gnarled old roisterers who tried to kiss her maids; her eyes for Ulysses, the teller of tales, sparkled jewel bright.

It was not till after ten that Ortho got the filly out of its stall at the Ship and for the second time started home. He rode slowly, steeped in delightful meditation, until he reached the high brow of Paul

Hill; there he swung his mare about and looked back.

Above him immensities of cloud pricked here and there with a glitter of constellations: the Bull with red Aldebaran and the twinkling Pleiades; Orion, bright sword on hip; the Goat, the Dog, Sirius blazing in its teeth.

Beneath him the low isthmus and the sea, dark as a gulf but for the dying lights of Penzance and, southward, the fisher lamps—a handful of tinsel strewn broadcast on black velvet. Stars above and below, his old recurring dream of floating in mid-air amid celestial diamond-dust.

Ortho drew a deep breath and kissed his hand toward the town lights. "Goodnight, my sweet and pretty!" He lifted the mare into a canter and went home singing. A poacher, crouched among his snares on Trevelloe moor, heard him go by and muttered, "Buck Penhale up to some devilry." Naomi Davy, awake with a troublesome tooth, heard him singing in the Bosula yard and ascribed his elation to brandy.

Miss Nicola Barradale lay asleep in the peace of Chapel Street, cheek pillowed on bare arm, and dreamed a dream in which Mr. Penhale appeared successively as the Grand Khan, a pirate and a post-boy against shifting backgrounds of palms, snow-mountains and painted elephants.

CHAPTER X

ORTHO PENHALE sat in the tap-room of the Ship & Castle and sulked. He had not seen Miss Barradale for three days and he had an idea that Mrs. Beckford and Vashti were combining to keep him off. Two attempts to get through the green door had he made that afternoon and each time been frustrated . . . Miss Barradale was sleeping . . . Miss Barradale had a headache—faugh! He had a shrewd suspicion that Miss Barradale knew nothing of her nap or her headache—or of his having called. Did those two fool women really imagine they could resist him, the irresistible? Faugh again! He slouched back on the bench, hands sunk in pockets, long legs straddled out before him, the picture of puerile spleen.

Young Carclew entered, stamping his feet. "Wind flown back four points and blowing a cracker," he announced; then he noticed Ortho and hooted. "My soul! Behold comrade Penhale! There's a sight to cheer a winter evening! Have you had all your teeth drawn to once, my poor friend? Or is the smart deeper? Has that miller's wench proved unfaithful? Shame take the ungrateful jade—and you offering her everything but marriage!"

"Oh, go to hell!" Ortho growled.

"I'll go where it's warmer, if that is your meaning," said Carclew, turning toward the fire. "Ho, Captain Kempthorne! Better ashore than afloat on a night like this—eh?"

The man addressed was a native of St. Ives, home on a visit. He was master of a barque trading to the Brazils and had recently won some measure of fame by not only beating but capturing a large Nantes privateer.

Then and there, in response to inquiries, he began to relate details of the exploit. Ortho's rancor increased. The fellow had been in Penzance for two days now and for two days had done nothing but chaw about his pettifogging skirmish. Now, ye gods, they were going to have it all over again! The fact that he, Ortho, had been allowed to wag his jaw for weeks on the subject of Rodney's battle did not weigh with him. He resented anybody but himself holding the center of the stage. He would shift over presently and give this small-beer hero a tweak or two.

Bohenna shoved his grizzled head in at the door and said the horses had been ready for an hour and were still ready. He, also, was told to go to hell.

Ortho, his lip curling in an ugly fashion, his black brows puckered, began to slide up the bench toward the fire. "Passed Steepholm with four feet of water in the hold," the captain was saying; "beached her at Pill." Ortho hesitated. Steepholm, that was an island in the Severn mouth, surely; and Pill a village on the Avon below Bristol . . . Bristol. He reflected for a moment and continued his sliding movement, but with changed motives.

Carclew, studying the stuffed mongoose over the mantelpiece, cocked his head sharply. "Hark!"

A general chorus of "What?"

"Sounded devilish like a gun."

Old Trebilcock, the attorney, nodded. "Now you say so, I believe I heard it myself; away to the west'ard."

The assemblage crowded out of the door, buzzing.

Ortho slid alongside Kempthorne. A healthy pink face, containing two sharp gray eyes and a mouth of extreme resolution, was turned upon him. Not at all the countenance of a man lightly "tweaked"; Ortho gave thanks that he had been deflected from his first purpose.

"Pardon me, sir, but do I understand you hail from Bristol?" he asked in his smoothest tones.

"That is my port of register."

"Are you by chance acquainted with a merchant by name of Barradale?"

Kempthorne chuckled. "Barradale? Nicholas Barradale? Yes, I am very well acquainted with him."

"What manner of chap is he?"

"What is that to you?"

"Oh, I may contrive a little business with him," said Ortho, airily.

"Are you in the African trade?"

"Me? Lord, no! Why?"

"Then I don't see what business you can do with Nick," said Kempthorne; "for that is the only trade he does that I know of, and a mighty fine trade too. He's got three ships and not one of 'em stows less than three hundred prime blacks—though I believe I did hear how he'd lost the *Fair Penitent* off St. Kitts last hurricane season."

"Slave-merchant?"

"Aye—sole owner, and a generous one. Best of gear and provision. Pays his masters six pounds monthly, besides primage, cabin privilege and seven shillings port allowance. A right good sort 'Wild Nick,' gay as a boy and free as a prince."

" 'Wild,' they call him. Why so?"

Kempthorne pursed up his lips. "Oh, he takes his chances. Ha'nt insured since war broke, I believe. Met him storming out of the Underwriters' Coffee House. 'What do you think them footpads want to rob me, George?' he hollers. 'Twenty-two per cent the round trip! By the Lord, I'll take my own risks and keep my own profits!' That's Nick all over. But his ships came home, mark you. They're armed like frigates and prime sailers. He's a lucky man, Nick is—though, like most of us, he's had his troubles."

"What troubles?" Ortho inquired.

"Married a wife, thought the world of her, and then in less than three years, damme, if she didn't go off. . . ." The captain jerked forward, hand uplifted. "That *was* a gun sure enough, a long twelve or I never heard one." He swallowed his toddy at a gulp and made for the door, Ortho beside him.

"You were saying that Barradale's wife—?"

"Eh?" said the captain. "Oh, yes, yes, a bad business. . . . Poor Nick! Poor Nick! Where is she, Harry?"

"Off Gwavas," Carclew answered, returning for his hat. "'Tween here and Mousehole. Come down to the front, Captain."

Ortho was left alone with the stuffed mongoose. Bohenna's hairy face came round the door-post again.

"Hey! Ain't 'e heard? There's a ship in trouble off Gwavas, dragging fast." He specialized in distressed ships; they were to him as manna from Heaven.

"Well, what of it?" said Ortho, feeling the mongoose's teeth with a fingertip.

Bohenna was shocked—such indifference to divine bounty! "What of it? Hark to 'en. Why, dang 'e, I don't s'pose thee'd scruple against a bit of free pickings, would'st? *She may be an Indiaman!*"

Ortho reached for his topcoat. He was not interested in the vessel, but there was no object in remaining in an empty tap-room. "Oh, all right," he
growled; "get the horses."

Though Bohenna was for a shorter route, Ortho
insisted on riding down Chapel Street. There was
a light in Miss Barradale's bedroom.

Not till they left the shelter of the houses did
he realize how the wind had risen. All the afternoon it had been blowing briskly but now it was
slicing out of the northeast like a whip-lash. It
whirled Ortho's coat-capes round his ears and kept
them there; flogged the horses along before it, tails
tucked in. Knots of people, bearing lanterns, dotted
the Green. Ortho hustled through them barking,
"Way! Way!"

Carclew saw him go by and grinned. "Friend
Penhale and henchman off to grab what they can."

"Yes," croaked old Trebilcock. "Did you ever
see those Monk's Cove rogues gut a wreck? I did
once. It's like magic."

As they cleared the crowd Bohenna forced his
horse alongside Ortho and pointed westward, shouting, "There y' are—her flare. Wind's got her
pinned under Penlee. Once her cables part—tchut!"

Ortho turned his head and saw a yellow light
flaring close under the black mass of land. "Why
should they part?" he snapped, still sulky. "There's
no force of water yet—"

Even as he spoke the flare disappeared.

"Yah!" jeered Bohenna and, driving his mount ahead, took the lead.

They blundered through Wherry Town, knocking a boy over; splashed through Laregan Stream; crossed the Western Green and came to Newlyn.

"Round or through? The tide's up," Ortho called.

There were two ways through the fisher hamlet: at low tide by the beach, at high by climbing halfway up Paul Hill and then coming down again.

Without deigning to reply Bohenna headed his horse down the slip into the water. Ortho, not to be outdone by his hind, flogged and spurred the scared filly after him. She slipped on the stones, fell, got up again and, terrified by the sudden drenching, tried to get out the way she had come. Ortho wrenched her back and they battled round and round, lashing the water up. At length, by sheer power of knees and will, he got her to face it and, half wading, half swimming, they floundered across and scrambled up the slip on the far side. Only then did Ortho realize that he was wearing his fine new suit and was soaked to the skin.

"Oh, curse you and your wreck!" he shouted to Bohenna; but the old man took no notice; urged his blown horse along the coast road.

By Ros Skelly they were stopped by a press of women who had flocked out of Newlyn, hastily wrapped in shawls.

"Is she struck yet?" Bohenna panted.

"Ess, this long whiles. Half her people's ashore already," a shrill voice replied.

"What is she, do 'e knaw?"

"Man-o-war, so I do hear," said the voice.

"Ach!" Bohenna's disgust drew a general titter. A girl jeered. 'What wer'st looking for, old plunderer? A rum ship?"

"Naw," cried another. "A Spaniard loaded with diamonds."

"Thee'll get naught but a passel of firewood this time, my beauty," said a third, 'and thee'll have to wait for that; she haven't started to scat yet."

"That her down under Penlee?" Ortho inquired.

"Ess, broadside to the rocks," the female chorus replied.

Ortho pushed on till directly above the wreck; then, leaving the filly with his disgruntled retainer, felt his way down the cliff. Since he was there and already wet through, he might as well see what there was to be seen.

The cliff was low at that part and sloped gradually. The vessel, lodged beam-on, formed a breakwater. Men were coming ashore fast, on hen-coops, gratings, studding-sail booms, swimming even. The waves swept them up the ledges and left them clinging to knobs and crevices where the fishermen secured them. Two or three had been stunned, but the majority had only bruises to show. Ortho met a dozen dripping castaways being helped up the cliff. "Sloop *Lapwing* from Gibraltar with despatches," he heard one say. "Thick weather. . . . Thought we were round the Longships."

Some farm labourers staggered by, carrying an unconscious lieutenant. Ortho felt his way to a group of lanterns by the sea edge. Five or six sailors who had just come ashore were sitting on the rocks surrounded by their rescuers, feeling their bruises tenderly and wringing the water out of their clothes. Two of them were continuing a vital argument they had been conducting when the sloop struck. They differed on the price of pig-tail chew in Malta. One, a negro, clutched a little monkey to his bosom; it had come ashore clinging to his wool. Another, a local man, had not been home for seven years. He asked if his old mother were still alive and on hearing she was, announced his intention of leaving forthwith. She was a holy terror, he said; had driven a knitting-needle through his arm last time he saw her.

Ortho passed on to the next group. It contained a phlegmatic Swede with a broken arm, and an Irishman, fantastically draped in seaweed, who complained that he had left seven shillings' worth of new bedding aboard the wreck and was with difficulty restrained from plunging back after it.

"Children," thought Ortho. "Drag them out of Death's jaws and they wrangle over the price of tobacco, moan for a lost blanket." There were plenty to conduct the rescue work. He turned to go home, then saw the third group and strolled toward it. What was here? Some brine-pickled, war-scarred infant bewailing a lost sheath-knife, a coloured scarf? He shouldered through the ring of fisherfolk and saw a tall man and a short man, sitting side by side. The tall man had an oblique cut running right across his forehead; blood masked his face, dribbled off his chin. Both expansive hands were locked about his companion's left wrist. His eyes were half-closed, dazed. The smaller man appeared little the worse for the dip, except that his coat was torn to rags. His complexion, even in the fluttering lantern-light, glowed ruddy as a pippin. He suffered the grip on his wrist without protest; his expression was that of amused resignation.

Ortho stared at him, jaw lolling with amazement. Was it? It couldn't be! Yet that bullet-head, those crumpled little ears! It must be! It *was!* What was he doing here? What had he been doing aboard a British man-o'-war? There could be but one answer. A fisherman lumbered forward and slapped the tall man on the shoulder. "Come, matey. Can't stop here all night. Best slip along to a doctor and have your head seen to." The sailor puckered his silly eyes and gathered his companion closer. "Bloody pirate . . . my charge," he mumbled. The small man winked and tapped his head significantly.

"He's silly," he whispered. "I'm sailing master of that sloop—silly."

"My charge . . . bloody picaroon," the sailor mumbled, his battered head drooping.

Again the little man winked. "Wandering in his mind."

The fishermen nodded sympathetically.

"Yes, yes, we'll see to him," said their spokesman to the idiot. "You let him go now and come along."

Ortho burst into the ring. "I know that fellow!" he yelled, pointing to the small man. "His name's MacBride, and bloody pirate he is. That's the scoundrel that picked me up off the Bishop eight years ago and sold me as a slave in Sallee—you dog, you!"

Up went the lanterns; a gasp of astonishment.

"Mr. Penhale!" Another gasp.

Everybody in West Penwith knew the story of Ortho's adventures in Barbary. Here was a dramatic climax indeed.

Ortho grabbed MacBride by the scruff of his coat and jerked him free of the sailor's grasp, shook him till his teeth rattled.

"Yes, I am Penhale," he cried; "and mighty fortunate I came, else you softs would have let this rogue escape—the renegade hound!"

He flung MacBride on his knees and kicked him to his feet again.

"You rest easy, mate; I'll take care of him henceforth," said Ortho, with a wave of his hand to the doddering sailor. "Mighty close care too—till the hangman relieves me. Come on, my bold buccaneer, march!"

He screwed his hand well into MacBride's coat and hustled him up the rocks toward the road. Darkness swallowed them. The fishermen turned to drag a fresh set of swimmers out of the surf.

Two hours later a boy climbing homeward along the upper ledges tripped over a pair of legs.

On examination the legs proved to belong to Ortho Penhale, Ortho Penhale lying stunned in a rock pool.

Of MacBride there was no trace.

CHAPTER XI

TOM Davy rubbed his boots on the scraper, entered the kitchen and, sitting down in the appointed place, just inside the door, removed them altogether. That done, he crossed to his chair by the fire in his stockinged feet. He was well trained.

His trainer knocked the hot ash from the bakepan and deftly extracted a trio of gold-brown tarts.

"Well, hast been to Church town?"

"Ess."

"Got my vinegar?"

"Ess."

"Have they caught that gert pirate yet?"

"Naw—but a Sennen woman spied 'em geeking at her out of the furze bushes."

Naomi was contemptuous. "Hugh! Some crabber's old donkey, more like! What would a sly rogue like he be doing at the Land's End? Believe me, he's most to John o' Groats by now."

"Well, that's what woman declared," said Tom, feebly.

"But they didn't find 'en, did they?"

"Na-aw."

"Pah! Course not. Every half-baked giglet

in the twelve parishes will be turning furze into pirates for the next month."

She dished up the tartlets and bustled into the next room. "How's your poor head, sir?"

Ortho looked up from his plate. "Oh, none so bad. Throbs now and again."

"You should have rested, sir," Naomi reproved. "Leaving your bed and riding round the country didn't do it no good."

Ortho grunted. "Hmm—maybe it didn't. But I've a score to settle with the man that cracked it."

Eli's massive form filled the doorway. "Been to market," he explained. "Great old clunk in town about you and your doings t'other night."

"And great old merriment too, I'll warrant," said Ortho bitterly.

"Didn't notice any in front of me," the brother replied, his square jaw hardening. "They hadn't better. 'Pears the sloop came on this MacBride in thick weather pounding into a Levant trader and lamed him before he could make off. Seeing he was undone, he blew his xebec up, but they dragged him and five others out of the water. He's a desperate fellow by all accounts."

Ortho nodded. "Desperate! Aye, he's desperate enough."

Eli continued: " 'Pears that when the sloop struck, the captain let him out of the bilboes, but put the bosun and a quartermaster in charge of him. In the confusion and all he gives the quartermaster

the slip and dives overboard quietly. But the bosun
dives after him. They came ashore swimming side
by side. Just as they struck the rocks up goes Mac-
Bride on the bosun's back. The bosun goes under
and gets his head knocked but MacBride washes
ashore smooth as a seal. He's a slippery one and
no mistake. How did he trick *you?*"

Ortho winced slightly, then shrugged his shoulders.

"There was I hustling him up the cliff before me,
him tripping and stumbling. Just as we're at the
top he trips and goes sprawling on his hands. When
I jerks him up he has a big stone in 'em and slugs me
with it between the eyes. I thought he was stumbling
because I was hustling him a bit rough, but now I
realise that he was feeling for a stone all the way."

Eli grunted with reluctant admiration. "He's a
sly one, ecod! But sly or no he won't last long.
I heard in Penzance that he's been seen."

"Where?"

"Zennor."

"He moves brear quick, then," said Naomi.
"Lightning's a fool to him. A few minutes past he
was in Sennen. He'll be in Scilly next—swum over
during the night. Who see'd 'en at Zennor?"

"A woman out gathering sticks by Trendrin Hill.
They're gone out after him with dogs and guns."

Naomi sneered. "Ess, I thought so. Geeking
at her out of the quoit stones, I s'pose. Well to-

morrow we'll hear that one o' the old Trendrin goats has gone to glory—shot as a pirate, the dear saint!"

Eli laughed and turned on the housekeeper. "Oh, now I remember. Mary told me to tell you to soak the master's bandages in brier-leaf water."

"Let Mrs. Penhale come and try it herself then," Naomi retorted. "For say what I will the man won't let me touch 'en."

"I can't abide a swarm of women pestering round," said Ortho testily. "I can shift my own bandages."

"Swarm o' women!" Naomi crowed. "That's me, s'pose. Do 'ee hear that, Tom? You'm married to a swarm like a heathen Turk—shame on 'e!"

Eli buttoned up his coat. "Must be getting home along. Take care of yourself, Ortho. There's no sense in raging after MacBride; he's gone—and good riddance. Oh, by the way, they've got four of the bodies."

"How many were drowned?"

"Six, I hear."

"And, who," said Naomi, "will tell me Satan don't cherish his own? Six poor innocents drowned like a litter of kittens while that old rapscallion walks off free as a king. T'eddn water will choke the likes of he, 'tis boiling pitch."

"Thee'd best go hot the cauldron ready for him, then," sail Eli, laughing. "Good night all."

Ortho sat before the fire long after supper was cleared away, scowling at the flames, sucking at his

long pipe. He supposed Carclew, Teage and the
other fools were having their laugh. "Ortho Penhale bamboozled, stung"; "Buck Penhale too clever
for once." He pictured the merriment in the tap-
rooms of the Star, the Ship, and lesser taverns, bit
through the clay stem and hurled the pipe in the
embers. "Oh, well, damn them! let them snigger!"

He took his top-coat from its peg, jammed his
hat on, and slouched out through the kitchen. Naomi
watched him depart, a lump of mutton halted half-
way to her mouth.

"Know where he's going?" she inquired.

"Kiddlewink, I s'pose," Tom replied, uninter-
ested, "or Roswarva."

His spouse scorned. "Roswarva—faugh! People don't go visiting wid' horse pistols sticking out
of their pockets. No he's after that pesky Mac-
Bride again, and he won't rest till the rogue's found.
And him with his brain laid open, out on a winter
night! Men . . . ! Do 'e know what he do want?"

"MacBride, s'pose."

"No, thou bufflehead! What he wants is what
thee's got already, a wife to put the fear of death
in him."

The mutton resumed its journey.

Ortho followed the Roswarva footpath till he
reached the hilltop and then turned sharp to the left
across Polmenna Downs. It was a bright starry
night, with little wind, but what there was had a
nip in it and there was a crispness of frost under-

foot. In the rushes by Polmenna pool a wild duck quarked. From the hillside came the thump of young rabbits at play. A curlew called. A furze plume gave a violent nod which was repeated by another some yards distant, accompanied by a slight rustling sound.

Ortho dropped on one knee, hand on pistol, sniffed and rose again—fox only. Something flung out of the heather quietly as a shadow and stood athwart his path, nose to the ground, back arched, rippling like a caterpillar—and then shot out of sight. A weasel, hunting—too intent to notice him. All wild nature was afoot in the darkness round about, up and about its business of killing or being killed. Otters brought trout quivering from out the Keigwin pools. Badgers scraped field voles from their holes. Owls swooped for mice—gray death falling downy-winged; and through tanglewoods of fern and bramble stoats went grimly on the blood-trail, red-eyed, pitiless. Up in the moor heather, down in the valley thickets, by bog and croft, pasture and hedgerow, battle and murder were running amok. Jungle law no less terrible, albeit in miniature, than that of dark African forests.

And over Polmenna, toward the sea, went Ortho Penhale, stepping warily, pistol at hand.

He reached the cliffs between Pedn Boar and Luddra Head, dropped down the broken turf terraces till he came to the sheer fall, steadied himself against a rock and looked over. The gale had blown out. The sea was smooth on the surface, but below that sleek veneer the ground-swell dragged and shouldered, outlining the coast with a gray blur of breaker, beyond which floated long ribbons of foam which writhed and contracted with undulations of the swell. Seaward of Pedn Boar was a detached blur of grey, a pale shade rather—the Twelve Apostles reef, whence came the murmur of eternal surf. Southeast, toward the Wolf, a ship's lights showed like pin-pricks in a black curtain.

Ortho mounted astride the rock. To the uninitiated he was on the edge of a sheer precipice one hundred and thirty feet high; but he knew better. There was a way down. Time and again as boys had he and Eli descended this very cliff, the incentive being gull's eggs. Bohenna had shown them the spot and they had made a point of raiding it at least once every spring. All that was needed was a steady head.

"Let's see where was that knob? Oh, yes, at the corner." Ortho fumbled along the rock, clutched the remembered fingerhold, and swung himself over the edge. Scraping along the rock-face with his toes, he found a niche, set his weight on his feet and felt for a second hand-hold—an oblique crack in the granite—inserted his fingers and lowered himself again. In this manner he descended some twenty feet and landed upon a little shelf, four feet wide and covered with coarse grass. The grass was very nearly his undoing: it was wringing wet and slippery as ice. Ortho's feet went from under him as though on skates and he came down in a sitting position, both feet dangling over the abyss. A cascade of small stones shot into the void and up rose a cloud of gulls, herring and black-back, squawking and wailing. He had not seen them before—they had been roosting in the cracks and ledges beneath him—but their number must have amounted to hundreds; it was as though a vast white sheet had been jerked off the cliff; the air throbbed with the thresh of their myriad wings.

Ortho wriggled back against the rock-face and drew breath. "Phew! that was close," he panted. "Nearly mince-meat that time." One hundred odd feet beneath him the swell broke in thunder—a dull reverberating boom, the swosh of tons of water overtoppling; then, in the second of peace between onslaughts, the gush and dribble of a thousand milky cascades.

Ortho rose cautiously and, digging his heels well in, sidled along the shelf to the left. It plunged sharply downward, broadening as it went, and turning a corner opened a tiny cove—the merest nick in the cliffs, barely fifty yards deep and seventy across, its entrance guarded by a fantastic pillar of rock worn by rain and spray into rough human semblance and known to local crabbers as "The Old Man"— "old" possibly from the layers of guano which whitened its poll. Ortho followed the shelf inward, treading silently in cushions of thrift littered with

gull-down and eggshells. Seams of feldspar striped
the cliffs, glistening frostily, and, in crevices, the
spicy samphire flourished. Seventy feet below, in
the black pit that was the cove bottom, the restless
water gurgled among boulders. One could imagine
some lost sea-monster prisoned in that pit, chafing
slimy flanks against the walls, gulping and bubbling.

The shelf stopped against a quartz barrier nine
feet high, but Ortho worked his hands and feet into
the crack where it split away from the main-fall
and hoisted himself to the top. On his right hand,
piercing the sheer wall, was a black hole, a cave
mouth, some twelve feet in height by five across,
hidden from above by the overhang of rock, from
the sea by "The Old Man." Ortho crouched, listening, every sense alert, but could hear nothing but the
slow drip of seepage from the cave roof, the suck
and gurgle of the tide below. He straightened his
back and, stepping into the tunnel, whistled three
times.

No answer.

He whistled again.

"Who's there?" came a hiss from the inner darkness. "Speak or I'll blow your brains out!"

"Me—Penhale."

"Step in and welcome," said MacBride.

CHAPTER XII

CAPTAIN Benjamin MacBride sat on the heap of dry bracken that composed his bed and puffed contentedly at his pipe. "Snug little berth this, Säid, my bonny," he chuckled, calling Ortho by his Moorish name. "What may it be?"

"Mine adit," said Ortho. "There was a shaft way back on the cliff, but it's fallen in."

"Been worked recent?"

"Not in mortal memory. The coast is honey-combed with these ancient holes, but its only round St. Just that they work 'em these days. Doubt if anybody knows of this one save me and my brother—and Bohenna."

MacBride grinned. "Aye, that hairy old ape knows it well enough; led me here straight as a compass t' other night. But, O my soul, what a ride, Säid! What a caper! Over hedges and ditches and all as black as a tar-barrel. I don't believe there's a part of that horse from jib-boom to taffrail, that I didn't sit at one time or another—Christy!"

"I didn't have any too gay a time myself, lying in a pool of water pretending to be stunned," said Ortho.

The captain agreed, "No, I'll warrant you didn't. I see you got bandages on still."

"Yes, to keep folk from seeing there's nothing beneath 'em."

MacBride laughed outright. "Well, you're a smart one, Säid, smart as a Newgate attorney. D'you know you foxed me the other night? Yes, you did, foxed me along with the rest. 'By Heck,' I says to myself, 'here's old Säid, what lived with me in Sallee, going to see me hanged,' I says. 'By Heck, there's gratitude!' I says."

"It was the only way," said Ortho. "I grant you'd nearly talked yourself out of that dazed bosun's clutches, but how far would you have got? Where would you have run to? There's a rare hunt afoot after you, Ben, and I'll confess that for the last three days I've been leading it—in the wrong direction. Listen while I read you something."

"Ho! So you're scholard now. Who learned you?"

"Started at school—before I ran; but the purser's clerk on an Indiaman gave me a fair wind in return for my grog ration." Ortho drew a scrap of paper from his pocket and crouched beside the lantern.

FIFTY POUNDS REWARD

The above will be paid to any person or persons who apprehend or give information that shall lead to the apprehension of the notorious evil-doer and pirate, BENJAMIN MACBRIDE, alias YUSSEF-EL-REIS, of

Youghal, Ireland, and Sallee in the Kingdom of
Morocco, lately taken by H. M. sloop *Lapwing* off
Cape Spartel and escaped near Mousehole, Cornwall,
on the night of January 24, 1783. The above is of
middle age, about five feet seven inches high. A ruddy,
full-faced man; wears his own hair and is blind of
the left eye. Had on a blue frieze coat, much torn;
two waistcoats, one of white flannel trimmed round
with black tape, one of watchet serge with bone buttons on each side; wore a brown pair of kerseymere
breeches and round pewter buckles.

N. B. Marked with the smallpox.

Ortho tapped the paper with his forefinger.
"What d'you think of that?"

MacBride snorted. "An insult, sir! At my age,
with my record, to be marked at fifty pounds!
Damme! the Spaniards offered that much for old
Pucheta, and the Frinch doubled it for that cross-
eyed sea-cook, Pierre le Borne, men that ha'nt taken
or sunk half the tonnage I have—no, nor a quarter!
Of all nip-cheese, miserly miserable penny-gluttons
these English do surely wear the crown!"

Ortho crammed the paper back in his pocket.
"Oh, don't sweat yourself on that score. They'll
put your price up as time goes on, never fear. Well,
you've heard the description. Now how to alter
yourself so's you won't fit it? Can you grow a
beard?"

"Beard is it," MacBride exclaimed. "Begob,

when I was in prison at Verdun I nourished a beard you could tie knots in. A brown beard that——!"

"Very good. Grow another," Ortho cut in. "Can't change your blind eye or pox-marks, but pox-marks are common enough. Those clothes must go."

"Brown breeches?" MacBride queried, a plaintive note in his voice.

"Unless you fancy being hung in 'em."

"Took 'em off a Portuguese count two months past . . . fitted me perfect . . . s'pose you're right . . . pity."

"Of course I'm right," Ortho snapped. "Don't play the fool or you'll get us both hoisted. I'll bring you a rig myself tomorrow, or send it by Bohenna. Now you lie low here and as soon as the hunt dies down I'll do what I can toward shipping you back to Sallee."

"Sallee?"

"Where else?"

MacBride shook his head. "I'm not going back to Sallee, my son——unless dragged. Had a bit of misfortune off Mogador last summer. Waiting for Canary wine-ships, I was, and met with a Spanish third-rate instead. Now there's another xebec gone. Do you know what they do in Barbary to *reis* who lose too many ships? A negro picks 'em up and tosses 'em backwards so that their necks is broke. If he misses the toss he gets thrown himself, so he don't miss often. A little pastime invented by His

Sublime Holiness Mulay Abdullah—whom Allah magnify! Nay, I'll not return to Barbary. I'd sooner have my neck stretched at Wapping amid speeches and good cheer than snapped by a black Sambo in Fez."

"If you won't go to Sallee, where *will* you go?" Ortho demanded. "Spain? France? I might run you to Roscoff on a smuggling craft."

MacBride spat. "France! Why, bless you, they *crapauds* has a longer score against me than England, and Spain longest of any—except Portugal—or maybe Holland."

"But, damme, you must go *somewhere!* Can't stop here forever!" Ortho exclaimed.

"I haven't any yearn to," said the unpopular seaman, calmly. "If you think I'm wishful to spend my reclining years burrowing into a cliff like a pesky rabbit you're swinging on the wrong chain. Säid, my heart,"—he slapped Ortho on the shoulder—"never you fret. I'll just bide here quiet-like for a spell and something will show up. Providence will show a light; Providence. Seems to me you young fellows now-a-days ain't got enough faith. Now I was raised strictly religious and have put my trust in Providence all my life, and believe me, Säid, the number o' times it has scooped me out of the jaws of the gallows are past counting, past counting.

"There was that time off Teneriffe. I got becalmed in the midst of the East Indies fleet, mainmast by the board and company run from quarters.

What did Providence do? Why sent a fog and I put forth sweeps and slipped away leaving the Indiamen banging at their own shadows. Then there was that *President* privateer. Didn't suspect her strength till we were yard-arm and yard-arm and I couldn't get clear. She tore me up cruel. Swept me fore and aft with swivels loaded with old nails and musket-balls. I was in a sorry plight. Then what happened? A nine-pounder on her quarter-deck blew up, killing her captain, first mate, steersman and three gunners. Providence once more. Again, when I was in the *Unicorn,* Guineaman, . . . but as I said before, they're past counting. I'll just lie-to and wait for the lamp o' guidance. Folk don't come this way much, I suppose?"

Ortho shook his head. "Nobody knows of this adit, I believe, and you couldn't tempt a Gwithian person across the Luddra after dark for minted gold."

"How so?"

"Said to be 'walked.' "

"Aha—who by?"

"A wicked huntsman who fell over here in the old times. You can hear him hallooing to his hounds, they say. You aren't afraid of ghosts, are you?"

MacBride scratched his chin. "Afraid, no—but a huntsman—what do he know about salt water and what do I know about dogs? I was hoping your ghost was one of these betrayed maidens—we

might have passed the long evenings consoling each
other in our misfortunes . . . ah, well! No, ghosts
don't scare me at all. The only one I ever met
was outside Dublin. I was stepping back to my ship
from Booterstown one night when a great white
soft thing tumbles out of a hedge atop o' me,
screeching, 'Repent! Repent!' 'Look where you're
coming to, clumsy,' says I, and gave it a dig with
my umbrello, expecting to see the umbrello come
out the other side. But instead of that the ghost
fetches a belch like he's stove in and doubles up in
the mud coughing, 'My Lord, where am I?' Know
what it was? Why, a Donnybrook sign-painter who
dreamed that Judgment was come, so jumped out
of bed and rushed to warn the world, wrapped up
in the quilt."

Ortho sniggered; then, feeling in his pockets, he
produced half a loaf, a wedge of cheese, some
onions, a twist of tobacco and two of Naomi's tarts.
These he laid beside the lantern.

"I'll come as often as I can and Bohenna will
keep you provisioned. Did he give you that fishing-
line?"

"Aye, caught two rock-ray and a small bass last
night."

"Well, don't venture out except after dark, and
then not far," Ortho warned.

"A body'd think it was *your* neck that was in the
noose," said MacBride, accompanying him to the
entrance.

Ortho turned on him fiercely. "Blast you! don't you see that *both* of us are in it now? You for being what you are and me for harbouring you. I wish to God I——!" He stopped short.

MacBride completed the sentence for him. "You wish to God you had let me go spin t' other night, eh? Wish you hadn't acted quite so hasty. Bit frightened, are ye? Heart failing? Stuck fast with a plaguy old barnacle and don't know how or when you'll get quit of him—that so? It ain't any use you denying it, Säid, my son, because I know you better'n you think." He patted Ortho on the shoulder. "Rest easy, boy, rest easy. Forty-eight years I've walked this vale o' sorrow and for the last eighteen of 'em there's been a price on my head. Nath'less, if you look, you'll notice that nobody ain't bought it yet."

As Ortho started to climb the granite barrier on his homeward way he heard a low chuckle behind him.

"What are you laughing at?" he inquired.

"Me?" said MacBride. "Oh, nothing to signify. Only something you said just now set me thinking. Good night!"

CHAPTER XIII

ORTHO saw the damson cloak disappearing round the corner ot Quay Street and followed hot-foot, plying the brass knocker one half-minute after Miss Nicola Barradale had closed the door behind her.

Vashti answered his summons and, seeing the futility of pretending that her mistress was indisposed, had perforce to let him in. Nicola received him with unconcealed pleasure; Mrs. Beckford with mild agitation. She was polite, but plainly wished him further. When Ortho inquired after Nicola's headaches she denied having had any and shot a glance at her duenna which made that poor lady quail.

So there *was*, as Ortho had surmised, a plot between the two retainers to keep him at arm's-length. He wished them joy of their conspiracy. As an excuse for his call he presented Mrs. Beckford with a bottle of lotion for Rupert's complaint (he had compounded it himself of black sulphur, oil and turpentine, and if it would do no good it would do little harm) and went on to say that he was anxious to buy a christening-gift for his darling niece, but being unversed in such matters besought the opinion of people of taste. Questioned by Mrs. Beckford (who, having had no babies of her own, was an authority on other people's) he came off shabbily. Not till he had spent three minutes checking backward on his fingers could he remember the day on which his darling niece was born, confessed ignorance of her intended name, and was equally blank as to the proposed date of baptism.

Mrs. Beckford started to read him a lecture on infant culture; but Nicola came to the rescue, promising to go shopping with him any morning he liked. She made many inquiries about the MacBride affair. How did it all happen? Was Ortho's head badly damaged? For the hundred and twentieth time Ortho explained how the sailor escaped him. He made light of his hurt. MacBride had struck him a stunning blow, but flat. When he removed the bandage—which he hoped to do in a day or so—he doubted if there would be anything visible beyond a slight graze. Miss Barradale sighed her relief. Mrs. Beckford rolled her eyes heavenwards. What an appalling man! And still at large! They would all be murdered in their beds. Only last night Rupert had been very restless: she was sure there was some one about. She had paid the watch five shillings to keep a special eye on the house and put an extra sixpence into Sunday's offertory. They were in God's hands.

Ortho hastened to reassure her. He did not think the villain could still be in the neighborhood, or in Cornwall even: they had searched every hole and corner. Would undoubtedly make for some large seaport, Plymouth, Bristol, London. There was nothing to fear.

Ortho was treated to China tea and sugar bis cuits and left soon after. Mrs. Beckford remained fixedly in the room all the time; nevertheless he managed to convey a note to Nicola without being detected. However, the duenna fired a parting shot which set him thinking—the long-expected Mr. Bar- radale was positively appearing at the end of the week. Turning into the Ship & Castle to fetch his horse, Ortho bumped young Carclew trailing a hound pup at the end of a whip-lash.

"Hello, my wounded hero!" said Carclew. "So they've got your man at last!"

"What man?"

Carclew scoffed, " 'What man'? Roast my liver, what man has set this Hundred buzzing like Bedlam and every old spinster squealing 'murder' if a mouse stirs? What man ironed out our intrepid Penhale flat in a pool for the night? 'What man'? Ecod!"

"You don't mean . . . ?"

"My faith I do," said Carclew, "A Pemberth fisherman gaffed him off Merther Point at dawn this morning and brought him in straightway. He's been identified."

Ortho reeled. "Did he blab—has he spoken— said anything?"

Carclew stared at him. "How the devil could

he, seeing he's drowned? You don't appear over-
joyed, my friend."

Ortho recovered himself. "Me? Er—no, to
speak the truth, I ain't; I wanted to tail that badger
myself."

"That I'll warrant," Carclew sneered. "Likewise fifty pounds would not have come amiss—to
pay for scalp-plaster—eh?"

Ortho pushed by him, got his horse and rode fast
out of town. MacBride was dead, drowned—and
his predominant emotion was that of relief. The
captain had sensed his feelings with disconcerting
accuracy. A moment's chivalrous impulse, combined
with the love of trickery, had driven him to save his
old friend and fool the crowd that night on Penlee
cliff. The moment passed, the trick turned, and
reaction set in. By sheltering a malefactor he was
risking his neck, and it looked like being a long and
arduous business. It frightened him; he was not
of the metal to withstand long strains. He was
ashamed of himself, for MacBride had been a good
friend to him. It was true that the sailor was
responsible for his original appearance in Sallee, but
it was MacBride who had saved him from the slave-
gangs and sent him to the comparative freedom of
the Moroccan army, furnishing him with horse and
musket. He remembered now that he had never
repaid the captain for that cow-hocked old barb;
he had always meant to, but never seemed to have
any money—or any money to spare. He consoled

himself with the thought that he had always *meant* to; that his intentions were of the best.

As he set his mare up Jack Lane he wondered how MacBride had met his end. Slipped off the rocks while going to fish, probably; slid on wet sea-weed or that treacherous grass ledge which had all but sent him, Ortho, headlong. The trusted Providence had not been quick enough for once.

MacBride being mercifully removed, the pendulum swung back again; Ortho became sentimental, shook up kind memories of old days in Sallee—the little house under the minaret . . . moonlight nights on the roof with Ayesha dancing and Schems-ed-Dah singing, MacBride lounging on the cushions, puffing his pipe, the soul of domesticity . . . MacBride coming home, pockets stuffed with sweetmeats, his three darlings twittering round him. . . . MacBride bellowing "Lowlands Low" in opposition to the shocked *muezzin*. . . . MacBride spurring his fat chestnut across the sands, every limb in convulsion. . . . Poor old MacBride! Dear old Ben! By the time Ortho reached Bosula he had worked himself almost into a state of tears. This, however, did not prevent him from eating a hearty supper; and by ten o'clock he was away again, striding over Polmenna Downs toward the adit, with the intention of cleaning up every trace of its late occupant.

It was a calm night, but misty. Detached wisps of fog wandered in from the southwest, streamed up the cliffs and spilled over the moorland. Boulders glimmered queerly, assumed curious shapes and seemed to waver; the very ground appeared to be sliding inland. Then the stream of mist would pass, and all, for the moment, become solid again. Ortho knew the moor like his own orchard, but even he, mistaking one landmark for another, lost his bearings and went slightly astray. When, at length, he swung himself over the cliff-edge it was to plunge into an opaque steam-bath, but by the time he had reached the shelf all was clear in his immediate surroundings. "The Old Man" stood up plain to see, a crumble of surf at his knees, the guano on his head faintly gleaming, but the secret cove behind him smoked like a crater.

Then, suddenly, "The Old Man" was gone and the cove yawned empty. The fog-veil bulged like a curtain masking covert movement; grotesque knobs and pinnacles of stone, sphinxes and gargoyles, peeped through fissures in the mist, nodded and were no more. It was as though the great rock-piles had come to life and were playing a game of hide-and-seek with the climber. Bits of the old folk-stories he had been reared on came back to Ortho's mind, of how, on certain nights the druid stones rose and danced and menhir bowed to menhir.

"Oh, pshaw! Grandmothers' gab, maids' whimsies!" he muttered, pressed on and then stopped dead, holding to the rock-face, utterly blindfolded, wrapped from head to foot in sliding coils of vapor.

The void beneath him suddenly exploded with eerie cries, the plaint of lost souls wailing in eternal darkness. Ortho jumped—then laughed shakily. "Blast those gulls!" The mist streamed clear ánd he felt his way onward, glad that this should be his last night journey to the adit. It must have been dreary for MacBride here all alone, with the water gurgling among the boulders and the tide fretting. Poor old MacBride!

In imagination he saw the sailor's finish, swaying wildly above the black abyss, hands grasping thin air, heard the breakers' exultant roar. Tears came to his eyes. Poor old Ben!

He crept cautiously forward, hoisted himself over the barrier and felt his way up the tunnel, fingertips touching the slimy sides. A stream of fog entered with him, sucked by the in-draught. Ortho fumbled ahead. The lantern must be lying up there somewhere; he would strike a light as soon as he reached the cross-cut. He stumbled on, kicking up the rubble with his feet, and then suddenly went cold all down the spine—*there was somebody ahead of him! somebody who groaned!*

Ortho flattened himself against the wall. What was that? He listened. Silence. Nothing to be heard but the drip of the roof and the murmur of the sea ringing in the cavern as in a shell. Fancy, he determined; a stone had fallen farther up, or a badger grunted and he had fancied the rest. That lantern. . . .

He moved a foot inward and the groan came again, right in front of him this time. "Oo-ah-a-a!" —long-drawn, human, unmistakably human. Who was it? Who could it be? Then he knew. Bohenna, of course! Had come there to provision MacBride and met with an accident. That was it. He hailed, "Hey there, is that you, Ned? This is me, Ortho. What's amiss?"

No answer but the drip-drip of seepage and the gurgle of the tide.

He hailed again, "D'you hear me, Ned? Where are you?" Then he swung about gasping—the moan came from behind him, from the way he had come! "Ah-a-a-a!"

Ortho's flesh prickled, his knees knocked. What in mercy's name was this? If there was a man lying in the passage, why had he not trodden on him?

Echoes? He thought of echoes and abandoned the thought. Echoes do not start of themselves. There was something devilish here. He started to slide for the entrance, back to the wall, one arm thrown up to guard his head, and then stopped, frozen solid by a series of dreadful whoops that rang down the rock passage as down a trumpet-throat. *"Wha-houp, hoo! Wha-ha!"*

Ortho fell on his knees, his teeth clicking together and, gathering himself, scrambled blindly for the entrance, crazed with terror. The huntsman! The huntsman! He heard the rattle of stones behind him, light danced on the green slime of the walls, a powerful hand grabbed him by the collar and jerked him onto his back.

"By James, you was nearly over the edge that time!" said Captain MacBride.

Ortho rolled over, goggling. That hearty red face, that heavy hand *must* be real flesh and blood. It *was* MacBride!

"Curse it, y-you're alive after a-all!" he stuttered.

Ortho paced up and down the cross-cut, biting his lip, hands thrust deep in pockets. MacBride lounged on his bracken bed, chafing sliced plug between capacious palms. The corners of his mouth twitched amusedly. Hanging from a peg was a freshly trapped rabbit. A six-pound rock-ray hung from another. On a red handkerchief spread on the ground was a small heap of limpets. The captain was learning to live off the country. He indicated the limpets with a jerk of his stumpy thumb. "Some night when you're stepping this way you might fetch a drop of vinegar, Säid. Limpets eat very grateful with a drop of vinegar—and pepper."

Ortho wheeled about and wagged an accusing finger in his face. "Lookee. I was in Penzance this evening and they told me you were dead!"

"So I am," said the captain; "and by this time to-morrow I ought to be safely buried. What more could you want?"

The finger wagged again. "They told me your body had been fished up off Merther at dawn and taken straight in and identified. *Identified*—mark that!"

MacBride nodded. "I thought it would be. You, as an old friend, didn't go and shed a last tear on my corpse, did you?"

"No."

"I think you'd of remarked that I'd growed a bit."

"What d'you mean?"

"It was this way. Two nights back I took fishing-line and climbed down into this cove here. It was low tide and most of the boulder-tops were bare and I went across, hopping from top to top. Presently I spies something dark jammed in the rocks on the seaward side. First I thought it was seaweed, then I thought it was a seal and I said 'Bo!' but it didn't shift, so I hopped across and had a look. It was a man, a drowned seaman."

Ortho clapped his hand to his knee. "One of the bodies from that sloop. There are two missing."

"That so?" said MacBride. "Well, there didn't appear to be anythin' to be done for the poor pugg— not by me, anyhow—so I searches his pockets to see did he happen to have aught of value or entertainment. He hadn't, though. A hank of lanyard and a broken pipe only. One o' they poor shiftless fellows only too common in our profession, I fear. So I leaves him lyin' and hops off again. Hadn't hopped more'n four boulders when a notion hits me between the eyes as hard as a caulking hammer and back I goes and takes a second look at him. He is a stout man of about my build, if taller by an inch or more—but we can't have everything in this world. 'Strikes me,' says I to myself, 'that seeing the hunting and harrying after false alarms those poor constables have had of late they'll identify pretty near anything to get peace and quiet again. Anyhow we must take our chances.' So I dresses this fellow up."

"What in?" said Ortho.

"In my old clothes, of course. Blue coat, flannel waistcoat, Portuguese breeches and all, according as the bill demands. Dresses him up and tows him round to the point where the tide would get a fair chance with him. Grasp the notion?"

"But his face, man?" said Ortho. "One eye, pox-marks?"

"Hadn't got a face," MacBride answered. "Seven days in the water, down to the bottom and up again . . . fish . . . crabs. See the beauty of it? I'm drowned now, dead and paid for—fifty pounds, blast 'em! Beginning to feel better now, Säid? Easier in your mind? Nobody'll go hunting for a paid-off corpse. If I was to swear to myself on a cargo of Bibles, they'd only laugh. 'Ben MacBride was buried in Penzance November Eighty-three,' they'd say. 'What mad-house has you sprang from?' See?"

"My stars!" said Ortho, slowly and with feeling. MacBride nodded. "I know what you're think-

ing of. And believe me, I didn't relish it myself.
Twice I gave up, but . . ." He looked at Ortho
very earnestly. "You can laugh if you wish, I don't
care, but you know what I told you t'other night?
Well, I believe it was Providence caused that poor
fellow to be washed up on those boulders. I do,
so help me! 'Matey,' says I to him, 'this may look
to you like a mean action for a living man to do to
a dead, but your old body ain't of no use to you any
more and if it'll carry my crimes it means new life
to me,' I says. 'I wasn't born a rogue, didn't take
to roguery from choice. All my life I've yearned
to be respectable. I verily believe Providence sent
you along to give me a second chance,' I says.
'Matey, I've *got* to take it.' "

The idea of MacBride, picaroon captain, yearning for respectability amused Ortho; a snigger
escaped him. MacBride glanced up.

"Aye, laugh hearty. You're young yet and you've
had luck—so far. Some day it'll turn and you won't
laugh so loud. You'll make some little slip and
you'll be over a cliff that you can't climb. D'you
think I put my neck in a noose for pleasure? Me
that was the youngest master in the Cork fleet and
might have been mayor of Youghal by now. D'you
know what sent me to the bad?"

"How should I?"

MacBride held up his hand, four fingers extended.
"Four barrels of pork."

"How?"

"I was master of the *Brothers* brig, of Youghal, at the time, trading to the West Indies. I owned a third share in her and was highly respected in the port. In Sixty-five, or was it Sixty-six—no matter—I was in Kingston, Jamaica, loaded up for home with pimento, broad mahogany .and cotton. Soon as I am ready to sail, my steward hops the twig. He had been carrying on with a mulatto bumboat woman. I searched the town, but find him I could not, she had hid him away too cunning. I picks up another steward and sails for the eastward. Off Pedro Bluff my mate comes to me and says he thinks some one has been at the provisions. I take a look with him. He is right. The run steward and the bumboat woman has been at the provisions. I hauls up for Savanna la Mar, drops the hook and goes ashore. There is a merchant there, a fat white chap lying on a mattress, fanning himself with a grass hat, and blowing. Provisions? Oh, aye, he can spare me some prime provisions lately in from Ireland. Very civil spoken, he is, and we have a glass of grog together while his negroes are getting my purchases down to the boat. Four barrels of prime pork I buy and some biscuit. Then I has another glass with the chap and I am gone, the wind being fair. The wind dies away once we are to the eastward of Havana and we go north drifting. We make a slow passage till we are to the south of the Grand Banks and there we catch the prevailing westerlies and matters improve.

"My mate comes to me. 'That pork you bought at Savanna la Mar is not prime at all,' he says; 'it is slave meat and there is more weevil than flour in the biscuit.'

"He is right. The pork is nothing but feet, tails and heads. 'Is it all the same?' says I. 'Broach the four barrels and see.'

"They are all the same except that *two* of 'em are *bad, stinking.* I understand. That fat chap has sold me condemned pork at prime prices. 'A chance ship, in a hurry to be off,' he thinks; 'they will never look and never come again.'

" 'I am sorry for that chap if ever we meet,' says I to my mate. 'Heave that filth overboard.' 'We shall have a reef in our belts before we see Tuskar,' says he. 'Not if this gale holds,' says I. 'No, if this gale holds we may just do it,' says he.

"The gale held till we were in Longitude West 15 and then slewed round and blew a dead muzzler. We were four days hove to. Then it shifted six points to the south and we made sail again, crowding. I crowded too strong. The foretopmast sprung and the fid parted. I was a day fishing the spar and fitting a new fid. Next day the wind flew back into the nor'east again. I spoke a Bristol snow and a Lancaster brig. Could they spare me any provisions? No, they could not; they are short themselves. The wind flies to and fro and sometimes we make headway. Twice we made landfall, the Blaskets and Dursey, but each time the wind headed us. There is a close reef in our belts now; the men are weak and sullen. They say there is Fate in it—what use to pull and haul? I do not see Fate in it; I see a fat merchant lying on a mattress in Savannah la Mar, puffing and blowing. I drove the men to the braces with kicks and curses.

"Still the wind held in the northeast, coming with snow and sleet. Thirty-eight years have I been seafaring and never have I known a nor'east wind hold like that. The men are getting too feeble to tack ship. Kick them as you would they *could* not haul, and the ship herself is strained with constant labor. 'Lay her on the port tack and let her stop there,' says I to the mate. 'I am not twenty leagues from the Irish Coast, but I might as well be twenty thousand. Lay her over and we will fetch something— France, Spain or Africa.'

" 'There is not a biscuit left,' says he, 'and there is a boy sitting in the hold watching for rats as I have seen cats watch. We shall see horrors on this craft, I'm thinking.' "

MacBride struck a spark on his steel, held the fuse to his pipe, and sucked noisily. His hand trembled somewhat. "Well, to make end, next day we spoke a Liverpool-Newfoundlander lying to. She was carrying salt cod and gave us all we needed. The men ate it raw, worried it like dogs.

"That voyage is over. I am in Kingston again, loading rum, sugar and coffee. I go ashore one night with a couple of Guinea masters. We enter

a tavern in Princes Street and, by Heck! there is
my chap of Savanna la Mar standing in a group
of town merchants, puffing and blowing. I thrusts
up to him. 'So-ho, my gentleman, we meet again!
I have a small account to settle with you concerning four barrels of pork,' I says, and I up and tells
how me and my crew is near starved dead through
his knavery, and I calls him every foul name I can
lay my tongue to. The town merchants are all of
a fluster, throwing up their hands and calling out,
'Enough! Avast, captain!' but the Guinea masters
are beside me, saying, 'Serve him slops, Ben! Have
at the lubber!' As for my chap, he is the color of
dough, backed up against a table, puffing and blowing so as he can hardly breathe. 'It is a lie,' he
gasps, and then his eyes roll in his head and he says,
'Ah!' and goes down on the floor in a heap, and
only then did I realise I had hit him."

"Dead?" said Ortho.

MacBride nodded. "Had a diseased heart—but
how was I to know? Before God I never meant to
hit him; but when he called me a liar my arm jerked
up of its own accord and I had done murder. I can
see him still, lying on the floor, a sort of green color
creeping over him, bubbles of blood on his lips. I
was like a man dreaming, but the Guinea masters
thrust me out of the door. "Run!" they said, and
told me where to run to. I have been running ever
since. He had two brothers, rich Kingston agents;
they raised all the islands against me, petitioned the

Port Admiral. I had no chance. Never have had any chance"—MacBride breathed heavily through his nose, grunted and then suddenly smiled—"till now."

"And what are you going to do—now?" Ortho inquired.

"Do? Why, bide here quietly till my beard grows, pondering on the future, and if anybody comes nosing along I'll slip the ghost loose on 'em— he-he!"

Ortho turned on him angrily. "Yes—what damned foolery was that, eh?"

"Foolery," said MacBride, pained. "That's an art, that is. Ventriloquism or belly-talking they call it. Learned it when I was in Verdun prison and grew my brown beard. There was a fellow with me that used to make his living by it at fairs. Locked up in a cellar half rats, half water, for trying to escape, we were. Used to practice it for something to pass the time away. When you spoke of this ghost huntsman hallooing folk off the cliffs it set me thinking, and I've been practising again. I thought you'd be surprised."

CHAPTER XIV

MISS NICOLA BARRADALE rode northwest out of Penzance on a livery hack, a
groom at her heels. She wore a pearl-green
riding habit with white silk lapels, and a pert gray
cocked hat edged with silver braid. Proudly she
held herself, brisking her mount with a gold-topped
switch. The gray horse cocked his tail and ambled
his best, conscious that he was bearing quality.

Old Trebilcock, toddling downtown for his morning gossip at the coffee-house, murmured, "Pretty,
pretty!" and went on his way humming. Young
Teage, riding in from Trengwainton, pulled his nag
to the side of the road and watched her till she
turned the corner. He was in a mind to follow,
but reflected that he would undoubtedly get that
switch across his cheek. Miss Barradale went uphill
to Madron. The parson, planting mignonette in
his front garden, involuntarily dropped the trowel
and swept off his hat. Miss Barradale impressed
his mistake on him with a frigid bow. The smith,
shoeing a colt outside his smithy, looked up from his
work and let a hoof fall on his foot. Miss Barradale consoled him with the hint of a smile. A pack
of children trotted through the hamlet behind her,

fascinated, dumb. She might have been a fairy princess leading them forth to realms of magic, never to return. At the village bounds they became conscious of this and stampeded home in a great flutter. Miss Barradale, erect, elegant, somewhat disdainful, went on toward the high moors. Yellow body and scarlet crest bright in the sunshine, a female woodpecker fluttered across the track. Over Trengwainton Cairn a hawk hung poised against the rolling clouds. There was not a soul in sight.

The groom began to drop back, grinning.

At the foot of the cairn the track split, one branch wandering northward through beds of sedge and watercress to Madron's holy well (babes immersed therein before dawn on May-morning were said to be cured of rickets), the other branch continuing westward and upward. Miss Barradale pursued the latter, passed round a wind-clipped coppice of dwarf oak and sycamore, checked her mount, and flushed charmingly.

Ortho Penhale rode out from behind the trees, hat in hand., They greeted each other formally and turned their horses uphill, side by side.

"You got my letter?" said Ortho.

"Else I should not be here. I found it as usual in my cuff when I returned from taking the air. Who drops *billets* in my cuff, sir? I never notice anybody."

Ortho laughed. "As well you don't. A hairy

thing more dog than man, dumb, middling honest and said to be idiot—which I contest. 'Cully John' they call him."

"And why do you select this creature?"

"Because, as I said, he is dumb and middling honest. Also he has a sugar tooth. When that tooth is hungry for sixpenn'orth of sweetmeats he will get a letter to you if it takes all day and night. The tooth satisfied, he leans against the Market House and would not move for a king's fortune. I fear next week will be his week for leaning. Is there any reason why I should not bring my letters myself?"

"There is Mrs. Beckford."

"And what has Mrs. Beckford against me?"

Nicola smiled. "Indeed, at this moment you are greatly esteemed. That lotion you gave her for her wretched little dog has worked wonders."

"Then why—?"

"Because I ask you," said Miss Barradale, urging her gray to a canter.

Ortho followed after, chewing the cud of his thoughts. Still farther in the rear lumbered the livery groom. Both parties paid him liberally to mind his own business; this was the third time the pair had met afield—he was doing well. His betters ambled along the ridge toward Lanyon, moors before and on either hand. The west wind came over the high country with a rush, setting the pale sedge-grass a-shimmer, ruffling the blue and white reflections in the rain pools.

Ortho brought his mare beside the grey. "When does your father appear?" he asked. "Saturday?"

Nicola pouted. Not till Saturday week. He had been delayed again—pressing business. Most provoking. But he was positively arriving on Saturday week, positively. She glowed at the thought of Barradale's coming. He was such fun, such a boy, avid for any form of amusement. The better to sing her paragon's praises she slowed her horse to a walk. Not only was Barradale entertaining, but handsome. She had rather walk the aisle beside him on Sundays than with any other man, young or old, in Bristol city. Not only was he handsome, but generous. She gave instance upon instance of his charity, of the sailors' widows and worn-out seamen he had pensioned off—and so on, a pæan of adulation. The hard-bitten sea-captain, Kempthorne, had chanted much the same tune. Flabby old Mrs. Beckford melted altogether when her employer's name was mentioned. *"Dear* Mr. Barradale, so courteous and considerate." Even stern Vashti relaxed. A charming creature evidently, to inspire such general affection.

Ortho thought he was going to like Barradale, and wondered how any woman came to leave him. Speaking of Barradale, Kempthorne said that his wife had gone off, but he had not mentioned with whom or why—the signal gun had interrupted him. Oh, well, no matter.

On the crest of the moors Ding Dong engine-house stood like a Border tower, foursquare to the winds, massive, lonely, a banner of smoke flying at its stack. Ortho pointed it out with his whip.

"The oldest and deepest mine in the world, they say. They dug tin there in the days of Roman Cæsar. Down there is Lanyon Quoit, one great flat stone laid on three upright, where the giants used to dine, and away yonder the Men-an-tol, a holed stone set on edge. I do not know what the giants did with that, but the old wives declare that if you crawl through it at moonrise your rheumatics will disappear."

"But I have no rheumatics, thank you kindly. Let us go up to the tin mine and speak with Cæsar's ghost," said Nicola, and rode forward singing:

"Sea-nymphs hourly ring his knell:
Ding, Dong.
Hark! now I hear them—
Ding, Dong, Bell!"

They passed a train of pack-mules carrying ore to the coast smelters, and a trio of cheerful bal-maids (women surface workers) linked arm-in-arm who deferred their twitting of the muleteers to stare at the cavalcade.

"That's Penhale," one whispered.

"No, is it?" said another, thrilled.

"Ess, a is," said the first. "Him that's been fighting all over the world. Seed en in P'nzance on Twelfth Night. Brear handsome great rogue, eddn a?"

She was not alone in her admiration. Swaggering down the street afoot Ortho was an outstanding figure, with his slim height and upright bearing, but mounted he excelled.

Flat-thighed, small-waisted, he clipped the saddle fast and balanced naturally to every movement of his horse. There was no violent heeling, no dragging at the bit; the mare went this way and that way, steered apparently by intuition, but in reality by quick leg pressure and deft shifts of weight. He cantered her out into the heather, wove her in and out among the boulders, making her change legs smoothly with each bend; vaulted off and on again; set her at an old prospect pit fourteen feet across, crumbling and overgrown, cleared it flying and cantered back patting the mare's veined neck, black eyes dancing, white teeth agleam in boyish delight. The yeoman half of him was uppermost for the moment, he was his father's son, out in the clean wind and sunshine doing the one thing he did supremely well.

All this was duly noted by Miss Barradale, but if her color heightened she said no word, but set her horse going again. They swept over the sheep-crop, side by side, the bay mare bounding light as a

greyhound, snatching playfully at her bit, flattening
her ears; the grey hack shooting his legs out like
piston-rods, stiff-necked, grunting. They passed the
engine-house, with the great stone-laden pump-beam
pounding the wind like some stranded engine of
medieval warfare, and came to a halt among the
old dumps.

To the north, northeast and southwest brown
moors rolled smoothly against the billowy sky,
jagged here and there with granite piles, and outcrops. Southeast the land sloped away to the blue
haze of Mount's Bay. A glint of foam tipped the
spear-head of Cudden, a bow of foam marked Per-
ran Sands. Grey rain-veils trailed along the western tors, Carn Brea, Bartinny and Sancreed Beacon,
but over Ding Dong the sunlight poured, and the
west wind sang lustily. It purred through the gorse,
bent the heather before it, whipped roses into
Nicola's cheeks, brought bright tears to her eyes,
set the horse tails streaming pennant-wise, blew
their manes about. Ortho's young mare backed and
sidled; even the livery hack cocked his ears and
pawed heather. There was no temporizing with
that boisterous gale: one must fight it or flee it.
Nicola elected for battle, turned her horse down
the slope, calling, "Come on! Come on!"

They swept downhill into the wide cup of the
moors. The groom, plodding past Ding Dong
engine-house, saw them far away, gay specks of
color in an immensity of brown, and plodded slowly

after them, head lowered to the wind. On they went, Nicola leading, splashed through a peaty stream, toiled up the slopes of Watch Croft and stood among the rude barrows of immemorial kings high on the backbone of the peninsula.

Fresh from untrammelled salt pastures, shaking the brine from its hair, the west wind fell on them in full force. It came rollicking up the hill, a mad shepherd, trampling the grass, buffetting the rocks, shouting, piping to its herds, the clouds and their shadows, the white sheep and black. The heavens were in spate, frothing with cloud; little white clouds that ran lamb-like, sag-bellied clouds that went heavily, trailing dingy wool. Eastward they poured, an unending stream, darkening the heather. The blast nearly lost Ortho his hat, all but unseated Nicola. She saved herself with a clutch at the saddle and crowed with surprise, "The sea!"

The tor fell sharply on the western side—a frozen cataract of bare boulders, bleached like bone—and then pitched headlong into the blue plain of the Atlantic. Flying mists of rain and spindrift hid the horizon, but inshore the water was many-colored; cerulean over the deeps, sapphire over sand-bars, rust-stained where it rolled over beds of weed, the whole sprinkled with the snow of breaker tops. Eight hundred feet down and three-quarters of a mile away the roller lines were plainly discernible. Spray-maned ridges following each other out of the seaward haze like cavalry squadrons, bursting over the outer reefs in dazzling explosions, romping on to burst afresh against the Morvah cliffs—"big green westerlies," as the fishermen have it, "coming home." The noise of them rose up on the wind, a sustained ringing, a deep drum-roll.

"The sea!" Miss Barradale exclaimed. "But why is it here so suddenly? I thought we had left it behind."

"There is sea on three sides. We have crossed the neck of land. This is the Atlantic." Ortho raised his whip. "The next parish is Newfoundland."

"Newfoundland! What do I care for Newfoundland? Cod, cold and whalebones! Where lie the Sugar Isles, the West Indies?"

He pointed again. "Over there."

Miss Barradale blew three kisses into the gale. "To my father's ships," she cried. "To the *Owner's Love, Fair Penitent* and *Barradale. Bon voyage,* my dears!"

Ortho glanced at her. She did not know the *Fair Penitent* had sunk off St. Kitts? Well, if her father did not choose to tell her it was none of his business.

"Egad, if they are Bristol-bound they have a fair wind for it," he laughed. " 'The nor'east wind is a broom to sweep the Channel,' we say, 'but the sou'west blows sweethearts home.' They should come booming, your dears."

He pictured them scudding, goose-winged, in a

haze of flying spindrift, burying their dripping figure-heads in a lather of sundered water, spouting at the scuppers, the faithful ships that paid Nicola's dressmakers. Well, they got their money's worth. Lovely she looked in her pearl-green and silver, coral cheeked, radiant eyed, the wind in her skirts and hair, streaming cloud masses for background. The gray horse leaned against the blast, rigid, neck arched, forelegs braced under him: a marble beast posed on the high pedestal of a king's grave.

The gale rushed up the slope with added violence. There was a virility, a madness in it infecting whom it touched. One heard the blare of trumpets, the rush of winged hosts.

Miss Barradale threw her head back, stretched out her arms as if to take flight over the whitening ocean. She sang, a wordless, aimless trilling.

Then she picked up the reins and forced the gray horse over the brink, down among the boulders. "I'll race you down to those cliffs!" she cried, plying her whip.

Ortho hastened after her shouting, "Take care! Steady!"

She went on unheeding, forcing the hack dangerously.

Ortho cursed. "She'll be down in a minute, down and crushed!" He loosed the mare's head and shook her out. The filly had run on Polmenna Downs as a foal; she went downhill like a goat, jumping from side to side, from grass patch to grass patch, grounding her hind feet where her fore feet had been. The gray tripped in a rabbit hole, pecked, recovered, slithered on a smooth rock, recovered again and cantered on, head erect, snorting. Miss Barradale trilled airily. They were in better going now, ground gorse and heather comparatively free from rock, but Ortho knew there was worse ahead, a hidden gully neither deep nor perpendicular, negotiable to a clever animal picking its own path and pace, but to that clumsy roadster destruction.

He yelled again, " 'Ware! 'Ware! Hold hard! Danger!" But the wind snatched the words from his mouth and tossed them backward. Miss Barradale, in a state of blind exaltation, went her way singing, plying her whip mechanically. "Tra-la-la lirra-le . . . !" Wild Nick's own daughter.

Ortho had a vision of a slim woman in pearl-green, suddenly pale and quiet, lying at the base of that gully with a gray horse on top of her, and drove his spurs home. The filly bucked in protest. She was making the best speed she could—in prudence. Ortho cut into her left and right, gripped her tight and bundled her at it, willy-nilly— to hell with prudence! He was her master. She straightened out, furious but resigned. "Oh, well, you fool, if you *want* a broken neck . . ." They went over the heather, bounding, gaining two yards in three, came upon the gray's quarter, drew level— but too late. In a flash Ortho saw that he could not stop two horses in time, would be lucky if he could stop one.

Miss Barradale saw the danger too late to help herself; the happy song snapped in her throat, her limbs went rigid. The mare saw the danger too late to stop, but not for nothing had she run wild on the moors in her youth. She clipped her hocks well under her and flung sideways to the left and at the same time Ortho's whole weight swung hard over with her, Ortho's weight and something added— he had dragged the numbed girl clean out of the saddle. But the gray hack went down, rolling. They skirted the gully rim and came to a stop, on firm ground, Ortho still supporting Nicola's feather-weight in the crook of his right arm.

"O my dear!" he panted. "O my dear!"

She flung her arms about him, dragged herself up and nestled her white face into his neck, shaking with hysterical laughter. "Ortho!"

The groom, looking down from the heights of Watch Croft, whistled softly to himself. Then he retired and, dismounting, sat down behind a rock. He was very discreet.

CHAPTER XV

HARD fortune that it was, by chain shot, by
  chain shot,
  Hard fortune that it was by chain shot,
  Our Admiral lost his leg,
  And of his men did beg,
'Fight on, my British boys, 'tis my lot, 'tis my lot,
Fight on, my British boys, 'tis my lot'.

"Whoo-sh, shoo-oo, sissss! Easy, my beauty,
stand easy!

"And then bold Benbow lay, crying, 'Boys,' crying
  'Boys'.
  And then bold Benbow lay, crying 'Boys,'
  Let us tack about once more,
  We'll drive them all ashore,
I value not a score all their noise, all their . . .' "

Ortho's voice failed lamentably. "Oh, murder!
Pitched too steep," said he. "Stand still, my treas-
ure, put it down."

The bay mare made a playful pat at him with her
near hind foot and then stood firm while he brushed
the fetlock out. "Sh-oo-oo, whiss-h!"

Eli, massive as a rock, clumped into the yard and
watched proceedings with a calm blue eye.

"Hello!" Ortho called. "How be'st? All well at Roswarva? Mary well?"

"Fine, up and about."

"Daughter?"

"Doing champion—at least so they say." His tone did not express complete conviction.

"So they say! What's wrong with her?"

Eli laughed. "Oh nothing, nothing—doing tidy, they tell me, but——" he scratched his head, "but to one unversed in babes she do seem powerful red and wrinkled for her age—dissipated, you might almost say."

Ortho chuckled. "Oh, that'll pass. They get younger as they get older. When's the christening?"

"Sunday week."

There was a silence. Ortho was waiting to be asked to stand godfather The invitation did not come.

"What 'cher going to call her?" he asked.

"Jennifer Mary."

Still no invitation. From the uncomfortable way in which Eli shuffled his feet Ortho inferred that none was coming. Did his own folk rank him as bad as all that? Mary's doing, of course. He was pained, for he respected Mary.

Eli broke the silence by changing the subject. "Mare's looking prime."

Ortho swept the beast's muscular quarter with his wiper and slewed her round so that the sun shone on her polished red hide.

"She should. There's precious few ladies get the attention she gets—eh, Lucy?"

Lucy gave him an affectionate poke with her muzzle, caught the rag in her mouth and tugged at it, mischievously.

"Step up along to Roswarva and file our old Ruby's teeth, will you?" said Eli. "They're too sharp, ain't chewing proper. You've got lighter hands than I have."

"Can't today. I'll run up tomorrow if I get the chance."

"Going to Penzance?"

"Yes—or thereabouts."

Eli shifted from one big foot to the other. "Seem me that Penzance sees more of you than Bosula—and Bosula is your living. Don't let the old place drop back, Ortho. No offense meant."

"Or accepted, my old heart," said Ortho. "I'm as fond of it as you are, trust me. P'raps I've my reasons for going to Penzance; p'raps I'll be surprising the life out of you before very long."

He had it on his tongue to tell his brother all, but swallowed the impulse. The time was not yet quite ripe, and to let Eli into his secret was to include Mary—and everybody. Eli was no tatler, but he was as transparent as crystal. Ortho shut his teeth on the great news and raked the mare's forelock out with an old comb; she played with his bright waistcoat buttons, lipping them gently.

"I don't know that I want to be surprised to

death," said Eli, "and I don't pretend to follow your smart business notions, but it do seem to me that if you've got a good farm the best thing you can do is to pull your coat off and farm it." He drew a deep breath and blurted out, "Why don't you settle down sensible and get married?"

Ortho smiled. "Suits you, does it?"

"Me!" Eli exclaimed, his tone that of pained amazement—that anyone should question his domestic felicity, his Mary! "Why, dang it I never knew what it was to have . . ." He caught the grin on his brother's face and grinned sheepishly in return. "Oh, you're joking me, as usual. Yes, it suits me very well."

"Take care it don't suit you too well."

"How?"

"Fat, my son; you're getting fat. You'd look a fool in the wrestling ring."

Eli gave a demonstrative pull at his belt. "Don't see any signs of fat yet and I don't notice anybody over-anxious to try a hitch with me. But, jesting aside, Ortho, you're rising thirty, and Lord knows you've had a wide enough run, why don't you settle?"

"Morning past, high noon now, time to snug down for evening—eh?" said Ortho, catching Lucy by the chin and wiping the oat husks from her muzzle. "Well, who am I to marry? Who's the fortunate party? Speak out, my pretty Cupid."

The pretty Cupid scratched his head. "Oh,

there's scores of tidy maids about. There's Crebo's daughter up to Skewjack. She's a wonder in the dairy, they say, and will have all Billy's property."

"She may be a wonder in the dairy, but I ain't butter," said Ortho. "Moreover she's got a mole on her cheek the size of a florin. What's the use of a wife you can only kiss on one side?"

"Well, there's Miss Tancock, of Bosavern. She've been to a lady-school at Truro and can play the harp very delicate, I'm told."

Ortho spat. "Can't stomach harps. My stars! ain't we going to get sufficient harping hereafter without wanting it here on earth? Look'e, Eli, whose idea is this matchmaking, yours or Mary's?"

"Mine," said Eli. "Mary don't think . . ."

"Don't think what?"

"That you'll ever settle."

"Ah-ha—and why not?"

"Don't know. She just laughed when I told her my notion. She said, 'Go forth upon Polmenna and tell the west wind to settle!'"

Ortho dropped the mare's head and turned upon him darkling. "Said that, did she? Well, you just give Mary my respects and tell her she ain't the only one that is laughing. Tell her that . . ."

Again he was on the point of letting his secret out and again refrained. Better to hold his tongue and taste the full dramatic flavor of the disclosure later on, to save his powder for one royal bomb-burst. It could only be a matter of hours.

"You tell Mary not to be too sure," he said, somewhat lamely. "She may know a lot, but she don't know everything." Then suddenly he jerked his head back and roared, good humor restored.

"What are you grizzling at?" Eli inquired in mild resentment.

"Oh, nothing. My duty to Mary, and tell her what I've told you. I'll square Ruby's teeth tomorrow."

He fitted a saddle to the mare, girthed up and disappeared into the house, whistling merrily.

Half an hour later he was ambling into Penzance, dressed in his very best, Lucy cutting exuberant capers. It was a fine day, almost the first since he and Nicola had climbed the Ding Dong moors, eleven days before; their last ride but one. Since then, with the exception of that solitary morning, it had been raining in torrents. The moor streams came down in spate, turning the bottoms into marshes; the tracks were bogs, the fields quagmires. Everything gushed and squelched and trickled. Ortho, forbidden Chapel Street by Nicola's decree, fretted and sulked at Bosula, making a nuisance of himself to Naomi in the house, wrangling with Bohenna in the barn. But the period of banishment was over. Barradale should have arrived on Saturday, and it was now Monday. Nicola would have had two nights and a day in which to break the news to her father. Ortho was to appear at midday on Monday; he was even then hastening to

the appointment. He did not anticipate trouble.
Nicola would have paved the way and he had
infinite confidence in himself, his handsome appearance and ingratiating manners.

Barradale might have looked higher for his
darling daughter; but, after all, he was only a
merchant, and a Penhale of Bosula was no beggar-
man. As he ambled along Ortho rehearsed a
statement of his possessions. A substantial ten-
roomed house; three hundred acres of arable land
with stock and buildings in proportion; part of
Polmenna Downs and a good stretch of the Keigwin
valley, mostly bog-land but fairly well timbered
and useful for rough grazing—an agglomeration
not to be sneered at even by a prosperous shipowner. From what he had heard of Barradale he
appeared to be both genial and generous. Ortho
hoped he would be free-handed with the settlements,
for his own ready money was running out.

A blue-gray heron stood in Lamorna stream,
watching the swollen waters for trout. Ortho's
halloo sent it beating slowly up-wind through the
trees. A solitary snipe went over. Ortho imitated
its cry with surprising accuracy and rode past Tre-
woofe and Trevelloe singing:

"No more shall buds on branches spring,
    Nor violets paint the grove;
Nor warbling birds delight to sing,
    If I forsake my Love.

The sun shall cease to spread his light,
    Ye stars their orbits leave,
And fair creation sink in night
    When I my Dear deceive."

It was an azure morning, mild for that time of the year. Away to the north the switch-back tors showed clear-cut and warm bronze against a robin's-egg sky. Southward was a glint of white fire, the English Channel. Birds cheeped in the hedges; there was a touch of yellow in the furze plumes. Spring was not far off, Ortho fancied, Spring with her crocuses and bridal white. His mercurial spirits rose still higher. Barradale would certainly do the generous thing. The lavish benefactor of widows and old seamen would not see his only daughter lack, even if she had gone behind his back in this affair. Ortho vaguely wondered why she had done so, why she had insisted on this secrecy. Oh, well, she knew her own father best and the likeliest way to handle him.

He was on the point of bursting into song once more when a head, slant-eyed, snub-nosed, thatched with a shock of strawcolored hair, rose above a wayside gorse-bush and peered at him with the furtive audacity of a wild animal. A Romany child, clad in a man's cast-off coat which hung down to its bare ankles. Behind the child was a dingy wigwam with a man squatting before it skinning a rabbit, also a straw-colored slattern bottoming a chair, her mouth full of reeds. A dejected donkey stood meditating among the ditch brambles, its forelegs hobbled with twine.

Ortho, ambling by on his bright bay mare, scowled at the miserable encampment. Poachers, roost-robbers, cow-drainers, night-slinkers, human foxes living by stealthy theft. Bohenna must be warned, the man-traps set. He glanced at the man so that he might know him again, and had a sudden impression that he had seen this before, *but from the other side*—that sometime, somewhere, *he* had crouched before a stick fire gutting filched meat for *his* woman and brats. Before he knew what he had done he had called out "Greetings!" in Romany. The man looked up and their eyes met, and behold! they were the eyes of brothers. It was all over in an instant. The instant past and Ortho was himself again, Penhale of Bosula, a lord of the soil, and the Rom had dropped his gaze and was fumbling with his cap, a ragged outcast.

Ortho blinked, startled. "My stars!" he muttered. "That was odd! What happened then? I saw . . ." But he could not remember what he had seen, the shutter had opened and shut too quickly. "Strange! Oh, well . . ." He lifted up his voice in song, came to the brink of Paul Hill and saw Mount's Bay far below him with the freed wind-bounders making sail toward the Lizard, white flecks on polished lapis lazuli. His eye lit on the thin spire of St. Mary's Church; behind that lay the

house with the green shutters and his china shepherdess, his Nicola, tinted like apple-blossom, pink-
lipped, fragrant. He laughed when he thought of
his brother's elephantine efforts at matchmaking;
Miss Tancock the harpist and that Crebo girl, the
dairy wonder—good Lord!

What would Eli and Mary and all of them say
when he brought Nicola home to the Owls' House?
Miss Barradale, the heiress, with her powdered
waves of hair, rustling silks and foaming laces.
What then? Successful in his previous bids for
fortune he might not have been, but this would wipe
out all foregone failures. This was triumph! He
would have sung again but that he was entering
Jack Lane and there were people about, so he compromised by bawling "Good-day" at every soul he
saw, and sent Lucy across Newlyn Green at a hand-
gallop. He hungered for Nicola; he had not seen
her for five days, not since that ride to St. Just.
Barradale! He'd manage Barradale—and, after
all, what could the man do *now?*

The dinner call had emptied Penzance sea-front
of visitors and town idlers alike, except for an
orange woman munching her own wares on a bench
at the Wherry Town end, and a black dot in the far
distance. Ortho, unimpeded, kept the mare at a
gallop, swept past the flag-staff, kicking up clods of
turf. The black dot resolved into two dots, big
and small, an old woman and a dog. Ortho came
abreast of them, passed, stared, and then checked.

It was Mrs. Beckford leading the afflicted Rupert—
Mrs. Beckford, but so changed he had to look twice
before being certain. Old age seemed to have fallen
on her in a night; the face she lifted to him was
piteous, the flat cheeks fallen, the pale eyes swollen
and red-rimmed. She appeared to have shrunk into
herself. "There's been a tow-row, and Nicola, or
Barradale, has dismissed her," thought Ortho.
"Dang it, they might have been gentle." He liked
the duenna and, despite the fact that she had tried
to separate Nicola and himself, he believed she
liked him—she was only obeying orders, he supposed; not her fault, poor old soul.

Swinging Lucy about, he jumped to the ground
and raised his hat. "Mrs. Beckford . . . nothing
amiss, I trust?"

She raised liquid eyes. "Amiss, Mr. Penhale!
Haven't you heard?"

Ortho shook his head. "I have been on my
farm—estate—these five days. What has happened?"

"Dead!" she wailed.

"Who? What—what d'you mean? Who's
dead?"

"Mr. Barradale. S-shot himself."

"Mr. Barradale shot himself," Ortho echoed,
horrified. "Why, in the Lord's name?"

"Ru-ined!" The flat face quivered like jelly, the
weak mouth sagged and tears came flooding.

Ortho let his reins drop and, catching the duenna

by an arm, helped her to a bench. The mare frisked off a few paces and then fell to nipping the turf, Rupert licked his sores and scratched his fleas, both blissfully impervious to their owner's troubles. There was a dinning in Ortho's ears: "Ruined! Ruined!"

"Here, calm yourself, bear up, madam," he said, as gently as he could. "There is no good done by crying. Did you say Mr. Barradale was ruined?"

Mrs. Beckford wailed into a sodden handkerchief. "Yes—all his ships lost."

"What, all at once?"

"No. It appears they have been going for some time, but he never told us anything. Now the last has gone, the *Owner's Love.* We heard from Bristol on Saturday . . . Kempthorne too . . . so he went into his bedroom and shot himself. Poor Mr. Barradale, so kind and courteous! They wrote to me, but I hadn't the courage to tell Nicola at once . . . so devoted to her father . . . I delayed, frightened, praying for wisdom. Dear Nicola, knowing nothing, goes out walking . . . meets Kempthorne . . . Kempthorne rushes up . . . condolences . . . and, dear me, poor Nicola!"

Mrs. Beckford sobbed and shook.

Ortho took her by the shoulders. "Steady! Steady! What is the matter with Nicola? Do you hear me? Nicola—"

"Gone!" moaned Mrs. Beckford. "Just like her poor mother . . . dreadful!"

"Gone where?"

"Off her head. It's in the family, Mr. Penhale
. . . her mother and uncle. It was always threat-
ening . . . the greatest care. She had two affairs
of the heart, at Bath and Tunbridge Wells, but
Mr. Barradale was adamant. 'No other man shall
suffer what I have suffered,' he said. Oh, Mr.
Penhale, I was afraid you were becoming attached!
Thank God, I kept you from any irrevocable step
. . . so kind to us in that dreadful post-chaise, and
to my little dog."

"Where is Nicola now?" said Ortho, grimly.

"At home. She is quite simple, like a child,
laughing and playing with Vashti . . . no mind at
all. And, O my goodness! what shall we do now?
She has nobody to look to in the world!"

Ortho turned away. The houses, the far hills,
were all blurred, unsteady, the very ground swayed
under his feet. His triumphal return with his
apple-blossom bride, his shining heiress!

Over those blurred hills was Bosula, his home,
Eli and Mary—quiet. He caught the mare,
fumbled for the stirrup. "A parson once bribed
can be bribed again; witnesses also," said the voice
of his gypsy mother, softly, slyly. "It means a
life sentence, bondage all the days of your life, and
you're young yet. Ride, ride, my son!"

He toed his stirrup, gripped the pommel.
"Shame! Shame!" said another voice, deep, ring-

ing, the voice of his yeoman father. "Who else in the world has she to turn to?"

Ortho let his foot drop to the ground, let drop the reins, turned slowly about, white in the face, stiff at the lips.

"I married Nicola at St. Just five days ago," he said.

CHAPTER XVI

PEACE reigned in the Roswarva kitchen. In the open hearth glowed a fire of salty drift-wood which burnt with occasional sputters of blue flame. Burnished copper pans on the opposite wall twinkled with fiery reflections. The sea-wind pressed against the window, tapping the panes with soft rain-fingers.

Old Simeon Penaluna lay in his rocker, head bowed upon his chest, snoring gently. Facing him sat Eli, head also bent in slumber. He had a book on his knees, a treatise on potatoes, their selection and improvement. For the last month he had been trying to read it, but had got no more than half-way through. Every evening he took it up with the best intentions, but sleep always mastered him before he had read more than a page or so. Mary was putting a patch in one of Eli's shirts. She glanced from her father to her husband, noted the book lying open at the same page as the previous night, bit off a thread and smiled. Tired as their own plow-oxen, they must be sent to bed ere long.

She listened for any cry from upstairs. All was quiet but for the low whimper of the wind, the tick of the grandfather clock. Mary liked to hear the wind, she felt lost without it. While there was wind there was life. She was born in a farm on the Bodmin moors; since she was twelve she had been at Roswarva; both exposed spots. Once, as a child, she had gone to stay with an aunt in the Constantine valley, a deep sheltered place of trees. On the first night she dreamed that she was dead, woke up in pitch-darkness and utter quiet and screamed in terror. Simeon came instantly and comforted her, but not until she was back again on the Bodmin moors with the familiar gale bustling round the eaves, rattling her window, did she again sleep happily. She listened to it now, wondering if her baby, born in this house of the winds, would demand the same æolian lullabies.

The dissertation on potato culture, which had been pursuing a downward course for some minutes, fell from Eli's knees to the floor. He started, yawned, stretched himself, and said he supposed he had "just dropped off."

Simeon woke himself with a shattering snore, sat up, and made precisely the same remark. Mary looked at him reproachfully. "Father, Father, be careful you don't blow the walls down like the trumpets of Joshua. Never did I hear such a shallah."

Simeon tweaked the offending organ and hunted for a candle. "Goin' to bed, I believe. 'Tis most nine o'clock. Be'st goin' to plow the Great Weeth tomorrow, Eli?"

"Yes—if I do live." Eli cocked his head sharply. "Is that a horse loose in the yard? Nobody can be coming at this time o' night. Hello!"

The latch clicked and Ortho entered, stood against the door, mud to the boot-tops, rain dribbling from his coat.

Simeon put his candle down. Mary drew a quick breath. Eli wheeled about.

"Ortho! What are you doing up here at this time of night? What is it? Fire?"

"It is no fire," thought Mary. "If it were he'd be the last to leave it; he'd work like ten. He's done crime or something dreadful—disgrace for us all. He'll drag us all down with him, this Ortho." Her heart leapt toward the mite upstairs.

"Come over here, man," said Simeon. "Don't stand there in darkness. What is it? We'm just going to bed."

Ortho stalked across to the hearth, turned his back on it, and stood with legs straddled, rocking from toe to heel. He looked haggard, pale; there was a queer twist to his mouth. Three faces bent toward him, yellow in the candle-light; anger was in them, bewilderment, dread. Three shadows converged on the wall behind. A log sputtered, the wind moaned. Even then, at the dead end of his hopes and dreams, Ortho's sense of the dramatic did not leave him.

"Would you like to hear a comic story?" he asked.

Simeon snarled, "Ach! Have done! Who have 'e robbed now?"

Mary gave a tiny sob.

Eli glared at his father-in-law. "None o' that, Sim! What is it, boy?"

Ortho laughed bitterly. "My stars, you do love me, you Penalunas! No, this time, you'll be pleased to hear, I have hurt nobody but myself; and, what is more, the hurt is like to last me my life—good news, eh?"

Then he told them all, without omission or excuse.

He started bravely enough, but as the dreary story dragged itself out he lost hold on himself. The pity in Mary's face was too much for him, the misery in Eli's. Simeon's dislike had braced him; sympathy broke him up.

"Curse it, don't look at me like that!" he cried, his lip trembling. "It's my trouble, ain't it? Mine alone?"

For answer Eli threw an arm about his neck. "Don't say that, Ortho boy—not with me here."

Simeon, pacing the kitchen like a caged beast, muttered, "No, we all stand together," in strangely modulated tones.

Mary laid a hand on Ortho's arm. "You say you bribed Passon Coverdale in the first place— couldn't 'e have bribed 'en again?"

"Yes, I suppose, but—"

"But you didn't?"

"No."

Mary laughed of a sudden, proudly, gladly. The men stared at her amazed, but there was a tear-bright radiance in her eyes, a sob in her laughter.

"Ortho, hold up thy head. There eddn no disgrace here, my dear. When first you came in I thought all manner of things—vi'lence, murder, misery for us all. But now—why, I honor 'e, I honor 'e!—and what burdens thee's taken to thyself we'm braer proud to share. Look up, brother!"

Kempthorne accosted Ortho in Chapel Street. Ever since the catastrophe he had been hanging about, Mrs. Beckford said, offering his savings, any possible assistance.

He marched up to Ortho and began to upbraid himself.

"My mind full of poor Nick . . . came round the corner straight into his daughter and the cat was out of the bag. Babbling fool . . . deserve to be shot . . . would have cut my tongue out first. . . ."

"No fault of yours," said Ortho. "It was bound to come sooner or later, in my opinion. There's a curse on me, I believe. Do you know how this ruination came about?"

"I do," said Kempthorne. "Piehorse, Nick's book-keeper, whote to me. They lost the *Fair Penitent* off St. Kitts last year. That left 'em the *Owner's Love* and the *Barradale*. They were both lying off Calabar, full slaved, when a tornado caught them. The *Owner's Love* and the *True Briton,* another Bristol ship, got to sea, but the *Barradale* went ashore, broke her back, and was plundered by the natives. Nick got word of this just when he was expecting to hear both ships were safe in the West Indies. They sat still and waited for word of the *Owner's Love,* the last hope, but no word comes. Piehorse says Nick gave no sign, carried on as gay as ever, but God knows what was passing in his mind. Then word came from the master of the *True Briton.* He said he sailed two weeks after the *Owner's Love* and made a fast passage. One night, when he was nearing Barbadoes, a boy reported firing ahead, but the rest of 'em could hear nothing, so he held on. Next morning, at dawn, he nearly ran down the *Owner's Love.* She was by the head, deserted and sinking. She sank within ten minutes of his sighting her. There could be no mistake—he had served aboard her as mate and knew her well. He said she was badly slashed about the rigging and had nettings triced up, and reckons she was taken by a privateer and her people carried to one of the French islands. He could get no word of 'em in Bridgetown, and as there was a trader sailing the day he arrived he sent word by her at once.

"Piehorse says Nick only laughed then. 'Oh, well,' says he, 'that is settled,' and sat drumming his fingers on the table. Then he picked his cane up and went down the stairs, stepping straight as a boarding pike. But in a minute he was back again. 'It escaped my memory,' he says, 'but how is your wife's health today, Joseph?' Piehorse says his wife is improving. 'That is excellent,' says he. 'I remember her when she was a girl in Bread Street—a very pretty girl. My duty to her, please. Good night.' With that he is gone—home to shoot himself."

"Was he in debt?" Ortho inquired.

"Piehorse don't think so. Not in his shipping affairs anyhow; he paid as he went. Piehorse thinks he was just clean swept."

So the great Barradale, that paragon of all the virtues had lacked one essential—courage. Ortho spat his contempt.

Kempthorne looked up, pained. "No, not that— not before me. You've got cause to think hardly of Nick, I grant, but he was a good man for all that, warm in his mirth and in his heart—as many a poor broken-down devil of a seaman will testify. I tell you he wasn't himself when he took that pistol up; he was crazed, off his head. Beggary don't matter much to me; I've been beggared more than once in my life and will be again, mayhap; but to Nick, who had always had all he wanted—money, houses, servants, carriages—it was the end of the world, I tell you."

"It is the end of the world for me," said Ortho, bitterly.

Kempthorne scouted the idea. "Not it. You're young, and from what I hear of you not one to drown yourself for love. And look'ee, Nick didn't get you into this pocket, you got yourself. Nick warned at least two suitors off his girl, though it nigh broke his heart to do so. If you hadn't been so damned secretive you'd have been warned as well. Remember that before you spit next time." He gulped down his anger and spoke more gently. "There, there, I've said more than I should—but he was my good friend. What I wished to say is that I am returning to Bristol tomorrow—ship refitting. If you empower me I'll see Joe Pie-horse and write to you. I'll do everything I can, believe me, for Nick's sake."

Ortho accepted his offer gratefully and they parted.

CHAPTER XVII

THREE days later Ortho moved the whole Chapel Street household out to Bosula, Nicola riding a-pillion behind him. The shock had wrought no physical change in her: she was as pink and white and exquisite as ever; but her mind was that of a child of six. The weakest link had snapped, leaving the rest of the chain unstrained. Fortunately she was a good child and trustful. Though she did not recognize Ortho she suffered herself to be lifted up behind him without demur and rode off waving her hand to Mrs. Beckford. She smiled charmingly at everybody they passed on the road, but said no word from first to last. Several times Ortho glanced over his shoulder at her, their eyes met, and she beamed at him. There was nothing fixed or idiotic in her smile, it was spontaneous and innocent, an expression of goodwill to all men; but it set Ortho's nerves on edge.

"Good God! is she going to sit grinning at me like that for the next fifty years?" he thought. "I shall go mad as well."

She grasped at his coat to steady herself, as the horse stumbled in a rut, and at her touch he softened. It was a sign of her utter dependence on him. Poor little soul! Let her smile; better that than tears—at all costs there must be no tears. As far as it lay in his power, her life should be a happy one, and Mary and Eli would help. Good food, good lodging, care and kindness should at least be hers.

Gwithian church tower stood black against a pale lemon afterglow as they came to the brink of the Keigwin valley; Boslua lights twinkled yellow among the bare trees.

"Thus I bring my bride home," thought Ortho, and laughed ironically. All his life he had been picturing the not impossible shes who might become Mrs. Ortho Penhale. As a boy, under the influence of sailors' tales, these ladies had been almost exclusively of color and blood royal. Goldenskinned beauties, daughters of cannibal kings, who fell in love with him, the shipwrecked mariner. Eastern princesses, silken and bejeweled, snatched from the harems of lewd old khans. He had lain on the warm turf out on Luddra Head, the gulls whirling round him, and imagined himself riding through Penzance with his bride, a barbaric but lovely person, dressed in pearls and ostrich feathers. As he grew older his fancy flew less high and nearer home. Some young duchess, rescued from pirates or highway men, would meet the case very nicely. All those boy dreams were over now. Reality was at his back, holding fast by his coat—a mad girl and a pauper. Nevertheless he turned and wrapped the mad girl's cloak closer about her against the dropping rain.

Eli was waiting for them at Bosula. He lifted Nicola from the pillion as she had been thistledown, and lowered her gently on the doorstep, where Mary gathered her into her warm arms. Naomi bobbed a curtsey and then, her good heart getting the better of her, rushed forward and kissed Nicola on both cheeks. This much Ortho saw, framed in the lighted doorway, then the three women disappeared within, Mary's arm about his wife's shoulders. He turned the horse and rode across to the stables. His bride was home.

Ten days later he saw a letter addressed to him stuck in the postmaster's window in Penzance. It was from Kempthorne, curiously spelt, but to the point. Barradale had left no debts in his shipping business; there had simply been a clean sweep. As for his personal affairs, the house was fully mortgaged and there were a few small debts which could be settled by the sale of his carriage, horses and household effects. Piehorse, if empowered, would see to all this. Kempthorne added that the shipowner's death had caused general shock and regret in Bristol, where it was understood he was a rich man. The fierce Liverpool competition had been whittling his profits for some years, but his pride had forbidden him to adjust his scale of living or decrease his charities by one farthing. His reserves had melted and when his ships went there was literally nothing left. Thus Kempthorne.

Ortho tore the letter up and, riding home, dismissed Vashti. Since there was no money coming with Nicola it behoved him to retrench. The childless Naomi had taken the girl to her bosom with all the warmth of her ardent, if arbitrary, nature; a circumstance which rendered the maid superfluous, and she departed for Truro and the Exeter stage riding pillion behind Bohenna.

Mrs. Beckford was also superfluous, but as she demanded no wages Ortho let her remain until another position could be found for her. Then he took his coat off, as Eli had advised, and set about farming Bosula. It was seeding time and there was plenty to do, but Ortho had not been at it a fortnight before he knew that he would never last. Muscle and energy were his in abundance, hard physical labour held no terrors for him. It was the pace that fretted him, the sludging, deliberate tread of his labourers, the mile-an-hour meander of the plow-oxen. To a man trained in the dashing school of smart ships and smart cavalry this was paralysis. He exhorted, cursed, goaded, but there was no mending the speed. The pace of the ox was the ingrained pace of the countryside. He must conform to it or break his heart. He gave in, feeling it was the first step in degradation.

Also there was the monotony. Ortho was thirty years old; with reasonable luck there were thirty

years more work in him. Thirty years of rising at
dawn, trudging up and down the same few acres all
day, and coming home at night to find Nicola sitting before the fire smiling and saying not a word.
The prospect appalled him. Thirty years of
drudgery, cooped up in that little gutter of a valley
—he who had fought and laughed and loved from
Bombay to the Antilles, who had seen the Western
Ghats and the shores of Yucatan! Had Nicola been
in her right mind he would have been compensated,
he told himself, would have rested at home content.
Now she added to his natural unrest. Her unsoiled
beauty drew him more than ever, her vacancy repelled him.

Sometimes at night he would watch her sitting
before the hearth in her rich dresses, the firelight
glossing her dark waves of hair, slim hands crossed
in her lap, the exquisite colour glowing in her cheeks,
and wonder if she were not playing some deep game
with him, if anybody so obviously healthy in body
could be broken in mind. Time and time again he
was on the point of snatching her in his arms, hugging her, kissing her, shaking her free of the spell.
Then she would look up at him and smile with that
dreadful innocence of hers and he would fling out
of the house and over the hill to Roswarva or down
the cliffs to MacBride's hiding-place; more often the
latter.

The captain's beard was doing well. It had not
the silkiness of its predecessor, that of Verdun

prison, its owner regretted, but what it lacked in texture it made up in vigour; and in another month, at the most—his heavy eyebrows plucked, his moustache curled—he would be ready to face the world. In the meantime he continued to live off the country, fishing from the rocks, snaring the cliffs for birds and rabbits; gathering driftwood and gorse roots for fuel by night; sleeping, cooking and amusing himself with ventriloquism by day. At the last he had become surprisingly adept and took impish delight in scaring Ortho half out of his skin by producing from the darkness behind his victim a voice which thundered, "Stand, in the King's Name!" "Ortho Penhale, I arrest you!" or some such nonsense. Apart from these small shocks Ortho enjoyed his evenings in the adit.

MacBride was a widely travelled person and knew how to tell of what he had seen. He would yarn away for hours, lying back on his bracken couch, pipe in hand, the driftwood fire lighting up the glistening wet walls of the cavern, drawing sparks from the feldspar, the surf rumbling ceaselessly without. Where he came from he did not know, he told Ortho; his earliest recollections were of the Dublin Foundling Hospital. At twelve he was sent to sea in a ketch trading coastwise. The master was an illiterate creature, who nevertheless made his way from port to port with marvellous accuracy, principally by means of the lead. When he was fourteen the master died as the result of a brawl with an

Irish porter in Water Street, Liverpool, and Mac-
Bride, not liking his successor, "hopped the twig,"
and signed on the Guineaman, *Unicorn*. It was
while on the Guineaman that he learned to read and
write, the surgeon—a kindly man, though addicted
to necromancy—being his mentor.

In three years he had made four voyages in the
Unicorn and was third, or trading, mate. Then,
when she was lying off Gabun and he was down the
coast in the long boat, slave hunting, the ship was
cut off by the natives and every man jack of her
company butchered. MacBride was four months
among friendly tribes, and then shipped as third
mate of the London slaver *Kitty's Amelia*, his predecessor having died of fever the day before. The
first and second mates succumbed to the same complaint on the voyage to Nassau, New Providence,
together with seventeen hands and a hundred and
eighty-odd negroes. MacBride made the voyage
home second in command, but as the owners refused
to confirm his rank he cursed them and looked elsewhere. From then on, till he became master of
the Youghal brig he made not more than a single
voyage in any one vessel, but among these were
numbered a Greenland whaler and two or three
privateers. It was while serving on one of these
that he was captured and imprisoned at Verdun.

Of his activities subsequent to the unfortunate
affair in the Kingston tavern he would not speak.
That was all over and done with, he said, but he

talked of the Yellow Sea, the Pacific and the islands thereof and Ortho inferred that he had spent some years plundering coastwise junks and buccaneering among the pearl atolls. The captain's reminiscences in nowise served to cure his unrest.

"They came swimmin' off as soon as we dropped the hook, blossoms in their hair, laughin' and singin'; brown girls in the blue water. 'By James!' says I, 'there's your mermaids!' You'd lie on the beach there under a palm eating fruit all day, and maybe, at night, take a torch and go fish-spearing inside the reef—fiery fish shooting through a sea of silver fire. . . . They've got rudders a fathom under their keels, mat sails and sterns painted up with dragons and demons all gold and red, and eyes in the bows to see with. The admiral was dressed in silk and had a fan in his hand and nails four inches long, so help me God! . . . They was all round us, mountains of ice, grinding and glittering, and the floes was black with seal calves bleating for their dams. . . . I shipped a skinful of yellow wine and staggered up the hill and fell down in a bed of flowers and went to sleep. When I woke up there was a little Portugee maid laughing at me out of a brush, tickling my old nose with a feather. Tamorica was her name; she gave me a walnut and I gave her a dollar. Aye, Funchal is a sweet place. You lie in the roadstead·there and all night there's bells ringin', ship bells and chapel bells. Very pretty it sounds, over the water. . . . He towed us four miles, the spray flyin' from our bows like we had wings. Then he charged us and broke two oars, that near he got. Then he sounded the depth of two lines and came up right under us, and over we went. A hundred-barrel bull-whale with a lump of ambergris in him as big as a cheese. Great days, Säid!"

Such stuff inflamed Ortho. To be cooped up for life on three hundred acres, with all the wide, colorful, clanging outside world calling him forth to try another fling. It was unbearable! He writhed and groaned and blurted his troubles to MacBride. The captain was sympathetic. To him a farmer was a clod, an unenterprising, brainless, sluggard, but one degree removed from his own beasts. He was not altogether sure that farmers did not eat grass—secretly. When his men stowed sail in a slovenly manner he called them "farmers." It was the most insulting epithet at his command, and he commanded several. The idea of a brisk young man, who had seen a bit of the world, settling down to grow turnips pained the captain, and he said so. But at the same time he comforted Ortho. Something would turn up soon, he was sure, some excuse to break away. And now that Ortho's wife had gone mad and barely recognized him he was under no moral obligation to stay with her. As for the farm, anybody could look after a farm.

But Ortho could see no light ahead. He had no money to finance any undertaking and no particular talents to sell, and without either he could hardly desert the Owls' House and leave Eli and Mary with the burden of Nicola. He saw no way out.

Then, on the last day of March, the unexpected fell like a thunderbolt out of a clear sky. It fell in the shape of a letter from the faithful Piehorse. Mackaffee, captain of the *Owner's Love* had reached Jamaica with a full complement of slaves which were sold by scramble at top prices. Furthermore, if he had lost one ship he had gained a better. His story was this: In getting clear of Calabar during the tornado he had run on and off a sand bank, straining the ship slightly. However, being full-slaved and finding the leak could be kept in check, he held straight on for the West Indies. He made a slow passage and, moreover, fell into a stark calm which lasted several days. This would account for his being caught up by the *True Briton*. However, the calm did not trouble him, as he had ample stores in hand and his slaves were in prime condition. The wind came on again and all went well until he was nearing Barbadoes, where he was chased by a large privateer schooner and, failing to outsail, clewed up his courses and waited. The Frenchman threw his boarders in right away, but they got such a reception that they hauled off and the two vessels remained side by side for over an hour, exchanging broadsides, much to the privateer's disadvantage. Mackaffee said she lost seventeen men killed and wounded in the attempt to board and one of her stink-pots, shot from the main-yard, fell inboard and disabled three more. This he learned later. As for the *Owner's Love,* she was somewhat cut about the rigging and had lost her first mate killed by a musket ball, one boy and three slaves wounded.

The privateer then tried to board for the second time, but while her people were swarming up the boarding nettings, Mackaffee ordered his crew to stand back and, with his own hand, discharged a swivel into the nettings. The swivel was loaded with copper dross and the boarders dropped into the sea "like dead sparrows." The Frenchman then hauled off again, having plainly got a bellyful, but to Mackaffee's horror the carpenter reported that the *Owner's Love* was "opening up like a basket, forward." The captain made an examination and found such to be the case. The working of the guns had aggravated the old strain and the ship was sinking. There was nothing to do but strike.

The battered Frenchman could hardly believe his eyes when he saw the slaver's colors come down, but once alongside he wasted no time in transferring slaves, stores, ivory and prisoners. That done he put some sinking shots into the unfortunate ship and stood away for Basse Terre.

The French captain had been killed, the mate lay wounded in the cabin, the command therefore devolved on the second mate, a Breton, possessed of small intelligence and less control over his wild crew, who, broaching the slaver's rum, made exceeding merry. On the second night Mackaffee, taking advantage of this continued inebriation, and having circulated a rumor among the slaves that the French were cannibals and they were being taken to Basse Terre to be fattened for the pot, rose with their help and took the privateer. He was now in the same predicament as his captors had been, with a large number of unruly prisoners on his hands and three hundred savage blacks who might be as easily swayed against as for him.

Fortunately, before he could be put to the test, he fell in with a British cruiser which relieved him of the prisoners. He then headed straight through for Jamaica, arriving there without further incident. In the meanwhile the *True Briton* had arrived in Barbadoes and reported the loss of the *Owner's Love*. Mackaffee reported that the French owners in Guadeloupe were not redeeming the *Charmante Hélène* and she had therefore been awarded to him by the prize court. He added that she was a fine large schooner, built in Bayonne only the year before, sailing like a witch and mounting eighteen guns, exclusive of swivels. He was loading rum and sugar and hoped to be home by June at the latest.

The letter set Ortho whooping like a school-boy, dancing with excitement. Nicola had brought him something after all, and no mean dowry—"a fine large schooner, mounting eighteen guns and sailing like a witch." The description rang in his head like a chime of the sweetest bells. What could he not do with such a craft? She opened the wide world to him.

He rode home like a whirlwind and broke the glad tidings to Mrs. Beckford, who, instead of rejoicing, dissolved into tears. "If only poor· dear Mr. Barradale had waited!"

Eli, who was plowing, also received the news with little enthusiasm. "Oh, well," he mumbled, "s'pose she'll fetch a tidy bit of money," and kicking a stone up with his toe, jerked it over the hedge.

Ortho frowned. "Who said I was going to sell her?"

Eli shrugged his huge shoulders. "Stands to reason. Nobody can captain a ship and a farm at the same time." He turned and regarded his brother with disconcertingly direct blue eyes. "You don't tell me that you propose to drop Bosula, home, new-wedded wife, everything you've taken on your shoulders and go roving again? You don't tell me that?"

"N-o-o—I—that is—"

"Then it stands to reason you'll have to sell the ship," said Eli, and, calling to his team, tilted the share and went on with his business.

MacBride, however, was of a different opinion. "There y'are," said he. "Told you something would happen . . . Providence! A Bayonne schooner of eighteen guns and a prime sailer—very handsome, *vee-ry* handsome! Those cursed Parlay-Voos know how to build—rot and wither 'em! All our best models were copied from them. Howsomdever it's a pity she didn't fall to you a couple of years back."

"Why?"

"War's over—or nearly. What's the use of a privateer in peace time? No more use than a talking horse at a Quakers' meeting."

"She'll do as a trader," said Ortho.

MacBride shook his head. "Not she. I know them Biscay privateers, fine run and over-sparred. Got no carrying room to speak of. Hm-m, hr-rr, let me think."

He paced up and down the tunnel, humming a tuneless dirge, tapping his corrugated brow—then spun about.

"Why, yes, of course, to be sure! What height has she between decks?"

Ortho referred to the letter. "Five feet, six inches."

The captain nodded. "Thought she'd be somewhere's about that. Put her in the Guinea trade."

"But I know nothing of the Guinea trade," Ortho objected.

"No matter. This Piebald knows one end of it and Mackaffee t'other. If Barradale died without debts the sale of all them slaves, teeth and gold will stand clear profit. You'll have enough to refit again and a good lump over."

"Yes, yes—but what'll I do?"

"Live like a gentleman on her earnings."

"But I've told you I want to get away from here."

"Very well, go with her as supercargo," said Mac-Bride. "You write to this Piecrust and tell him you're wishful to carry on the Barradale trade with this new schooner and you want him to look after your interests. April, May, June—she should be in the Avon by early June and out again by early August. You write tomorrow."

Ortho duly wrote and received a reply from the faithful clerk saying that while he himself was only too delighted to serve anybody connected with the Barradale family it would be necessary to find a new ship-master. Mackaffee being of a ripe age and having amassed a comfortable competence, was retiring. He intended to retire to his native Skegness and dedicate his reclining years to astrology and the flute. The first mate was earmarked to succeed him but had unfortunately been killed and Piehorse could not recommend the second mate to so responsible a post. The man, an Irishman, was a fearless seaman, but utterly unreliable in port, disappearing for weeks on end. Piehorse reported that, now peace was practically established, Liverpool, Bristol and London were hastening to fit out slave ships and consequently experienced masters were at a premium. He said he would do his best but admitted, at the moment, he knew not where to look.

MacBride received this dismal intelligence with jubilant noises. "I've been prayin' for that," he chuckled, "and I'll tell old Piedish where to look"

—he tapped his own broad chest. "Here! I know the Coast from Senegal to Angola and the West Indies likewise. Ever since you told me you'd got this schooner I've been thinkin' things over and this fixes it. You sail as captain and owner and me as mate—see?"

Ortho gasped. "Me, captain! But I know no navigation."

"Pshaw, I'll soon teach you the principles," said MacBride. "We've got four months ahead of us. You can learn to use a quadrant as easy as a soldier learns to use his musket, and as for working out a position, it's plain rule of thumb and the same sum every day. There's men that never had a day's schooling taking ships round the world, and half the grand Navy captains don't know longitude from latitude—their masters sees to that for 'em. You've done several voyages, you know some seamanship, and moreover I'll always be there to tell you."

"Why don't you go as captain? I'll go super-cargo," said Ortho.

"For two reasons. I don't hardly feel ready to take so conspicuous a position just yet. Also when I'm captain of a ship I'm captain, king and God Almighty, and I don't take no dictates from my supercargo."

Ortho protested. "But I should never—"
MacBride cut him short.

"Oh, yes, you would. Not the first voyage perhaps, nor the second, but by the third you'd know more'n the rest of us put together—or think you did. That's settled then."

Ortho bought a second-hand quadrant, an epitome and a chart or two and the lessons began forthwith, but he gave no hint of his project to Eli or anybody else, working steadily on his land by day as though reconciled to the life of a farmer. Spring came, whitening the Keigwin valley with the snow of hawthorns, gilding the hillsides with gorse flower, spilling pools of purple hyancinths in the Bosula woods; but Ortho Penhale had no eyes for beauty blossoming under his hand—he was looking farther. He saw illimitable forests steaming under the morning sun and a marigold river sliding through the mangroves. At the river mouth there was a stockade with canoes hauled up the beach and seaward a black schooner rolling at her anchors. He saw the same schooner, stunsails set both sides, stemming the ridged sapphire, "sailing like a witch;" saw Barbadoes, green and purple, rise over the sea-line and the whole chain of the Leeward Islands—Martinique, Dominica, Guadeloupe, Montserrat—unfold before him—the peacock islands! He had no eyes for present loveliness.

"June, July, August," he said to himself. "We should be away by August."

CHAPTER XVIII

TRUDGING homeward in advance of Bohenna
one noon Ortho heard a great snapping of
twigs and boys' voices calling. He was on
his own land, close to the orchard, so turned aside
to see what the young trespassers were about. Two
of them were standing at the base of an ash, the
merest brats of eight or nine years of age, bare-
footed, ragged, with flaming copper heads—twin
brothers evidently. From the showers of falling
twigs, the agitation of the leaves, a third marauder
was somewhere in the ivy, struggling upward. Their
impudence annoyed Ortho. He set no value on
nests, but that these young scamps should pursue
their quest, without any "by your leave," almost
to the very doors of his house, was altogether too
much. They would be robbing the orchard next.

He determined to give them a fright and crept
toward them stealthily, using the tree-trunks as
cover. Just as he was getting within pouncing distance he stepped on a dead bough and it snapped
with a loud pop. Instantly, without even glancing
round, the two little red-heads plunged into the
thorn thicket—they reminded Ortho of two fox
cubs darting to earth—but, quick as they were, he

managed to grab one by the seat of his pants as he was on the point of withdrawing himself down a rabbit-run. The little creature clasped both hands over his head, as though expecting a blow.

Ortho had all he could do to keep from laughing. "See here, young man, what are you doing on my property?"

The infant squeaked and whimpered, pawing the mold with his bare toes.

"What is your name?"

No answer.

"Do you hear me? What is your name?"

Still no reply.

Ortho shook him. "Come. If you don't tell me I shall box your ears. Where does your father live?"

The boy cowered, but beyond the continued whimpering made no sound.

Ortho lifted his hand. "I shall beat you if you don't. . . ."

"Lave un be!" cried a shrill, vibrant voice behind him.

He turned about and beheld a third boy; from the bits of lichen and ivy adhering to his tatters, the climber.

"Lave un be, to once!"

Ortho laughed. "Well, I'll be damned! And if I don't—what then?"

"I'll make 'e!"

"*You*, you'll make me! Well 'pon my soul! Ha-

ha !" He looked at the small champion with admiration. A curly-headed, blue-eyed lad, not more than ten years old, yet sturdily built, with a superb little chest and straight, strong legs. His eyes sparkled defiance, he panted with rage. "What a man he'll make !" thought Ortho, and at the same time was vaguely reminded of Eli, Eli as a boy.

"Lave un go ! Do'est hear me."

"Yes, my lord, I heard well enough," said Ortho, and twitching the red baby across his knee, lifted his hand again. He had no intention of hurting the child, but was curious to know how the elder boy proposed to effect the rescue.

He was speedily enlightened. Something crashed against his forehead, filling his eyes with noisome yellow fluid.

"Run, Tim !" squealed the rescuer, and a second nauseous bomb burst on the bridge of Ortho's nose.

The red baby wriggled like a snake, but Ortho clipped him fast between his knees and cuffed him lightly over the head. In an instant the elder boy was on him, pommeling him furiously in the stomach, kicking at his legs. One sharp little boot-toe caught him on the shin-bone, another above the instep, and at the same moment the red cub bit him in the hand with teeth like needles. Ortho, uttering a yelp of pain, released the infant and, gathering the ten-year-old to him, laid in. He was really angry now. His shin ached, his hand stung, the contents of two ripe pigeon's-eggs clogged his eyes.

and dripped from his chin. Moreover, he felt supremely ridiculous. He laid in in good earnest. But his captive did not take the thrashing quietly; he fought with all his strength, unyielding, untamable; kicking, scratching, pommeling, squealing with rage.

A rough hand gripped Ortho's upraised arm. "Here, have done! Hear me?"

It was Bohenna, grizzled head sunk between his shoulders, an ugly glitter in his fierce little eyes. "Drop un to once!" He caught the boy by the arm, wrenching him free. "Run, you—run away quick!"

The boy beat a slow retreat up the hill, rubbing his chastised portions, blazing unutterable hatred at his chastiser.

Ortho swung on Bohenna. "What in hell d'you mean by interfering? What's it to do with you— eh? I catch that young devil down here robbing nests and—"

Bohenna spat. "Robbin' be damned! How can the child be robbin' his own place?"

"His own place! What d'you mean, you old fool?"

"Old fool, is it?" Bohenna roared. "Old as I be, I b'lieve I could twist your neck yet—but lave that be. Ess, I'll tell 'e what I do mean." He waved a trembling hand after the retreating urchin. "There goes a better Penhale than ever you'll be, you black gypsy, you! That's a colt of the old

stock, that is, a throw-back, the dead spit and image
of his grandfather, my old master, my John. Go
thou up, little Penhale," he shouted, his voice shaking with emotion. "Go thou up and bide awhile.
Thou shalt come back to thy own place in God's
good time!"

Ortho caught him by the sleeve. "Will you tell
me what you are talking about?"

Bohenna scowled at him, but there were tears in
the little fierce eyes.

"Ess, surely. De 'e mind a maid called Tamsin
Eva, a 'red Dane' girl, daughter to old Phineas Eva,
parish clerk o' Gwithian? Can 'e mind her at all
among all your fancies?"

"Yes, but—now I remember there was. . . . But
you don't mean . . . ?"

"Ess, I do mean," said Bohenna. "She married
Trevaskis o' Joppa after you left her and that boy
do go by his name, but he's yours for all that, and
the only son you'll ever have, seem me."

Then, without another word, he shambled off
toward Bosula. Ortho sank down on a windfall
and remained there for over an hour, staring into
space—the only son he would ever have.

Thomas Trevaskis of Joppa Farm was trimming
his hedges, slashing down brambles and thorn with
a long-handled bill-hook, when the old pied mongrel
leapt up barking and Ortho Penhale jumped his bay
mare over the bank.

"Good day!" said Ortho, pleasantly.

Trevaskis growled. If there was one man on earth he hated it was this same Penhale. Eleven years previously Ortho had stolen his sweetheart from him—and had his will of her. Now he came riding over Joppa fields smiling and shouting salutations. Trevaskis had a sudden desire to dash his bill-hook into that smile, to ruin that handsome, insolent face forever. His grip tightened on the handle.

Ortho's eye met his, twinkling, amused, and the grip loosened. Hate Penhale he might, but he feared him even more. His word it had been, that set the Preventive on Ortho's track and drove him overseas. He had hoped the squire would never come back, but now he was back and he was not sure how much he knew. The uncertainty tortured him. Also there had been a local man killed in that affair, a Baragwanath of Monk's Cove. There were six Baragwanath brothers left in the Cove, a lawless, vindictive tribe. Ever since Ortho's return his sleep had been haunted. Not a night passed but he saw the squire and the six brothers slinking along the dark hedges toward Joppa, armed with bludgeons— and a rope. He hung a loaded blunderbuss over his bed, telling his wife, Tamsin, it was for foxes. And now here was Penhale come to visit him! He felt sick with apprehension.

"Get off my land!" he stammered.

For answer Ortho sprang from the mare and

swaggered toward him, thumbs in embroidered waistcoat pockets.

"Shoo-hoo! not so fast, neighbor. If it's a matter of trespass, two can talk. My hinds, Bohenna and Davy, out and about t'other night on the west side of Tumble Down—which adjoins your fields, I believe—well, they found some gaps very cleverly netted for hares. They sat them down quietly by the likeliest and by and by puss came into the net, close driven by—" Ortho's gaze wandered till it rested on the mongrel, "by a pied dog with one toe missing on the near forepaw."

Trevaskis started. "I—I never—'

Ortho held up his hand. "No, your dog did it all by himself, eh? Hung up the nets and all? A monstrous clever dog! For all that, you'd better tell him that the penalty for poaching is transportation. However, I shall say nothing unless you drive me to it, for I know you have a large family to support and matters have not prospered with you."

"Wha—what do you w—want?"

"I want the eldest boy."

Trevaskis gaped at him and then broke loose, frothing. "The eldest boy, saith 'a! I'm to raise, feed, and clothe your bastards till they're fit to work and then you'll ride up and snatch 'em from me, will 'e?" He swung the hook menacingly. "Get off my land, you gert black rogue, get off to once or I'll spaal 'e wide open!"

"Then thee'd best turn thy weapon t'other way about," Ortho advised, removing a snip of thread from his cuff; "thee's got it back to front. That's better. Now spaal away."

Trevaskis dropped the hook, cursing.

Ortho twinkled. "Now look'ee, Tom, I'll speak you fair. I'll give you fifty pounds down for that boy and eight pounds a year till he's sixteen. You can hire a grown man for that and be the gainer."

"But what of my feelings?" plaintively.

"You can stop that right away," said Ortho, "for, by all accounts, when you're not kicking him, you're beating him. Fifty pounds down and eight pounds a year for six years."

"Will 'e put it in writin', signed and sealed?"

"Hand him over to Trebilcock, the lawyer, to-morrow and you shall have the fifty pounds in your hand and a writing for the rest."

Trevaskis grunted, undecided, but the glint in his narrow eyes betrayed him. "Umh! what are 'e goin' to do with 'en?"

"That's none of your business, but I don't know that I mind telling you. I'm going to send him to school and later into the Navy as an officer and a gentleman. Is it a bargain?"

"Make it sixty."

"I'll make it nothing if you say another word!" Ortho thundered. "Stand up to me, would you, you bilge rat! You always were frightened of me and, by the Lord Almighty, I'll make you more so before

I've done. Why, dang it! you daren't even plunge that bill-hook at me, and me unarmed!" He towered over the shaking farmer, hands upraised, black brows crumpled together, showing a wicked snarl of teeth. "I try to treat you fair, but that ain't enough for you. Well, then, I'll treat you rough and see how you like that. Now, for the last time, which'll you have, money or bloody war? Which, you filth?"

"Money!" Trevaskis gasped, cowering against the bank.

Ortho nodded. "I guessed you would."

The *Charmante Hélène* docked in Bristol at the end of June and was refitted under Mackaffee's supervision. By mid-August she was ready for sea again and Ortho went north to join her, leaving a letter for Eli giving his destination and purpose— he dared not face his brother.

The slaver towed down the Avon on August 18th and that evening, after dark, her first mate came aboard, brought off by a shore boat from King's Cove. He sported a bushy brown beard and called himself Fortunatus Gold.

CHAPTER XIX

ORTHO PENHALE and Oko Ephraim Jack Jack sat in the shade of the palaver-house publicly wishing each other long life and everything of the best, privately consigning each other to Hades. Both were dressed in their finest; of the two, Oko Ephraim the more impressively, which was right, for he was a king. He sat on a carved stool, naked to the waist, pock-marked, immense, the fat wreathing his massive trunk in greasy collops. A kilt of tarnished brocade hid his swollen thighs. Round his bull neck hung a string of cowrie shells, and suspended therefrom was a copper kettle-lid burnished to great brilliance. The whole was surmounted by a naval cocked hat in advanced stages of dilapidation. Slave-born, he had worked his way to power first by intrigue, then by astute poisoning, finally by wholesale massacre.

A splendid wild animal, a bronze Hercules in his day, prosperity had played havoc with him. At the age of fifty-three he weighed twenty stone, the elastic muscles had softened to blubber, his eyes were pouched and bloodshot, he breathed with difficulty—the savage run to seed. But he was still king. When he spoke, the head-men squatting round him

instantly hushed their parrot-chatter. When he gave
an order, men leapt to obey. Unwieldy, breathless,
obese, there was still potency in him.

The hollow compliments dragged to a close. Both
principals drew breath for the impending duel.
Ortho took stock of the compound. He had not
been there before. When the first trade was opened
he was down with fever and MacBride had done the
business, and since then the trading mate had carried
on—or tried to. It was a strong place of seven
stockades, set one within another. The fences were
of bamboo, pointed at the ends and eight feet high.
One entered by a narrow gate at the north corner
and walked round and round until one reached the
innermost yard where Oko Ephraim sat in splendor.

A six-pounder ball would smash through from
end to end, Ortho reflected, but it would be an awkward place to get out of. On his right hand was
the royal palace, a square hut daubed with mud and
thatched with palm-leaves. Over the door hung a
string of goat skulls and some calabashes smeared
with red ochre—fetish charms. On his left was a
palm-thatch supported by bare poles, beneath which
sat the tribal ju-ju, a crude idol about four feet
high, carved out of mahogany. It had outstanding
ears, slant eyes, no nose to speak of and a gaping
mouth curved up at the corners so as to produce
the most imbecile expression imaginable. Ortho
could barely refrain from laughing.

"See that bat-eared image over there, Sam?" he

whispered to the surgeon. "My stars, there's a thing to pray to!"

The little Jew, who had been paring his nails, looked up, blinking through horn spectacles.

"Hm-m, yes—somebody has been praying to him recently. He's clotted with blood and palm-oil libations. Hm-m!"

Ortho sniffed. "Devil-dance last night, belike." He turned to the interpreter. "Hey, you Robin. Tell the king that when I came three moons past I advanced him goods to the value of nine prime slaves. I want them now."

The mulatto translated. Oko Ephraim made an almost imperceptible motion of the head. One of his wives, ever watchful, held up a silver soup tureen. He spat into it and the great mass of flesh rumbled internally.

"King say he no 'member," said the interpreter.

"Then I will remind him." Ortho produced the count book from his pocket. "King Oko Ephraim Jack Jack. Twenty pieces of chintz. Ten pieces Chelloe. Ten Bandanoe. Four Niccannae. Six of Cushtee. Fifty handkerchiefs. Six muskets. Two brass pans. Twenty kegs of powder. Five bags of shot. Seven hats. Three iron pots. Twelve gallons of brandy. Nine ankers of rum. Thirty knives. Beads. Hawk-bells. Bar iron. It is all here. Count book speak true mouth as the king sabby very well. Tell him."

Came another pause. Oko Ephraim was thinking. Ortho watched those gossips among trees, the feather-headed wine-palms, nodding before the sea breeze, their split leaves rattling harshly; watched a kite wheel up into the blue, poise and then swoop. A pretty gecko lizard flicked out of the palace thatch, stood panting in the sunshine and flicked back again.

Oko Ephraim rumbled once more.

"King say powder him no good."

"Tell him it was good when I gave it to him. Ask him if he will stand before a musket loaded with that powder?"

Oko Ephraim made a motion for his soup tureen and squirted it generously.

"King say brandy him no good."

"He should have said so before he drank it."

A flight of gray parrots dashed out of the river mangroves and thrashed overhead, squawking like fools. A rank stench of uncovered mud told that the tide was ebbing. The mounting sun brought out more smells, smells of rotting vegetation, decayed fish offal, of warm black bodies smeared with palm-oil. The shadow of the palaver-house lay like a dark stain on the sand.

"King say five slabe too much."

Ortho smiled indulgently at his majesty and held up both hands, one thumb turned in. "Nine! Job would have been no success in the Guinea trade," he said to Mordecai. "He had not sufficient patience. This black whale knows he owes me nine Eboes and knows he will have to pay sooner or later, yet we must talk till our jaws drop off. Nine!"

The heat increased perceptibly, minute by minute. Sweat broke out all over the royal carcase, dripped and hung in the heavy creases. Flies settled on him, an attentive wife scourged them gently with a fiber switch.

"King say no havy slabe," the interpreter droned. "King say nex' time captain fit for come havy plenty slabe, pay ebryting. Berrah good."

Ortho frowned. "You tell the king he does not speak true mouth. He has slaves and I cannot wait. I have been eight moons on the coast and my men are sick."

"King say he speak true mouth. Him too much sorry you mans sick."

"That was a mistake telling him the men are down," Mordecai whispered, still at his nails; "now he will not fear you."

"My guns are very healthy, though," Ortho retorted. "I'll knock his filthy village—"

"Hush!" the surgeon warned. "The linguister is his man. Let us get out before we threaten."

Ortho's eye roved round the eight-foot stockade and lit on the gaping idol. The flies were busy about the ghastly libations, black on the dead fish at its feet. Somehow it did not appear as comic as it had been.

"You're right," he whispered, under cover of his hand; "my long twelves shall take up the palaver."

Aloud he said, "Tell the king that if he don't pay me I will jam no more trade with him. I will tell other captains that he is a bad man and they will not jam trade with him either. Then where will he get the brandy, gin and rum he loves so dearly?"

Oko Ephraim's heavy eyelids flickered, the rumblings were deep, as of a mountain in travail.

"King say he speak true mouth by Gor A'mighty, no havy slabe. Eboe peoples take fright too much, run along bush, no can catch. Captain come back nex' year catch plenty slabe, fill ship. I bound she no stand long before she full for go away."

"Next year!" Ortho exclaimed. "I may be shark meat by next year. I want nine primes *now*, or look you, I'll take elephant's teeth instead."

The interpreter shook his head sadly. "King say no havy."

Mordecai stood up. "There is no more to be said, then."

Ortho nodded. "Not by *us*. Hey, you, palaver finish."

The interpreter clutched at his skirt. "Please, captain, King say please dash him rum. No havy rum. All drink—woh, woh!"

Ortho burst into a roar of laughter. "Well, damme, that's rich! D'you hear that, Sam? This smug-faced rogue refuses to pay me for one advance and now asks me to dash him some more. Heard you the like?"

"King say you come back nex' year pay you ebry-ting. No havy Eboe today."

"And next year he'll tell me to come back the year after, eh?"

"No, Captain. Nex' year catch 'em plenty prime boy, by Gor A'mighty!"

"By Gor A'mighty, *no!*"

"You no dash King rum, Captain? King sick. King no havy—"

"No!" roared Ortho, springing to his feet. "Pala-ver finish. Come on, Sam."

His last impression of the palace yard was the clack and buzz of many excited tongues rising to fever-pitch, the idol leering through its mask of flies and Oko Ephraim spitting violently into the soup tureen, tears rolling down his cheeks.

They found the pinnace tied to a root below the village fish-traps, its crew stretched out in the shadow of a palm, roused them up and dropped down-river on the ebb.

Dark green mangroves lined either bank, black-belted with mud, their gray stilt-roots showing above water. The bank mud stank, the mud-loaded river steamed and stank. In midstream a ten-foot croco-dile drifted, sleeping, amid a litter of palm refuse and logs. Ortho spat viciously into the tepid brown soup overside. "My stars! to think I left a good farm for this! Stench and fever, fever and stench, bars, tornadoes and black swine that bilk you! Pah!"

"If you still have that good farm, why not return to it?" said the Jew, dryly.

"Why not?" Ortho hesitated. He had an instant's vision of the summer woods above Bosula, green dells of oak; ash and sycamore; the stream bubbling and creaming under delicate sprays of fern; trout basking amid flickering water-lights; the enamel-blue flash of a kingfisher—everything green and cool, green and cool. Tears came to his eyes. "Why not? Because . . . because there's the ghost sitting at my hearth at home, warming her hands and smiling and I . . . I can't bear it. And, moreover, I want to make money."

"What for?"

"To spend, of course . . . and because I want to show I can."

"Well, have you not made money?"

Ortho spat again. "No. Six years I've been at this trade, and I've not made more than enough to keep me going, what with the Yellow Jack perishing my cargo in '86 and Sherrow and Watts' failure last year. Money! No, all I've gained out of this so far is fever and gray hairs."

He took off his hat, wiped the sodden band and flicked the trickling sweat from his brow and chin. "Give way, my hearts. Bend your backs. Let's get clear of this pestiferous swamp."

The boat's crew dragged sulkily at their oars and the pinnace swept on. The river took a sharp twist southward and met the sea in a tumbling ridge of surf. Beyond the bar, etched against the intense blue sky, rose the slaver's tall masts, rolling drunkenly. They crossed the bar, hoisted sail and tacked toward her.

"The mate is back," Mordecai commented, wiping the moisture from his spectacles. "There's the longboat astern of the schooner."

"I wonder what fortune he's had?" said Ortho.

"Good."

"How know you?"

"I know Mr. Gold."

Ortho smiled to himself. "Ah! I wonder how much you do know of Gold?"

"I know him to be a very determined man. As for his previous career—four years' experience of Guinea traders has taught me that one may speculate but not inquire."

"That four years has tarred you with the same Guinea brush, my friend," said Ortho. "Remember that."

"I remember—and claim the same immunity," said Mordecai, blinking through his spectacles.

Ortho grunted and, putting the helm down, ran alongside the *Charming Helen.*

The slaver lay at anchor a short mile seaward of the surf, a trysail on her mainmast to steady her. A fleet of native canoes, loaded with yams, fish and coker-nuts, bobbed on the foam-striped swell around her. Awnings were slung over her poop and fo'csle and under them lay sick members of the crew gasp-

ing what air they could. The slaves squatted on the
main-deck under a strong thatch of bamboo and
palm, the men shackled to chains running fore and
aft. Some, the more recent acquisitions, lay inert,
terrified, seasick or merely sulky, but the majority
talked, laughed and sang, thumped on drums fash-
ioned from old powder kegs or extracted appalling
noises from mouth-harps and horns. Many had
been seven months on board. The few women went
unfettered, one nursing a baby born only the day
before. Looking down from the poop barricade
the main-deck was a packed mass of black flesh.
The chatter was deafening, the smell overpowering.

O'Keefe, the second mate, met Ortho as he came
aboard, a pistol in his belt, a cutlass at his thigh.

"Mr. Gold is just after comin' from M'bo, sor,
wid tin primes an' one pickaninny," he drawled.

"Ten! My stars, that's good! Where is he?"

"In the galley, brandin' thim."

MacBride (alias Gold) came along the main-
deck carrying a boy in his arms, shouting crude
jests in the Eboe tongue. The slaves shouted back,
gleefully, hailing him as "Daddy One-Eye." He
set the infant astride Ortho's Great Dane, Hero,
and rode him round the poop.

"What d'you think of this? Bought him for
twelve gilt looking-glasses, four umbrellas and a
pewter basin. He'll look pretty dressed up in a
turban an' a silver collar followin' some fine lady
round. Eh?"

"Ten you got," said Ortho. "Well, you've had easier trade than I."

MacBride's smile stiffened. "None so easy. Grandy Dapho wouldn't sell at all at first, but I talked to him—I talked to him for three days. Then he trotted forth a woman touched with the sleepy distemper, and then a couple of men. They came boundin' into the barracoon, hoppin' like fleas an' howlin' like wolves, very spry. 'Berrah prime boy,' says he. 'You are right, Grandy,' says I, 'an' I'll tell you what they were primed on—palm-wine. An' I'll tell you why they had their heads shaved—to hide the gray wool. An' I'll tell you why they're shinin' so nice an' sleek—they've been groomed with palm-oil. I'm tellin' you a few trade secrets, Grandy, old shipmate,' I says, 'but I wouldn't tell everyone; they might act unscrupulous.' Grandy an' me we looks at each other eye to eye. 'Take dem away,' says he, and they was took, still hoppin' and howlin.' 'Now shall we talk sense?' says I—and we did."

MacBride prodded a scrap of cheese into the child's gaping mouth with a blunt forefinger and handed him over to a negress.

"How have matters gone here?" he asked.

"We buried the cooper this morning and that lame boy the day before," said Ortho, "and there's four blacks died. If we stay much longer we'll all rot."

"Then why stay? We must be full-slaved."

"I want that nine from Oko Ephraim."

"H'ant he paid yet?"

"No. Starkie has been three times and I've been myself this morning. Swears he has none—will pay next year."

Mordecai spoke. "He says Grandy Dapho and Duke Cookey Gam raided so ferociously the Eboes ran into the jungle and he could capture none. It is my belief he speaks the truth."

"Why?"

"The man was perished for a sup of rum. He's been drunk for years. He wept for it."

"I'll make him weep for something else ere sundown," Ortho growled. "I'll pitch him an iron pill or two that'll make hot swallowing."

MacBride took some ground-nuts from his pocket and fed them to a gray parrot perched in the mainshrouds. "Pshaw! You're out of range by a mile, Captain, and if you're goin' in over the bar you'll have to wait till next spring tides. The fat Beelzebub was athirst, eh, Sam?"

"Burnt up."

"D'you give him any rum?"

"No, b'God, that I did not," said Ortho, angrily. "He owes me for nine ankers already. No!"

MacBride shook his head. "You should have, then—just a sup. With him parched like that a sup or two would have produced a cravin' for more and you'd have got any slaves he had—or maybe some of his own people."

"Well, if you're so clever you'd best try it yourself!" Ortho snapped. "It was you opened the trade in the first place."

MacBride took it calmly. "Begob, and I will try it myself. I never open anythin' I can't close. I'll take the long-boat and a couple of ankers and start now."

An hour later he was gone, in the long-boat with four hands. Mordecai saw him over the schooner's side. "Be careful how you raise the devil," he warned.

"Oh, pshaw!" laughed the mate, and waved his hand cheerfully.

The surgeon watched the long-boat till it had seesawed over the bar, watched till its white sail disappeared among the mangroves, and then went below, persuading himself that Oko Ephraim was a joke, that the mate was more than a match for a host of Oko Ephraims—nevertheless he was uneasy.

The burning afternoon wore out. The slaves were roused up and ordered to dance, and dance they did, rolling their white eyeballs, clapping their hands, stamping to the time of monotonous native chants. The chains thumped the deck. The fetter links clinked a doleful accompaniment. The sick and sulky were enlivened with a rawhide whip—they had to be exercised somehow.

Astride of the fo'csle barricade sat the sailmaker, sawing a cracked fiddle. A boy, shaking with ague, banged the ship's drum. Ortho Penhale stood at the poop ladder exhorting the blacks to further efforts, promising tobacco to those that leapt the highest. But they were listless that evening, kept the whip singing.

"What they need is the mate and his droll ventriloquistin'—that makes 'em laugh," said a voice at the surgeon's side. He turned and saw O'Keefe.

"Yes. He lived amongst 'em once; speaks their tongue."

"Shure—but it's not only that."

"No-o."

"If we lie off this divil's dhrain of a river much longer we'll all be dead," O'Keefe grumbled, "black as well as white."

Mordecai nodded. "If the mate gets satisfaction from Oko Ephraim we lay for Barbadoes immediately."

"Please God he does," said the Irishman piously. Then, altering his tone, "There's a swate juicy little Eboe gurrl over there by the fore-hatch, d'you see? How d'you think she'd look dhressed in a yard or two of red bandanoe? I believe I could find room in my cabin for—"

"You leave her be!" said the surgeon, with heat.

O'Keefe feigned surprise. "What! Lookin' for her yourself, are ye? O Saint Samuel! Saint Samuel!"

"You know I am not."

"Begob, I know nothin' of the sort. You quiet

ones are often the deepest in divilry. Tell you what, I'll play you fair. I'll dice you for her."

"Women will be the ruin of you one day, O'Keefe —and us too, most like," said Mordecai, bitterly.

The Irishman laughed at him. "Faith! they've been the ruin of me already; but I protest 'tis very agreeable ruination . . . a yard or two of red bandanoe. . . ."

The Jew turned away in disgust and looked shorewards. The mate must have reached the village by now. How was he faring? He had a mental picture of that sun-beaten stockade; the king sweating on his carved stool; Gold knocking the bung from a rum keg; the idol leering through its mask of flies. "Be careful," he muttered to the surf and the palmtrees. "Careful."

The drum and fiddle stopped. The bosun hung his whip round his neck. Down on their haunches sank the negroes, panting, dripping from the exertion. Food was served out, a good broth of shrimps, flour and yams boiled together; then the slaves were hustled below and packed in the stifling 'tweendecks for the night.

The sun went down into the South Atlantic, bulging sideways as it sank, a bursting pomegranate, crimson ripe. The western sky was a bed of red roses smoldering at the edges. Then, in a moment the flush and the fire were gone, flooded by a tide of green water deepening into star-pricked blue. Night. A cold wind blew offshore, rank with the

smell of fetid swamps and rank jungles. Mist
floated up through the palms and mangroves and
hung above them in a low cloud. Mist rolled down
the river in a wall, rolled lazily over the bar and out
to sea. Dew fell cold and heavy, soaking everything. The schooner lurched round to meet the
land breeze, pitching sullenly.

CHAPTER XX

ORTHO sat at supper in the stern cabin, muffled to the ears in his big deck coat, gnawing at a tasteless native fowl. Mordecai sat on one side of him, O'Keefe on the other. They spoke but little. A horn lantern swung to and fro with the lurches of the ship, casting barred shadows along paneling hung with small arms. From below came the swish of water breaking against the rudder, then gurglings as the schooner squatted stern-first into a trough. Ortho abandoned the hopeless struggle with the fowl, flung the carcass to Hero and turned on O'Keefe.

"Those small arms are rusting through. Turn the men on them tomorrow."

"Aye, sor—what men, sor?"

"Don't question me! See to it!"

O'Keefe raised one significant eyebrow at Mordecai and bent to his food. "Very good, sor."

Silence again but for the swish and gurgle below, the big dog scrunching the carcass. Then from behind the paneling came a long-drawn moan, followed by a scream and the noise of fists beating on wood.

O'Keefe grimaced. "Starkie—havin'. Two

nights ago he thought there was hairy brown
demons chokin' him. Last night he was walkin'
Clifton Downs wid his true love, all in the merry
springtime O. He kissed my hand, before God, he
did, an' called me 'darlint'—*me!*"—a snigger.
"Tonight it must be the demons again." He
scraped his chair back, sighing. "I'll go—"

But Mordecai was before him.

O'Keefe waited till the cabin door had closed
on the Jew, and then jerked his thumb.

"Now that man is an everlastin' plague and
puzzle to me."

Ortho glanced up, surprised. "Sam! A better
surgeon never walked the deck."

O'Keefe nodded. "Shure—as you say, sor. An'
that's what plagues and puzzles me. Why is he
walkin' a deck? Why is he tendin' sick negroes
in these stinkin' black-cattle ships when he might
be snug ashore cossettin' rich owld wimmen at a
guinea a visit or bleedin' apopleptic dukes at a
shillin' a drop?"

"Well, somebody must come."

"Granted, sor—but it's not the likes of him that
comes. Thim that comes comes because they must.
The surgeon of the owld *Columbine* had fits the
way he'd frighten ye. Parkyns drank like a bale
of sponges. Delbouys of *Brookes* was wanted for
debt, and Hillas of the *Owner's Love* for worse
than that. He'd go ashore at Pill, when we hauled
up Bristol River, and stay hid till we sailed again.

I've been thradin' to the Bights tin years,—God preserve me!—and I know the slaver surgeon. There's always a weak sthrand somewhere, and up to now I've always found it; but Sam, I confess, is a puzzle to me. Why is he here?"

Ortho shrugged. "I do not know. Why are you?"

O'Keefe pushed his plate back. "Pride, sor— an' the money to indulge it. It is my conceit to live like a gentleman, and whin I step ashore afther a round voyage I can do it—for a month. Salt-horse I may be *now*, but whin I am ashore nothin' but the height of fashion will content me and the best the town affords in company, wine and women, sor. I have visited Bath, Tunbridge and Sadlers Wells and ruffled it with the quality callin' meself a rich planter of St. Kitts—and none suspectin'. I may be but a poor second mate, sor, but in my day I have dhrunk the rarest an' kissed the fairest —and by God I will do so again!"

Ortho laughed and poured out a stiff dose of brandy. "Here's to that day, Mr. O'Keefe. Help yourself."

The Irishman lifted his mug to the east. "With your permission, sor, I would sooner dhrink to Mr. Gold, his success, for methinks the one will depend upon the other." Then he went on deck to relieve the bosun.

Ortho was left alone with the swaying shadows, the dog and the cockroaches. He tried to light a pipe, found his tobacco damp, cast the clay from him and took another swig of brandy. The irresponsible O'Keefe had amused him for the moment, but mention of the absent mate revived his anxieties. Should he have allowed MacBride to go ashore, and how was it going with him? Was the rum-bait working? They should know something by noon at the latest, a flag or smoke signal. The long-boat should be back by the following evening —all being well.

Ortho rose and paced the cabin. There were fungi growing in a corner under a deck beam, he noticed, and the powder flasks were covered with green mould.

Curses be on the negligent O'Keefe! Curses be on this curséd coast! Everything rusting, moldering, oozing damp within and without. He had a sudden poignant longing to be gone, a craving for open sea and the clean breath of the Trades.

Mordecai came out of the third mate's cabin, finger on his lips.

"Fallen asleep—but he's very weak. How much longer are you going to keep us here, Captain?"

"We shall sail the middle passage as soon as Mr. Gold returns," said Ortho.

"Whether he has been successful or not?"

"Whether or not."

Ortho's steward roused him out at eight bells and he went on deck to relieve O'Keefe, whom he found blissfully asleep against the poop rail, one arm hooked about a backstay. He woke up with a start, smiled his disarming smile, and reported all well.

"Slaves quiet?" Ortho inquired.

"As the dead, sor."

"The wind has freshened. Blowing offshore now. Did you veer out any more cable?"

"No, sor. I thought she was ridin' aisy enough."

"Humph! You can go below."

O'Keefe hesitated. "The bosun reported he heard dhrums, but I'm slit if I've heard annythin' —that surf would deafen ye."

"Drums! Where away?"

"Dead upriver, sor. An' he said there was a kind of red glow in the mist, like the reflection of a big fire, just for the minute."

"In the bosun's watch? That must have been all of four hours ago?"

"All of that, sor. I've seen or heard nothin' since, nor has annythin' been reported from forrard."

Ortho remained for some minutes staring shoreward. The freshening wind was bringing the fog off. It floated round the schooner in banks and streamers of clammy, malodorous steam, ghostly glimmering in the light of the old moon. Ortho could see nothing and there was nothing to be heard but the creak of tackle as the schooner pitched and scended, the everlasting thunder of the surf.

"Oh, well, Mr. O'Keefe, that'll do—hello! what's amiss with the dog?" The big Dane had reared up, forepaws on the rail, and was growling uneasily.

"What is it, Hero?"

"Moonlight and fog," O'Keefe grumbled. "Begob, he's not the only one that sees things on a night like this. I was thinkin' meself only just now—"

Ortho snapped, "Oh, quiet! He's no fool, if you are. What's the matter, son?"

The dog sprang to the main-deck at a bound and galloped forward. Ortho found it on the fo'csle astride a cat-head, barking in good earnest.

"There's something moving, I believe," he said to the sailmaker, "but I'm damned if I can see—can you?"

The man cursed the fog and said he could not. "Send a boy aloft."

The dog's barking increased in fury. The hair stood up on his neck, every muscle was rigid. Ortho strove to quiet him without avail.

"There *is* something there," he affirmed. "Is that boy aloft? Hie you, boy! Where are you?"

"Astride the topgallant-yard, sir."

"Can you see anything?"

"I can see a patch of water here and there—the fog shifts . . . difficult. . . ."

"Which way are you looking?"

"To windward, over the jib-boom, sir."

"Can you see anything coming off?"

"No, sir."

"Damme, the dog must smell something!" Ortho exclaimed.

"Maybe a dead beast drifting, sir," said the sailmaker, waggling his gray head. "There's a mort o' wisht stinks blowing off with the wind. I'm nigh consumed with 'em meself. That river's fit to poison a shark."

Came a hail from the invisible boy. "Please, sir, I think . . . I think there's some'ot black right ahead . . . I think it's a log, sir; about a half cable distant. No it's . . . it's a canoe, *two canoes!*"

Ortho hailed the poop. "Mr. O'Keefe, there's two canoes coming off. Turn out the after guard and stand by."

"Aye, sor!"

"Turn out all hands, *armed*," he said to the sailmaker. "Quick, jump to it! Are those canoes any nearer, boy?"

"Yes, sir, close aboard."

Ortho cupped his hands and hailed. "Canoes ahoy! Who are you?"

There was a moment's silence; then came an answering shout, and Ortho recognized the voice of Oko Ephraim's interpreter.

"Captain Pen'ale, dat you, sar?"

"Yes. What do you want?"

"Canoe from King. Bring slabe, sar."

"Slaves! At this time of night?"

"Yes, sar. Daddy One-Eye say you live for get away one time, sar; too much sick mans along you."

"Where is Daddy One-Eye?"

"Make rum-palaver along King, sar. Long-boat she live for come big—by'mby, presently."

Ortho whistled with satisfaction. So MacBride had turned the trick after all! And all the while he had been fearing unmentionable things. Not a wink of sleep had he had that night for thinking of MacBride. And now they would be away at sunrise, off and away into open sea, crowding for the West Indies. His men were tumbling up, half clad, priming pistols and buckling on cutlasses as they came. It was on his tongue's tip to order them back. Instead he hailed the canoes.

"Hey, you, Robin! Paddle up to the port side. I'll throw a ladder over. Hear me?"

"Berrah good, Captain."

He saw the two craft cross his bow just under the bowsprit. They seemed packed with men. Somebody aboard the first began to flog a drum with great violence.

"Avast that noise, Robin!" Ortho shouted, but the drumming went on.

"Oh, curse you! Well, as long as you've got the slaves—"

There was a sudden frightened shriek from the forgotten boy aloft. "Sir! Captain! Canoes, hundreds of 'em, to starboard, close aboard— O my God!"

As at a signal the swaying mists to starboard throbbed with the boom of war-drums answering the first.

"Cut off!" Ortho muttered to himself, quite quietly. "MacBride baited 'em too far. They've come for more rum—well, well!" It had come, the nightmare dread of every Guinea captain—cut off. He saw the *Charming Helen* at dawn, skimming the sapphire meadows like some white albatross? —ah, no! Beached, stripped, afire, smoking to heaven; swarming with debauched savages that ate through her like ants through a carcass, dancing, vomiting, staggering under their loads of plunder. He saw himself and his men lying in the scuppers, naked, gory, defiled beyond words. His *Charming Helen*, his little pretty—his sick men!

"No, by thunder, not yet!" said he. "Mr. O'Keefe, I'm going to cut and run," he yelled. "I leave the poop to you. Get your party behind the barricade—and hey! douse that trysail and close haul the starboard braces."

An uproar amidships told him that the interpreter's party had boarded and were being dealt with. But he paid no attention to that. O'Keefe would do everything possible; he could be trusted in an emergency, if at no other time.

"Boy—are you there?"

"Y-yes, s-sir,"—a small shivering voice.

"Loose the topsail and topgallant-sail—for your life! Thompson, down with you and cut the cable at the manger—quick!"

The headsail gaskets he cast off himself, running out along the bowsprit to do so. A man in a canoe fired a musket, and a hurricane of pot-leg whirled by within a few inches of his face. The canoe fleet was at hand. The headsail halyards were belayed to the foremast bitts, also the topsail sheets and topgallant jeers. To get sail on her he must reach the foremast somehow. Mustering his men, he dropped down the fo'csle ladder and charged along the main-deck, the Great Dane baying at his heels; fell headlong over one wounded negro into another, bearing him to the deck. The dog tore the black's throat out. As Ortho rose he saw the mulatto interpreter rush for the port bulwarks and attempt to vault them, but they were too high and he fell back to be impaled on a boarding pike.

"All gone, sir," the bosun reported, licking a cut on his tattooed forearm.

"Gone!" Ortho echoed. "They're *coming*, man, droves of them! Hark!"

A pandemonium of yells and drumming rose up out of the mists to starboard, the splash of flying paddles, the thud of canoes bumping against the schooner's side. To increase the confusion, the slaves below decks raised a chorus of jubilant howls, hammered on the planking, rattled their shackles. The din was indescribable.

"Will I fire a pistol down the hatch to quiet 'em?" the bosun inquired.

"No, you fool," Ortho blazed. "Sheet the topsail home and hoist the headsails! I'll cover you as long as I can."

"Boardin' by the foremast chains!" came the voice of O'Keefe, tingling pleasurably, followed by the crash of a poop swivel and the rattle of musketry. A woolly head rose above the bulwarks, then another and another.

Ortho and his men charged them cheering, piked, hacked, battered them down. More rose and were beaten under. The swivel crashed repeatedly. O'Keefe and his party were peppering the canoes to some order.

"Jibs and forestaysail aloft, sir, and topsail sheeted home," the bosun reported. "Will I sweat up the topgallant-yard?"

"'Ware boarders to port, *port!*" O'Keefe warned from his vantage, and Ortho swung about to see a wave of black break inboards into the waist.

There was no withstanding this. This was inundation. He turned and ran for the fo'csle thrusting his men in front. A huge Koromantyn, marked with hideous cicatrizations, slung a war-club at him, he felt the wind on his face. Another, cutting round the foremast, lunged wildly with a spear. The Great Dane, upleaping, took it to his heart and Ortho reached the barricade unharmed, to find more negroes climbing up the dolphin-striker.

But things were easier now. All of the slaver's company were either on the poop or the fo'csle, both strong places, designed to resist slave out-breaks and provided with swivel-guns kept peren-nially loaded. Moreover, the schooner was free, and under her backed topsail paying off before the wind, the headsails were taking hold. Under pressure from ten-foot boarding pikes the negroes on the dolphin-striker and martingale dropped into the water and struck out for their canoes. Those that attempted to climb the barricade were cut to ribbons; but they packed the main-deck from side to side, yelling, gesticulating, brandishing spears, and more were swarming up every minute.

"Please God, they don't let the slaves out!" Ortho muttered, discharging his pistol through a loophole.

"Or cut the halyards," said the bosun.

The sailmaker shook his head. "The swine don't know enough for that."

Crash! O'Keefe had discharged the port swivel right into the jammed mass amidships. A piece of grape, going wide, rang against the barricade. An-other sang overhead, ripping a hole in the fore-staysail.

There was utter silence for a second, then the

wail of a man in mortal agony, followed by shrieks of terror, as the survivors rushed to the starboard side, fighting, treading each other down, in their endeavors to reach the bulwarks.

Crash! O'Keefe discharged his starboard swivel into *them*.

Ortho hoisted himself astride the barricade and cheered across the poop. "Hooray! my bonnies, my hearts of oak, they're running! They ain't cut us off! Swing the yards over and hoist that trysail! She's away, away! Cease fire, Mister, they've had sufficient. I—"

A wounded man, lying in the shambles of the main-deck, lifted himself painfully to his knees, flung a spear and rolled over with a grunt of content. The spear pierced Ortho in the shoulder-joint and he toppled backward into the bosun's arms.

"I don't think it's poisoned, but we'll let it bleed on for a short while," said Mordecai, dropping a crimsoned swab into a basin. "The flesh is badly lacerated and must be painful, but there's no great harm done."

"Oh, I'm well enough," Ortho grumbled. "What other damages?"

"That boy you sent aloft is off his head with fright. As for the others, some minor cuts and scratches only. We were lucky."

O'Keefe entered the cabin, black with powder,

but on excellent terms with life. "She's under plain sail, sor, and all well. I'm afther examinin' the boarders. Nineteen dead and eight wounded. I've thrown thim overboard. None was worth keepin'. Thim that could crawl jumped for the canoes." His face sobered. "Oh, I picked this up. One of thim divils must have brought it aboard—that Robin, most like."

He placed a small flint-lock pistol on the table. It was of common type, but the wooden stock had been cross-nicked to provide firmer grip. All three men knew the pistol. A vision came to Ortho of that same cabin one bright morning off Isla de Pinos, two years before, and MacBride seated at the table nicking the stock with a sheath-knife, reading the gray parrot a homily on its lack of morals the while—and his eyes grew misty. It was Mordecai who broke the silence.

"I have known as much since the canoes came. Let us pray it was over quickly."

"He was the best friend I ever had," said Ortho, bringing his fist down on the board. "Six years he stayed with me and my folly when he could have bettered himself. And now it is in my business he has got killed. But hear me! I swear by Heaven I will avenge him ten times over. Not now—I am too weak and short of men; but some day, an' I live, I'll come back to this river and I'll shoot, I'll raid, I'll burn, I'll—I'll—"

It seemed to Ortho that the lantern was contracting to a pin-point, that the cabin was growing dark—strange, when dawn was breaking! He made an effort to grasp the table, missed it, and fell forward. "I'll—"

"Excitement and loss of blood," said Mordecai. "A swoon, merely."

CHAPTER XXI

A MAN slung aloft tapped his scraper against the mainmast and hailed the poop. "Navy pinnace makin' for we, sir."

O'Keefe regarded him coldly. "Is it a lookout ye think ye are? If you was on watch and the two Americas bowled before ye shure ye'd never notice them at all. But now you're supposed to be scrapin', sorra a thing ye miss, ye scut!" He clicked "T'luc! t'luc!" as though in despair of obtaining satisfaction from an ordinary seaman, slouched to the rail and took a lazy survey of Kingston Harbour in general and the approaching boat in particular. It was nearing rapidly, propelled by six rowers. O'Keefe's spy-glass revealed an officer in the stern-sheets.

He slouched to the companionway and shouted down it, "Steward! Stew-ard! My compliments to the Captain and tell him there's a Navy pinnace headin' for us."

Mordecai, who had been dozing under the poop awning, opened one mild brown eye. "What is it?"

"Trouble."

"Why?"

"How should I know? We've neglected to salute one of their plaguy beef tenders, belike; or you was

walkin' in Kingston yesterday and didn't haul your
luff for a purser's mate. We'll know in a minute.
Which death d'ye fancy? Flogged round the fleet
or plain keel-haulin'?"

"Speak him fair when he boards; there's no good
got by arguing with these officers," said the Jew.

O'Keefe spat. "Faugh! Bow, scrape, dip and
smirk before some plaguy little new-weaned louse
in his first pair of breeches, is it? Not I! Not if
I go to Port Royal and be hanged for it."

Nevertheless he hailed the bosun, telling him to
clear the port gangway and throw a ladder over,
and then swaggered down to meet the officer.

The pinnace foamed alongside. The rowers
tossed their oars smartly, the bow-man hooked the
schooner's foremast chains, and up the ladder
bounded a midshipman, a singularly attractive lad
of about seventeen, with frank blue eyes, a broad
pleasant face, and shoulders that would have done
credit to a grown man.

"'Day!" he greeted, and smiled with the utmost
good-humor.

O'Keefe, susceptible as mercury, melted instantly
before that smile and beamed in return. "A very
good day to yourself, sor!"

"Master of this schooner?" the boy inquired.

"No, sor—mate. I'm just afther callin' the master. He'll not be a minute."

"Thank you," said the cordial midshipman.
"What craft is this, Mister?"

"Charmin' Helen. Bristol Guineaman; just discharged."

The boy nodded. "Guineaman—I thought so from her lines and rake. Make a fast passage?"

"Cape Coast to Old Harbour, Jamaica, in forty-four days."

The midshipman whistled. "My soul, smart travelling! No snugging down at sunset aboard this packet, I'll hazard. Fly your kites all night, eh?"

"All day and night—till they carry away."

"And then?"

"Bend a fresh suit."

"Bold work!" The boy laughed admiringly, and lifted a professional eye to the slaver's lofty network of spars and stays. "Well, you've got a pretty little fairy here, Mister. As I was only saying to my coxswain as we were approaching, she's as pretty a thing as I've seen on the West Indian Station, and those Bahama schooners are no lame ducks."

O'Keefe's heart warmed to the boy still further. His admiration of the *Charming Helen* was so genuine, his smile so winning. The mate dragged a coil of tobacco from his pocket and thrust it forward.

"Will you do me the honor, sor?"

The midshipman declined. "Thank you kindly, but I don't chaw."

"'Tis very preservin' for the teeth."

"And very disruptive for the stomach. It can

serve me worse than a Biscay roll. D'you see that?"
He pointed northeast.

"See what, sor?"

"Those heavy clouds edged with rainbow colors
over the Blue Mountains. That spells hurricane
weather, Mister. 'July—stand by,' you know.
You'll have to get back to the Guinea anchorage."

"We hauled out to clear the floatin' garbage, sor.
We're safe enough here."

"You may be. But the men-o'-war are coming in
from Port Royal tomorrow and this is their berth.
I've come to warn you."

"Will you speak to the Captain, sor? He's just
behind you."

"Certainly." The midshipman turned about and
found himself face to face with Ortho. A startling
change came over the youngster. A flush mounted
slowly from his throat to the roots of his hair. The
smile died from his pleasant face; it became anything but pleasant. He stepped backward a pace,
then two forward, his fists doubled.

There was a moment's pregnant silence, then he
snapped out: "You are master of this—" a dis-
gusted sniff "—this cattle scow?"

"Of this schooner," Ortho replied.

"Sir!"

"Sir."

"D'you know you're occupying a berth assigned
to His Majesty's Navy?"

"I did not."

"Sir!"

"Sir."

"Well, you know it now, and if you're not out of here and back among your own Guinea scum by sunset I'll haul you before the Port Admiral. D'you understand?"

"I do."

"Sir!—blast you!"

"Sir."

The boy, scarlet with fury, swung about, marched to the gangway, halted and sniffed again.

"'Tis a pity you blackbirders don't wash your ships sometimes," he sneered, "—or yourselves."

With that he was gone. From overside came his vigorous voice barking to the men to give way and be smart about it.

O'Keefe gave tongue to blasphemous amazement. "Well, now, did ye ever? An' me just sayin' to meself what a civil-spoken, dacent young buck of a boy it is, when— Well, I be condemned!"

"I can give the explanation, I think," said Ortho, strolling to the rail and watching the diminishing pinnace. "That young gentleman and I are acquainted. I dusted his tail pretty shrewd some years ago for stealing eggs in my woods. It would seem he has not forgotten."

CHAPTER XXII

"I SHALL land below the fish-traps, grab what men I can, fire the village and come off again," said Ortho, stuffing a pistol into either pocket. "You understand your orders, Mr. O'Keefe?"

"I do, sor," the mate grumbled. "But I wish ye'd lave Packard an' take me. I'd take great delight in—"

Ortho cut him short. "I've told you one navigator must stay, so that's an end on't. As for you, Sam, you'll be ready? I don't look for any resistance, but in case—"

"All has been ready this hour," said the Jew. He stepped forward and laid a hand on Ortho's arm. "You are intent on this enterprise, sir? Nothing will dissuade you?"

Ortho scowled. "How many times must I tell you? No, nothing. Three years ago I swore I'd be avenged on Oko Ephraim, and be avenged I will. Do you think I've worked down to this thrice-cursed river to creep away again, frightened?"

Mordecai shrugged. "Oko Ephraim has been dead of drink these years, most like, and all your burning will not restore Gold to life."

"Maybe not. But I'll teach these treacherous dogs I am not a man to be played with."

"They learned that when they attempted to cut you off."

"They shall learn it twice, then." Ortho swung overside, dropped into the pinnace and pushed clear. The long-boat, a brass swivel mounted in its bow, cast loose from the schooner's stern and followed in his wake.

Ortho hailed it. "All ready, Mr. Packard?"

"Aye, sir."

"There's a rowlock squeaking. Muffle it. No talking after we cross the bar. You'll know the landing by a break in the trees on your port hand. If there's any resistance, fire the swivel into 'em. Now follow me close."

The breakers gathered them into their drag, slung them forward on hissing ridges of foam, dropped them into sliding valleys sparkling with phosphorescence, and hurled them over the bar into calm water beyond. Dawn was not far off. There was a perceptible glow eastward over the dark forests. The cold was waking birds in the mangroves; they whistled their long, fluty calls. A crocodile, paddling against the stream, his mouth open to embrace incoming fish, gave vent to a whining bark.

Ortho let his rowers take it easy. The flood-tide was carrying them swiftly enough; another quarter of an hour should bring them abreast of the village. He wanted to arrive when there was just sufficient light to see by, yet before the chill was out of the air, and the villagers would be huddling together for warmth, heads under blankets. He considered that he had timed himself to a nicety. That he had not been seen from the shore he was almost certain. Greatly daring, he had waited for sundown before bringing the schooner in. The attack could not be suspected. There were no signs of alarm, no frantic booming of gongs and war-drums, no horns roaring in the black jungles. All was quiet—a silent river flowing through silent swamps.

It should be a quick affair, he determined. A dash through the sleeping village, the stockade ablaze, and then back to the boats dragging what salable captives he could. Oko Ephraim must be settled, of course—a bullet through the head. He could not escape, too fat. He would lie helpless among his women and be slit like a pig. It should be quite a simple affair, providing it were done smartly. Now that he was committed, Ortho wished he had brought O'Keefe instead of Packard. The mate, roused from his indolence, could rival forked lightning. However, it was too late now. Something splashed among the mangrove roots. Ortho started, and then sank back again—a hopping fish only. The stroke oarsman sneezed abruptly and violently, prepared to do so again.

Ortho grasped him by the nose and held on till the spasm was over. "Quiet, you fool!"

He listened for signs of alarm, but all was still, still as death.

"Pull on," he whispered, and the men dipped their blades.

Light was breaking fast, coming up out of the east in a pale haze. The palms nodded their feather heads against it, rustling softly. A marmoset wailed in the tree-tops, an eerie, heart-wrenching cry, and was answered by another across the river.

Ortho, watching the palms for the remembered break, saw it suddenly open on his left, backed water and waited for the long-boat to come up. It had fallen some way behind. He could dimly see it, blundering along in midstream as if uncertain of its bearings. As he watched, it yawed toward the right-hand bank. Cursing Packard under his breath, he stood up and waved. The boat swept past unheeding. In a moment it would be out of touch. Ortho hailed it as loud as he dared, hailed again, and heard Packard exclaim. The boat swung round and forged headlong for the landing, the loose rowlock squeaking like a thing in pain. There was a blaze of fire on the bank ahead, a deafening explosion and the air about Ortho's head was rent by a thousand shrieking furies.

It was so unexpected it took him fully five seconds to realize what had happened. The landing was manned and not only manned but guarded with cannon—*cannon!* That storm that had just passed over was grape—no less. Niggers with cannon, firing grape! How dare they? It was a white man's prerogative. Niggers with cannon! Good Lord, what was the world coming to?

A bullet carrying off his hat warned him that this world's destination would not concern him much longer if he didn't act quickly. He ducked under cover of the gunnel and bawled to Packard to row for his life. But the second mate needed no urging; he was already foaming seaward as fast as inspired oars could drag him. There was a chorus of triumphant howls from the bank, and a volley of musketballs droned overhead, ricocheted off the water.

"Pull!" Ortho yelled; and as he did so there came a blinding flash, the pinnace buckled under him, cut in half, and he fell forward, hitting his head on the thwart, and went under, the roar of torrents in his ears.

"Thump-thump, thump-thump," went the hammers in Ortho's temples, "thump-thump"—as though to split his skull. He felt cold, sick and dazed. What was the matter? Was he down with fever again, lying in his cabin off that accursed river waiting for Oko Ephraim to pay up . . . Oko Ephraim to pay up. . . . No, that was years ago, surely. Something had happened since then. A raid. What was the outcome of it? Disunited incidents floated across his memory—the squeaking rowlock . . . the break in the palms . . . a sneeze . . . that fool Packard . . . grape. . . . They jostled about in his brain like kaleidoscopic segments and then, suddenly, clicked into pattern and he remembered everything.

Where was he now? Aboard the schooner? No, his bed was steady under him. The long-boat had not picked him up. He was ashore; the blacks had got him—Oko Ephraim! Horror possessed him. But he did not move, not by the flick of an eyelash. As long as he lay still they would not touch him, he thought, since there was no sport in torturing a supposedly unconscious man. He must lie still and think. What was he to do? Brazen it out? Maintain that he had merely come to trade? The idea was conceived to be dismissed. Trade in the Bights was not opened by armed boats creeping in with the dawn, oars muffled, but with the payment of "comey" tribute, gun salutes, banquets and much elaborate ritual. That would not do. Should he try to ransom himself, offering, if necessary, all he possessed aboard the slaver for his life? That he dismissed also. Who was to approach the ship? O'Keefe had strict orders not to allow a native canoe within gunshot. Rescue? Not even O'Keefe would risk landing with a single boat's crew where two had failed.

Ortho thought of everything and abandoned everything. The great bloated beast who had murdered MacBride would show him no more compunction. Sooner or later—that evening probably—he would be dragged to the sacrificial bowl, beheaded and dismembered. His eyeballs would go to the necklace of some foul fetish priest, his bones bleach on the pile in the ju-ju house. Now that death was inevitable he felt little fear, only a profound disgust. The black swine!

White men had gone that way before and gone manfully. MacBride, for instance. He was sure MacBride had gone out unflinching, mocking his captors. It seemed to him that his old mate was very near to him at that moment, jovial, ruddy, four-square in his worn blue coat, a reassuring ghost. If O'Keefe got safely to the West Indies there would be some money for Nicola—and in any event those two steadfast things, Eli and the Owls' House, would shelter her. She would not miss him—poor Nicola! And the boy. He pictured the boy as he had last seen him, on the *Helen's* deck in Kingston Harbour, smart as paint in his Navy uniform, arrogant, pouring scorn upon him, the "blackbirder." A clean boy and handsome. He should go on and up, and be Admiral of the Blue some day. Ortho wondered if he would ever discover who his father had been. Well, he had tried to make amends.

The nigger dogs should not frighten him. Lords of his body they might be, but not of his spirit. They should not make him quail.

For all that, he wished he had his hands free that he might make one last fight, choke the life out of one black throat before he went down under a hail of spears. Subconsciously he stirred a hand and, to

his astonishment, found that it was free. He shifted
a foot, and behold! that also was unbound. Cautiously he opened one eye, then the other. He was
lying on a grass mat inside a hut. By his side was
a gourd of water and a bunch of plantains. What
the deuce did it mean? "Thump-thump, thump-
thump!" That noise again, but this time Ortho
recognized that it emanated from outside his head
rather than inside.

Stealthily he raised himself so that he could see
out of the door. He was inside Oko Ephraim's
holy of holies. The first thing that met his eyes
was the imbecile idol, but instead of being crowned
with blood and palm-wine the bat-eared image now
wore a wreath of flowers. Against the opposite
fence two native women were pounding rice in a
hollowed log, and on the other end of the log
lounged the *Helen's* sailmaker, smoking his pipe and
drying his jacket in the sun.

Ortho sat bolt upright. "My stars!" he exclaimed.

"By Heck! It's like old times to hear you callin'
on your stars again, Säid," said a familiar voice;
and from a pile of mats at the far end of the hut
rose a square figure, scantily, if picturesquely, clad
in a striped flannel shirt and a beaver hat. Ortho
stared at him, mouth gaping, eyes goggling half out
of his head.

"MacBride!"

"King One-Eye the First, if you please."

"But what— How did you? . . . God bless my soul, man, are you *ever* dead?"

"Very seldom," said the king, pleasantly.

"That's an ugly lump over your eye. I'll get you a slice of raw meat for it." MacBride clapped his hands and a smiling young negress entered. She wore a white turban and a piece of flowered chintz wrapped about her opulent body.

"The Queen—that is, one of 'em," her lord explained, spoke in the local dialect and the girl nodded and went out, returning with a strip of goat's flesh which she bound over Ortho's swollen brow.

"I regret the mistake at dawn," MacBride continued; "but how was I to know? I thought it was those rascally Spaniards come again. I've been on the lookout for 'em this long whiles. Two Cadiz ships tried to open slave-palaver with me, and when I wouldn't trade, forced a landing—them three-pounders is what they left behind. Some o' my boys, bream-spearin' on the bar, heard a vessel drop anchor and I made sure it was the Dons, and got ready. I had no notion it was you. Howsomdever, I fished all your crew out of the river, save one blown to bits, and one the crocodiles ate. 'Tis fortunate 'twas no worse."

"I came to avenge your death," said Ortho.

"So I hear. A monstrous friendly notion, and I take it very kindly—only, you see, I ain't dead."

"I can see that plain enough—but why the dickens ain't you?"

MacBride wagged a solemn finger at him. "Providence, my son. Providence. The Power that has kept old Ben MacBride from the gallowses of seven European nations for eighteen busy years wasn't goin' to see him be poured out as a sacrifice before a heathen image. It had more proper respect for Itself, so stooped down and rescued him once more."

"But how, man, how?"

" 'Twas this way. I admit I made two mistakes. I knew Oko Ephraim when he was pull-away boy to the Governor of Dick's Love Castle and even then he was the greatest liar on a coast stocked with liars. When he said he had no slaves I didn't believe him, but for the first time in his life he was telling the truth. The second mistake was to take some of the rum myself, being parched by the long run from M'bo. Not much did I take, but enough to fog my judgment and keep me from seein' how quick matters was movin'. A club came down on the back of my head, and when I woke up I was lyin' in this hut, trussed like a roast suckin' pig, and all hands was armin' to cut off."

"They did not," said Ortho grimly.

MacBride smiled. "I know. I seen 'em crawlin' in next mornin'—them that could crawl—lickin' their cuts and lamentin' pitiful. You was trucks down to the west'ard, I heard 'em say. There was a great palaver after that. Of course 'twasn't nobody's fault they hadn't cut you off, the witch-doctors declared. The ju-ju was in it. Ombuiri was angry, Sasabonsum, or the Great Shark. Blood must flow in sacrifice—mine. They dragged me forth that evenin', dragged me into the ju-ju house, face to face with the idol. It was a notable to-do. Wood was piled on the fires and they blazed up red. The fetish priests gamboled round me, smeared with chalk, feathers and leopard's whiskers stuck in their wool. They clanged trade bells and frothed at the mouth, and all the people howled like mad dogs and hammered on tom-toms. Oko Ephraim was there, sittin' on his stool, sweatin' and gaspin', a sick man. Everybody was there, head-men, free-men, women, slaves and pickaninnies, all howlin' and bangin' and packin' the compound from fence to fence. 'By Heck!' I says to myself. 'This may not be much of a death, but the wake will be nothin' to complain of.' They forced me down on my knees before the blood-pit, forced my head back, and the uproar of gongs, bells and drums ceased at a beat. You could hear that great multitude suck in breath like one man. The stockade was as silent as the grave.

"I looked up, thinkin' of you and Sam and O'Keefe and all, crowdin' for blue water, looked

up and saw the image right in front of me, grinnin'
away like a fool; and as I looked, suddenly it spoke.

" 'Aha l' it screeched. 'Aha l' and 'Aha l' again.

"By James, you should ha' seen them poor blacks l
Some of 'em screamed, some of 'em stood still and
shivered, some of 'em tried to run. They got as
far as the gate and jammed there, fightin' and
bawlin'. The priest with the knife let it drop into
the blood-pit. His mate fell flat on his back, legs
in the air. Then the idol began to talk in earnest.
None o' your Coast pidgin but right good Eboe.
Their troubles had come through the wickedness
of Oko Ephraim and their shockin' treatment of
their best friend, Daddy One-Eye, he said. The
High Spirits were furious. Sasabonsum and Ombuiri would lay in wait for 'em in the bush paths
and tear 'em to rags. The Great Crocodile would
foul their fish-traps; the Shark God overset their
canoes in the surf. Sleep-sickness should fall upon
them; blight strike the oil and wine-palms; their
wives should bear twins with front teeth cut. Oh,
he lashed into 'em proper, did that image, broadside upon broadside. They lay on their faces in
the dust and moaned and groveled, sobbin' for
mercy, promisin' to be good boys for ever and a day.

"All but Oko Ephraim. The sweat was runnin'
off him in streams, and the breath was whistlin'
through his nose; but he stood up and tottered forward, one step, two steps, makin' straight for me.
Not for nothin' was that great whale a king, I tell

you. His priests were low, his headmen, warriors and people. There was magic in the air he could not grapple with, but with me he could, and he tottered forward, chest pumpin' like a bellows, the fat shakin'. Two steps, three steps.

"I stood up to meet him. The matter rested between us two, now. Me tied hand and foot, he carrying thirty years of rum and sin. Five steps, six steps.

"'Back, Oko Ephraim!' screamed the image. 'Back, on your life!' But he waddled on, one hand at his throat, one outstretched for me. Seven steps, eight steps. Then he stopped, gasped, tried to speak, choked, and crashed like a tree, blood from his burst heart spurtin' from his mouth, drenchin' the sand.

"'Aha!' screeched the idol. 'Aha!'"

"Your old ventriloquisting, I suppose," said Ortho.

MacBride nodded. "Aye, what I learned to pass the time away down among the rats in Verdun Prison—little thinkin', little thinkin'."

"And you made yourself king?"

"I did—the image aidin' and abettin', you understand."

"But you'll come back with me now?"

The old sailor shook his head. "No, Captain. When I was four-and-twenty I was wishful to be Mayor of Youghal, Cork. Four barrels o' pork overset them young fancies. Now, in my old age, instead of mayor of a village I find myself king of a country. Me that was born nameless and raised in a foundlin' hospital! A king I'll stop."

"Will you keep a barracoon?" said Ortho, eagerly. "Stock slaves and trade with me only? I'll fetch you any goods you name. Wine, powder, guns, tobacco—anything you choose."

Again MacBride shook his head. "No, Captain."

"You'll not? You'd make a fortune. Why? What d' you mean?"

"See here," said MacBride. "The King of England don't sell his subjects for slaves, do he? No more does the King of France or any other respectable monarch. Well, no more will I. For though I may not have a first-rate kingdom I mean to be a first-rate king. You can laugh if you like, but that's how I see it, and if you or them Spanishers or anybody else comes here thinkin' to force me, I'll serve you the same as I served you this mornin'—only hotter. Elephant's teeth, gold-dust, gum and wood I'll sell you as much as I've got, but there'll be no slaves go from here as long as I live."

"You old fool! How long will you live?" Ortho scoffed. "Some day some young buck with ambition will drive a spear through you or bribe one of your women to poison you. They'll kill you like a dog."

MacBride nodded. "I know that. But not just yet, I think. I have the talkin' image on my side, you see. And even if they do kill me, what matter?

A man can't live forever. As you say, some young upstart—some Oko Ephraim—will lay me low and rule in my stead, and, like Oko Ephraim, sell his soul to the white men for rum, and torture his people for tribute, and let loose the slave-hunters and fetish-priests and witch-smellers again. And who will the people talk of then? Why, me. 'These things never happened to us in the reign of Good King One-Eye,' they'll say. 'In the reign of Good King One-Eye a man was free; he could keep his wives, children and goods about him and walk openly in the sunlight, unafraid. We were happy in those days.'

"There never will ha' been any reign like mine in the mouths of them that never lived in it, and I shall go down from tongue to tongue and year to year like Alfred the Great and the Golden Caliph and Prester John. I shall be a Historic Personage."

"You will not come away? That is final?" said Ortho, rising.

"It is," said MacBride. "But you can go when you please—my state canoe shall take you out." He hesitated, embarrassed, scratched his ear violently, and grinned. "Look you, when you come again—if you ever should come—bring me the finest crown you can buy for a reasonable sum; I will pay you in elephant's teeth—likewise a mirror to admire meself in."

CHAPTER XXIII

EXTRACTS from the log of the slaver *Charming Helen*. Penhale, master. Ambrize Roads. West Africa. 1793.

Light breezes and cloudy. Sent Mr. Packard to Marsoola for slaves. Employed washing ship. Receeved on bord five slaves. viz. 1 man, 1 woman and 3 girls. Number on bord 271.

Fresh breezes and clear. Mr. O'Keefe with pinnace employed taking water and provision. Receeved on bord 1 man. 1 boy slave and one elefants tooth, weighs 119 lbs. Total on board 273.

Ditto weather. Employed taking water and provision. Arrived Brigg Florimel of London. Capn. Edward Leech, from Gabun. Reports war is broke out agen between England and the French Republick. Pleese God we get safe to Jamaica. Returned from Marsoola ye long boat with seven slaves. viz. 4 men and 1 woman with childer 2 boys. Going to Marsoola ye long boat was overset in the surf when James Rigg and Mathew Peasgood was drowned. Dyed this day 2 men slaves of ye small pox. Total on bord 278.

Ditto weather. Mr. O'Keefe employed with long boat and pinnace taking water and provision, Mr. Packard being to his berth very bad in a cold he took from his wetting. Mr. Mordecai, surgeon, sick also. Arrived ye *Prince of Orange,* brigganteen, of London, commanded by Mr. Michl. Curtiss. We saluted him. He saith ye *Alice Galley* of Lancaster is lost at Benito and all her company killed, her slaves having rose on her. God preserve us from such knavish tricks. Dyed one girl slave after sickness of nine days. Total on bord 277.

Light airs and cloudy. Mr. O'Keefe employed as before. Carpenter employed making Womans room bulkhead. Receeved from Factory four slaves. viz 1 man and 3 girls. Men scarse and mighty deer. Dined ashore with Govenor who is a native of Dundee in Scotland and is married with a Spanish mulatto of Fernando Po by whom he hath several childer, the eldest darter of which is none two bad appearance having very bright eyes and abundant shiney hair. Made Govenor a present of beer, cheese and six bottel brandy. Departed this life Benj: Fasham, gunner, of ye small pox. Dyed 2 boy slaves of same. Total on bord 275.

Fresh gales and heavy swell. Veered to a full cable.

Modrate weather. Hove in to half cable. Long boat and pinnace emploved watering. Departed this life James Brady of ye small pox. He was, I think, a felon, walking very wide between the legs as if he had the gyves on. Dyed one man slave of same. The pox is very bad amongst us. I give thanks we are near full slaved. Ye Govenor dined abord us. A civil man speaking little but merry in liquor. Saluted him with six guns.

Heavy weather with rain. Parted our small bower ankor. Dyed of ye pox 1 woman and 1 girl slave.

Modrate and clear. Swept for small bower ankor. Dyed of ye pox 1 woman and 1 girl slave.

Modrate and clear. Swept for small bower and got him up. Mr. O'Keefe employed as usual. Dyed one man slave. Dined ashore with ye Govenor. His darter played ye guitar very sweet, sang also. Made present of botteled porter.

Light airs and clear. Careened ship and scrubbed both sides as best we might but she is parlous foul below being so long on the Coast. I fear she will sail very sluggish. Mr. Packard is mending. Mr. Mordecai still sick. Mr. O'Keefe did not come off last night, reported ye surf two heavy but it did not appear so from ye ship. Departed this life Tobias Mundy, cooks mate, of ye pox. A very religus fellow forever singing hyms. I heard he was wanted by the Hereford constables for unlawful preeching. That is ye end of ye pox I hope, there being no more sick of it that I know.

Ditto weather. Mr. O'Keefe employed ashore with long boat and pinnace watering. Receeved from King Bessie Osuku twenty two slaves, viz 6 men, 4 boys, 4 women, 6 girls and 2 childer. One of the men is own brother to King Bessie who has sold him in fear he will usurp the throne. Total slaves on bord 292. I shall lay for Barbados tomorrow.

Weather moderate. Mr. O'Keefe has run the ship. He went ashore in a canoo last night and tho' I have been ashore I can find him nowhere. Robt. Tancock tells me that all the time the water party has been filling casks Mr. O'Keefe has been dallying with the Govenors darter, she with bright eyes, and that they could have come off easy t'other night but Mr. O'Keefe would not let them, he having bisness of his own. Methinks she has hid him away and I can get no satisfaction from ye Govenor for all I obleeged him with beer, cheese, brandy and botteled porter. I can wait no longer or I shall have this small pox agen. I will raise Mr. Packard to mate and the bosun shall take a watch. As for the Govenor dam him I say he is not what I thought him, and as for Mr. O'Keefe dam him two, he will live to regret he played me false for the Govenor will see he acts honest by his darter and these mulatoes are well enough when they are young but by the time they are twenty-five they are as big round as a capstan and have mustachios like a French dragoon as well I know. Dyed one slave woman in a fit. Total abord 291.

At Sea.

Course WBN½ N. Wind SEBS. Lattd. pr Obsn. 3° 36' South. At 7 a.m we sighted a ship SbW about 6 leagues. Proved to be ye *Prince of Orange* which sayled from Ambrize five days after we. This schooner is so foul she can hardly crawl, the weed trayles a foot long and her bottom is like a rock for barnacles.

See *Prince of Orange* but from topmast head only. Washed the rooms and slaves.

Prince of Orange out of sight ahead these twenty hours. Speared two dolfins with the grains. Steeped in brine and broiled with much pepper and salt they are prime eating.

Modrate gale, set studding sayles but they carried away. Made poor progress.

Wind fair and steddy. Set studding sayles on starbord side also ringtail below the spanker. Made good progress.

Wind fair and steddy. Mr. Packard reduced sayle without telling me fearing squall which did not come. Reprimanded him. He went off muttering I do not know what.

Light airs inclinable to calms. Exercised the men with small arms.

Weather ditto. Exercised the great guns.

Flat calm. Clewed up all sayle to prevent chaffing.

Flat calm. Scrubbed the small bower cable.

Flat calm. Scrubbed the best bower cable.

Flat calm. Men employed scraping and greasing masts.

Flat calm. Men employed on masts.

Flat calm. The small pox has struck in again. Peter Kerwen, being seezed with rigor and fever also pains in the head and back. Also three negroes. Have placed the negroes under an awning on the main deck to keep them apart from the others. Mr. Packard said I should throw them overbord. Told him I was captain and I would put him overbord first.

Flat calm. Have now been eleven days idle in the doldrums. The heat is very great melting the pitch in the deck seams but despite that have deemed it best to cut down the water allowance one half except to the sick who suffer dire thirst with their complaint.

Flat calm. Departed this life Peter Kerwen, sailmaker, of the pox. A servicable man who had been with me five years and served on ye *Nonsuch* 74,

Capn. Truscott, at the Battle of the Saintes. Buried him also two slaves. Many yearning. Total 289.

Flat calm. Cannot judge of any currant and cannot say if we are in the sphere of the south equatorial drift or no. Saw a starr shoot which continued in the heavens some minits like a flaming sword. The men are complaining at the lack of water and I think that dog Packard is with them but he dare say nothing before me.

Have caught the NE Trade wind and am hauling to the northard in hopes to fetch it stronger. From the topmast head saw a brigg which stood NE. Think she is a Guineaman also.

Wind coming light and puffy. By my reckoning I am in the lattd. of Georgetown but I wish I had that knave O'Keefe or other navigator to check me. Next voyage I will purchase Mr. Harrisons chronometer clock such as is now used in the Navy and by which longitude may be esstimated to a degree they say. The Guineaman is now out of sight. It is the first time this schooner has been out paced on the middle passage but she is so foul she cannot travel to her credit.

Modrate gale and we made fair progress. Have restored full water allowance. Am touched with my old Coast fever. The small pox continues without abate but several of the negroes may mend.

Weather ditto. Sighted a frigate hull down to the westard but she continued on her way. We are in poor shape to meet privateers. With so many men sick we should be hard put to handle the great guns. Carpenter reports that rats have ate holes in two water casks. I take it the ship dryed up in the doldrums and there was no sweatings for they to lick. Could ill spare those casks did the wind fail. Plenty lightning last night spreading over ye heavens in sheets of blue light.

Light airs and puffy. We are full in the region of the Trade but it will not come on. Caught a dolfin measuring four foot and a half. Have now at this day noon 64 slaves dead and many more sick. Am feverish agen, a day on a day off, the intermitant Mordecai calls it who is the same himself and so week he cannot properly attend the sick tho' he will try to as long as he can stagger. Mr. Packard is with the men two much, dicing and carding. O'Keefe, for all he served me scurvy, would never lower himself in such manner.

Flat calm. Last night the moon came up red as rose into a green sky, she being at the full and flushed with sunset. A slave man leaped overboard and was taken by a shark.

Flat calm. By observation we are in the latitude of the Grenadines by judgment all of sixty leagues east of Barbadoes but of this there is no saying for drifting and idling day by day the log is useless. We are now 69 days from Ambrize the longest passage I have ever made or hope to make. Departed this life Gustav Thorwaldsen, a Sweed, of the small pox. Dyed five slaves.

Calm. We are undone. The great part of the water brought abord at Ambrize is stinking, brackish and full of small white worms. There are but 3 barels of good water left among 217 blacks and 15 whites. Had I O'Keefe beside me now I would strangle him with my own hands law or no law. Have cut down all hands to half a cup a day but unless ye wind comes on and we meet with a ship we perish miserably. God knows it is no fault of mine but that dog O'Keefe sitting comfortably with his wench on the castle wall at Ambrize, her playing the guitar to the sea breeze. I would I had my hands on him, the false dog. Departed this life Matth Quarrier and Hugh Quarrier of Redstock England, brothers. Dyed eight slaves.

Calm. That dog Packard has left the ship along with all the sound men taking with them one barel of good water. They went last night in the mates watch when I was in my berth with fever so Robt. Tancock says. Yesterday Packard asked me where we was at and I says 30 leagues east of Barbadoes to comfort him, but in truth I do not know. Now he is gone in ye long boat making for Bridgetown. I hope the sea swallows him up. O'Keefe for all he is a scurvy hound was no coward like him, he would never have left me alone in such a pass. Robt. Tancock says that O'Keefe showed the men where to water and then went away with the Govenors darter she playing her guitar very seductive in the bushes. When he was gone the men went and drank palm wine and debauched with the negro girls filling the barels from a swamp nearby the boats. Robt. Tancock says he dared not tell for fear of his comrades vengence, likewise he thought there was sufficient good water to fetch us across which there would have been had not the ship sailed so sluggish and ye Trade failed. By such a small thing are we brought miserably to our ends—one mulattoe wench with bright eyes! Departed this life Benjamin Wade of the small pox. Robt. Tancock will not last the morrow, his features is swollen beyond knowing.

Calm. Departed this life Robt. Tancock of Penzance, Cornwall, my own good townsman. I buried him overside sewn in my own blanket. Now left abord this ship of the white men only the surgeon and me and him two sick to move.

Calm. Many slaves are dead but I dare not venture into the tween decks for fear the living would tear me to shreds they being raving with thirst. From the noyse below some have got loos of their fetters and are beating on the hatch and I fear will soon burst it. The heat is like a furnace and the crys of ye sick most pityful to hear. There is no sign of wind and no ship in sight and even if there was she could not come at us. This is the end.

Mordecai—hollow-cheeked, wasted, the ghost of a man—opened his eyes as Ortho entered the cabin. "Well," he rasped, "is there any land in sight?"

Ortho shook his head.

"Or sail?"

"Nor sail."

The Jew sighed and lay back among the blankets. Both door and port were open, but no air entered the stifling cabin. Outside a sea of glass shimmered under a brazen sky.

"Have you any notion where we are?" he asked, wearily.

"East-southeast of Barbadoes, about forty leagues, at a guess, but I cannot say."

"Forty leagues only?"

"At a guess— but we might as well be forty thousand. There is no wind or any sign of it."

"Water?"

"Two days more for you'n me. As for the slaves, not all the rivers of the world could save them now."

Mordecai groaned. "I can hear them crying out. I wake from tormented sleep to reality that is more dreadful still. Hell can hold no terrors worse than we have shown these poor blacks."

"Before God it is not my fault," Ortho protested. "You yourself can bear witness that I have never overcrowded, starved or mishandled my cargoes as some men do. It is no fault of mine. Blame that hound O'Keefe."

"I do not blame any one man," said the surgeon, gently. "O'Keefe, if he has unwittingly betrayed us now, has saved us before. During the Yellow Jack scourge who so fearless and tender as he? And in that typhoon off St. Thomas—you remember? It is the Guinea Trade I blame—the fat merchants that coin money and more money from this unholy traffic and live safely in great houses ashore—not their wretched tools, the poor, fever-racked seamen of the slave ships." He propped himself up on his elbow. "But the time has come for us to make an end of these horrors, Captain; time for us to play the man. There is four days' water for you alone, you say. The pinnace hangs by the stern. Lower it, take the water and go."

"You spoke of playing the man," said Ortho.

"I did and I will tell you your part. This ship is all you have. She is your career, your love, and I know it, I have watched you handling her. Nevertheless I ask you to give her to me."

"Why?"

"To destroy. There has been enough agony, I say. Now I will end it as mercifully as I may. Trim the magazine, lay a powder train to my bunk-side, and begone."

"You—you will blow her up?"

"Yes."

"And yourself with her?"

Mordecai shrugged. "In any case I should not outlast the morrow."

Ortho stared at him—the waddling, soft-spoken little surgeon, butt of his coarse wit for six years.

"You will? You!" he cried, and remembered MacBride, the king, doggedly determined to rule well though it brought no recompense but the assassin's spear. "My God! Is there nobody frightened of death but me?"

"Believe me, there are times when death may appear a very good friend," said the Jew. "You will do as I ask, Captain?"

"No," said Ortho, slowly.

Mordecai propped himself on his elbow again, his fevered eyes ablaze. "You grudge me your ship, eh? You will hold on and hold on, hoping for wind and the sail it might bring, with all these poor chained creatures wailing in torment about you? Are you devil?"

Ortho shook his head. "I do not grudge the ship, but I will blow her myself. I am man enough for that."

"Your hand, Captain—forgive me," said Mordecai. "But go you must. You have stood by your command long enough to satisfy honor. There is no reason why you should sacrifice yourself."

"I will not go," said Ortho; but even as he protested he knew that he would do as he was bid; for all his high words he was not *man* enough. Ruined, worn with anxiety, weary beyond words, the will to live surged in him even as he spoke, drowning his nobler resolutions. He was only forty. Death appeared no good friend of his; it was Life that beckoned, cherry-lipped, snowy-bosomed, wonder-eyed, promising exquisite moments, heart-thrills, passions and raptures. Forty leagues across a windless sea in an open boat, alone—the chances were he would never see Barbadoes. But if he did—Life!

"I—I will not go," he repeated, wavering.

"You must," said Mordecai. "I have nobody but myself, but you have a wife and son. You must."

"I had not thought of them," said Ortho. Then an idea occurred to him. "I have it. I will set a slow match which should give us time to pull clear, and you shall come with me to Barbadoes—an' we ever reach Barbadoes."

The Jew shook his head.

"You are thinking of the water?" Ortho asked.

"No matter of what I am thinking, I will not come."

"I will make you, carry you bodily."

Mordecai glanced up, and for the first time called Penhale by his Christian name. "Ortho, since first I came aboard this vessel I have served you faithfully, doing as you bade, asking nothing. Now at the finish I ask you one small favor—namely, to let me stay to the end with the people I have tried to succor these eight long years. One small request, friend."

Ortho, understanding dawning, stared at him with eyes going blind with tears. "Sam," he said, softly, "what sent you into the Guinea traffic? Tell me that, and it shall be as you wish."

A flush mounted on the Jew's shrunken cheek, his eyelids fluttered. "I—I am a surgeon," he stammered "I—I Conceived it my duty to go —to go where there was most suffering—that is all."

A ray of westering sunlight penetrated the cabin port and fell upon the speaker. It seemed to Ortho to reveal another man. Not the stout, short-sighted, ungainly little Jew he had known so long, but a being transformed, glorified. He fell on his knees beside the bunk and buried his face in the tumbled blankets, clutching at the wasted hands.

"I am going, I am going; but for all I've said and done these years past and for what I am doing now, forgive me, Sam . . . O Sam!"

Crouched on the bottom boards of the pinnace, palms held tight to his ears, Ortho awaited the explosion. Mordecai had given him half an hour, yet hours seemed to pass, an eternity of suspense. In imagination he saw Mordecai strike the fatal steel, the train catch fire, the flame race, sputtering, across the cabin and down, down to where the broached barrel lay up-turned, in the deep heart of the magazine. For he had laid that train well, though to do so was torture. Ten perilous years the schooner had carried him faithfully from landfall to landfall. To him she was an animate being. He loved her. She was his own. Now he had laid the train that was to rend her to matchwood, wipe her off the face of the waters. A murderous act, an act of the foulest treachery.

Memories of her arose before him, dancing foam-footed through the blue flying fish weather; fleeting ghost-pale under a ghostly moon, striking fiery sparkles from the tropic sea; working to windward off the Grendee Shoal in a smother of weather, two Dane ships ashore and breaking; dashing through the packed, yelling war-canoes in the Kameroon River, grinding them under, stamping them deep—his loyal love, his little pretty! And now he had betrayed and deserted her, while Sam stayed to the end, Sam alone. A flood of shame welled through him. No, he would remain faithful to his ship, his trust. He, too, would play the man. He sprang to his feet, arms outflung, shouting:

"Stop, Sam! Hold fast, for God's sake! *I'm coming back!*"

Too late. A cone of solid flame leapt from the schooner's deck to her foretopmast-backstay, bursting her in halves. The boom of the explosion rolled across the water like a clap of thunder. Bits of splintered planking whirled into the evening sky. The two tall masts nodded apart and crashed overboard. Smoke poured from the schooner in dense black clouds, enveloping her, and, wrapped in a pall of smoke, she went under.

Too late!

The sun dipped, smoky red, into an empty sea. Night swept on, blue-robed, crowned with a splendor of stars. About the lonely boat in which Ortho slept exhausted, the lazy sea-fire flashed and sparkled. A shark cruised by, his fin outlined in silver. Time passed, hours. Then the stars to the eastward dimmed, the stars overhead. A flock of chubby dark clouds appeared, streaming leisurely into the west. More followed, pressing faster. The sky was covered with them. The heated air cooled and began to move. There was a whisper in the night. Catspaws dimpled the sea-floor. Ripples lapped the boat, chuckling to themselves. The whisper grew louder, louder. The ripples swelled to little waves that slapped at the boat, rocking it. "Come on," they seemed to say. "We have been idle long enough!" The whispering voice rose to a hum. "Come on, this way!"

The northeast Trade was blowing.

CHAPTER XXIV

IT WAS in the afternoon of the next day that Ortho saw the island—an indigo smudge on the western horizon—and knew that he had been nearly one hundred miles out in his longitude. He had under-estimated the equatorial current. Ah, well! there was nothing to be gained by vain regrets. That phase was closed forever. Now to get the boat to Barbadoes. There was a landing on the windward side, he thought, St. Andrews, north of Ragged Point. The stream was in his favor and the wind plumb abaft. Nightfall should see him safe ashore. He put his foot on the sheet, crooked a knee over the tiller and made a full meal of bread, cheese and salt pork, sluicing it down with a long draught from the water beaker. Now that land was in sight there was no longer need to stint himself of water.

The Trade blew strongly, humming a merry tune, and under her big lug-sail the pinnace ran like a thing of life, tossing the sundered water from her bows, swooping, soaring. A cloud of flying-fish skimmed the wave crests, a rainbow glimmer on their fins, and after them came a school of porpoises, golden glistering as they leapt into the sun-

light. Then gulls began to appear, boatswain and
men-o'-war birds, and one little web-footed fellow,
dark gray with a white head, who fluttered aboard
and remained perched on the bow-thwart till rested.

By sundown Ortho was close under the island.
He did not recognise it, but that was understand-
able, for he had hitherto approached Barbadoes
from the south. Neither could he see any sign of
a settlement. Nevertheless, impatient, he held
straight on, and, beaching the pinnace in a small
bay, stepped ashore, his one remaining possession
of value, a small ivory tusk, under his arm. There
was a hut of bamboo and palm-thatch hidden under
the trees, a fisherman's hovel, but there was nobody
in it, nor did it appear to have been inhabited for
some time. Ortho picked a hatful of fruit, ate
it, and pushed inland beside a small stream which
came leaping down over a saddle of the hills. A
path there had been, but it was long disused and
difficult to find now that dark had fallen. Twice
he blundered off it and was severely handled by
thorns, and a hanging liane raked his hat off. But
he was ashore. There was solid land under him
and abundant water rushing, gushing, splashing
deliciously close at hand. The nightmare of drought
and disease was over. He was alive and ashore.
He pressed on lustily, beating the thorns and lianes
aside with his tusk, dragging fruit off the bushes
and munching it as he went. Myriads of whistling
frogs shrilled all about him, fireflies spangled the

bushes with glints and glimmers of living emerald, and the warm night was heavy with flowery incense, angelim, magnolia and, sweetest of all, frangipani. Ortho snuffled draughts of it, and memories came thronging, poignant, wistful.

"My stars! On St. Lucia, eight—nine—ten, ten years ago, that morning I deserted—the same old scent! Ten years ago!"

He leaned against a tree, panting from his climb. A decade gone down the wind, and what had he to show for it? Nothing—but a few gray hairs over his temples and a few more scars. He looked back in the lost years and saw nothing but struggle and hardship. Nights on the poop, lashed by hail, swept by roaring seas, black chaos all about. Months off the Guinea coast, shaken with ague, racked with anxiety. Year upon year close beset by those four constant perils: the negroes, the plague, mutiny and the sea. Ten years of vigilance and endeavor gone for naught. It was no fault of his, he told himself, it was Fate. Fate, that sorry jester, that arch cheat. Forty years old—husband without a wife, father without a son, captain without a ship. Forty years old and the whole battle to begin over again! High noon was past, gone the golden prime.

Reaction set in; a great physical weariness came upon him and a sense of utter defeat. He sank against the tree, face buried in the bend of his arm, tired out spiritually and bodily. Why had he troubled to come ashore and begin all over again, when to go down with the *Helen* would have been so simple? What use to play against Fate with its marked cards and loaded dice?

The fireflies wove their sparkling patterns about him; a pootoo bird called from the cottonwoods; sweetly, cruelly, blew the scent of frangipani, bringing its memories.

In a spasm of rage Ortho beat at the bushes with his tusk of ivory, thrashing the red blossoms to the ground, crushing them under his heel. The scent of the bruised flowers rose up all the sweeter. He fled from them, plunged into a thorn thicket and, wrenching himself free, found he had topped the hill-saddle. Far away up the valley glowed one small bead of light.

Instantly his spirits rose a point. "There's a house up there; a pen maybe. I'll get a drink of rum and a night's lodging in all events," he muttered, and stepped forward.

He was out of the tanglewood now, in a savannah cleared for pasture and sugar-cane, which ran from east to west between hill spurs. There was a road across the flats, furrowed deep with the tracks of cane carts. Up this Ortho plodded, stumbling in the ruts, but making fair headway. The guiding light was high up. The house must be built on some eminence, he decided; also, as he progressed, he could see other lights lower down on the right. These, he thought, must mark the overseer and

slave huts. Intent on the bigger game, he bore
left-handed, crossed a log bridge and, climbing the
hill, came to the gate. The gate was open, disclos-
ing a square *patio* in which a few orange-trees
flowered, filling the air with scent. A light showed
through the shutter cracks of a window opposite;
the door also was ajar.

Ortho stepped cautiously under the arch, crossed
the court on tiptoe. Nobody challenged, no dog
barked. "I wonder if there is anyone in?" he
thought, and hesitated. Explanations might be
difficult were he discovered in the house alone. Better go straight to the slave village, perhaps; that
at least was peopled—in the distance he could hear
the rub-a-dub of Eboe drums and the squeal of a
pipe. He stood for a minute undecided, then
marched boldly up to the door and knocked. The
door swung open at his touch bringing him face
to face with a man.

Ortho, surprised, stepped back a pace, was about
to explain, when he saw that the other face was in
a mirror and somehow uncannily familiar. When
had he seen that man before? Where? A wild
rascal, ragged, bull-curled, bold-eyed, with a week's
stubble of black hair on his jaw and lips—where?
when? In a flash he knew. It was himself as he
had seen himself in that dread house on St. Lucia
ten years before. He was facing his own youth!

And the mirror! The mirror with the rope-pat-
tern frame and the gilt Cupid atop. It was the same

mirror! Could he ever forget it? He shot scared
glances right and left. The *prie-Dieu!* The great
mahogany *garde-robe* with brass hasps! By heaven,
he was in that same house! That same accursed
room! Not only had he been out in his longitude,
but forty miles out in his latitude. He was not
on Barbadoes at all, but on St. Lucia, on St. Lucia
and in the same room!

"O. P.!" said an astonished voice at his side.
"O. P., by all that's marvellous!"

Ortho backed up against the lintel, gaping. "The
same woman!"

She had been sitting with her back to the window,
fanning herself with a tinseled fan, a French romance in her hand, held up to catch the light of two
silver candlesticks. He had seen her youth crumble
before his frightened eyes that night ten years before, and here was the result, an old woman, white-
haired, yet prinked out like a girl in a billowy dress
of sprigged satin, with rouge on her haggard cheeks,
a streak of rouge on her shriveled lips, and great
Spanish horn combs set coquettishly in her faded
coils—the effect was ghastly.

"You!" he gasped.

"And who else did you expect?" she inquired,
recovering from her amazement sooner than he.
"What have you come for this time?" Then, with
a titter, "Are you still intent on that duck?"

"I—I did not think. . . . I did not know. . . .

I—I—" Ortho yammered, staring at her in a sort of horrified fascination.

"You are trying to tell me that you have only returned by mistake?" said the woman. "I guessed as much. It was Destiny brought you, O. P. Destiny working in its mysterious way. But, since you are come, pray make yourself at home. There is no danger now. That—that is long forgotten."

"Not by me!" Ortho retorted, hotly.

The lady raised an eyebrow. "No? Well, I wish you joy of the memory." She looked at him curiously. "Matters do not appear to have improved with you in all these years, my friend. Ten years ago you strayed in out of the night, bearded and tattered. Tonight you come again, bearded and tattered. Tell me, are you still—er—deserting?"

"No!"

"Not deserting? That is excellent. Nor fleeing from—er—justice?"

"I am not fleeing from anyone!" he snapped.

"Excellent again. Then at least your way of living has mended if your circumstances and manners have not. Still, let that pass. Since, on this occasion, you are not fleeing from anyone, we have the night before us and may take up our conversation where it was so rudely interrupted last time we met. Tell me of your fresh adventures. Have any more hennaed ranees in the East fallen to your spell, or Moorish houris passionately succumbed? Last time I could not properly attend, being under a certain strain, as you will understand; but now I am all ears. Come, Don Desperado."

Ortho sneered, "Last time is not this time, madam."

She felt his narrowed, contemptuous eyes on her silvered head, her shriveled neck, and a flush burnt her cheek under the rouge.

"I am not worth your trouble now—that is what you would say, eh?" Her eyes dimmed as with tears; she bit them back, but a note of anxiety trembled in her voice. "Am I indeed so distasteful? Do you think a man that loved—. Do you think— If a man—."

"I mean that I am older now—and wiser," said Ortho.

Instantly she was on her mettle again and flashing at him. "Older, I grant. Time has not left you untouched either, my gallant; he has his hand on your shoulder. There are wrinkles about your eyes and gray hairs here and there. Make haste, O. P., make haste!"

"I am but forty and, by heaven, I am as good as ever I was!" he defied.

The woman sneered at his rags. "You never cut any great figure then! But I think you deceive yourself. *Once* you had a sound coat on your back, I know, for I gave it you."

"Madam," said Ortho, prickling, "I will have you know that until yesterday I was a captain owning my own ship."

Her lip curled. "Yesterday!—a thing of little value, O. P. It is but yesterday I had all Kingston —aye, all Jamaica—at my feet. And what will my brave yesterday buy me now? One sigh? One tiny glance of admiration?" She flung her hands out, despairingly. "It cannot even win me civility from a broken ship-master."

"Do you consider that he owes you civility?" said Ortho.

"Still harping on that night?" the woman cried, tapping angrily on her palm with the fan. "That night! That night! Shall I ever know the last of it? What is it to you? Who bears the guilt— if guilt there is—you or I? Fourteen years I suffered death-in-life with Olaf; he—one minute. I care not that, I tell you!" She snapped her fingers in his face, blazing, and then on the instant suffered one of her astounding changes and was all smiles, all honey. "But enough of this. Let us be friends, if for tonight only. I am so lonely here. I feel I could shriek and shriek till the roof fell on me— and you are in need. For mercy's sake, do not leave me yet; and I will help you when you go—we can help each other." She sprang to her feet. "Ah, how could I be so thoughtless? You must be famished and I have offered you nothing. Forgive me. You shall be seen to at once. Let me see, what have I on hand? There is a fresh mullet, a capon, some excellent madeira, and—"

Ortho rose slowly, his hand uplifted. "Hold!"

"A capon, a fresh mullet,"—it was complete. He felt a fatal net tightening about him, doom looming near. The past was rounding into the present, the Wheel turning full circle. Presently they would be back where they had started and horror upon them. The past was there complete. Himself drawn in, unwitting, from the wide seas; the woman bidding him to sup on capon and fresh mullet; the moth-dance round the candles; the distant rumble of drums. The tragic stage was set once more. Presently the third actor would come to his cue, a face would appear in that gilded mirror—whose?

"Stop!" he cried and his voice was hoarse. "What devil's trap are you setting for me now? Who am I to rid you of this time? Raoul? Your precious Raoul? Tired of *him* now, are you?"

Another lightning change transfigured the woman. It was as though the very name of her lover were a spell to charm her. Her feverish eyes brimmed, grew wistful; her cynical mouth relaxed, quivering. "Raoul," she whispered, "Raoul," and her tongue caressed the name, made music of it.

As he watched, Ortho's dread of her went from him, his disgust also. He saw that her bitter raillery was only a pose, her calm only a mask, that, for all she snapped her fingers and boasted bravely, the memory of that night ten years before would go with her, waking and sleeping, to the grave— and beyond it. She was no longer a withered old woman, daubed and prinked, laced and padded, but the saddest thing he had ever known.

"No, not Raoul—or anybody else," she whispered. "I am all alone now. Raoul is not here. He—he left me."

"Why?" said Ortho gently.

"He did not believe my story. Everybody else did, but not he." She choked, and when she spoke again her voice was shaking. "Sad, was it not, that the one man I thought *must* believe it would not?"

"Why would he not?"

"The knife. Your knife with O. P. carved on it. He said the murderer would not have left that behind, whatever he left."

"And then?"

"He went away in misery, left the island. I don't know where he is. I—I hope he will come back some night, and I am dressed like this, ready if he should come—he used to like this dress." She turned her head stealthily, and when she faced Ortho again the haunted light had returned to her eyes.

"Tell me, is there—can you, can you see anything, anybody, lying on the floor there, by the *garderobe?*"

"No, nothing. What should there be?"

She sighed. "Ah! I imagine—I thought for the moment . . . I often think I see Olaf lying there, sprawled out . . . but it must only be my fancy. It is terrible, though—horribly red and his eyes rolling—ach! I hate this house, but I dare not **leave;** Raoul might come back and not find me."

Suddenly she braced up, as though inspired. "Why should he not come tonight? *You* have come. Destiny brought you here out of the sea; it will bring him, my own dear! It is the night of Destiny! He will understand and forgive me, now. He will not mind because I have grown old in waiting. Raoul!"

She clasped her hands over her bosom, her face shining with the white fire of exaltation, turned and fled from the room.

"Where are you going?" Ortho cried.

"To the orange groves where we used to meet," she called over her shoulder. "Where else will he be?"

"Mad, poor soul," said Ortho to himself. "He is not there. Dead years ago, most like. She'll break her heart." He hastened after her shouting, "Come back! Stop a moment!"

But she had gone. Far down the hill among the scented orange-bushes and weaving fireflies he saw the sprigged dress glimmer, running on, hither and thither; heard her calling, "Raoul, dearest, I am coming! Wait for me . . . Raoul!"

Ortho looked upon the Great House standing dark and silent on its hill, the slave fires winking red eyes in the valley below. The Eboe drums rumbled like surf on a desolate coast; the pipe wailed like a wounded thing. He shuddered, and,

turning away, set his face westward. He had not
gone half a mile before he remembered he had left
his treasured tusk behind; nevertheless he did not
go back, but stumbled on over the wild hills and
ridges toward Castries, the ships, and the blue sea
highways, dawn leaping golden at his back.

THE CORNISH LIBRARY

Cornwall has a literary heritage quite out of proportion to its geographical size. Since Richard Carew of Antony first published his *Survey of Cornwall* in 1602 its native writers have consistently produced outstanding works of history, biography, poetry, and fiction. At the same time the Cornish landscape and the peculiar character of the Celtic peninsula – part English county, part independent nation – have inspired visiting writers to works of extraordinary power and imagination.

The Cornish Library is a new publishing venture, dedicated to presenting in attractive, paperback editions some of the best and most lasting books on Cornwall and the Cornish, both fiction and non-fiction. In print, or shortly to be published, are:

Up From The Lizard	*J. C. Trewin*
A Cornish Childhood	*A. L. Rowse*
Freedom of the Parish	*Geoffrey Grigson*
School House in the Wind	*Anne Treneer*
Rambles Beyond Railways	*Wilkie Collins*
A Pair of Blue Eyes	*Thomas Hardy*
The Owls' House	*Crosbie Garstin*
Twenty Years at St. Hilary	*Bernard Walke*
Troy Town	*Arthur Quiller-Couch*
Short Stories	*Arthur Quiller-Couch*
Cornish Verse	*Ed. Anthony Mott*
High Noon	*Crosbie Garstin*
The West Wind	*Crosbie Garstin*
Hands to Dance and Skylark	*Charles Causley*
Confession of a Rebel	*Jack Clemo*
The Splendid Spur	*Arthur Quiller-Couch*
The Ship of Stars	*Arthur Quiller-Couch*
Love in the Sun	*Leo Walmsley*
A Cornishman at Oxford	*A. L. Rowse*
Cornish Years	*Anne Treneer*
Hawker of Morwenstow	*Piers Brendon*
A Short History of Cornwall	*E. V. Thompson*

All the books in *The Cornish Library* will be numbered to encourage collectors. If you would like more information, or you would care to suggest books that you think should appear in the series, please write to me at the following address:

Anthony Mott
The Cornish Library
50 Stile Hall Gardens
London W4 3BU